Praise

"A high-speed chase of a mystery, filled with very likable characters, a timely plot, and writing so compelling that readers will be unable to turn away from the page."

– *Kings River Life Magazine*

"Will keep you turning pages late into the night and make you think twice about the dark side of the Hollywood Dream."

– Paul D. Marks,
Shamus Award-Winning Author of *Vortex*

"Radio host Carol Childs meets her match in this page-turner. Her opponent is everyone's good guy but she knows the truth about the man behind the mask. Now Carol must reveal a supremely clever enemy before he gets the chance to silence her for good. Great read!"

– Laurie Stevens,
Award-Winning Author of the Gabriel McRay Series

"A story of suspense, raw emotion, and peril which builds up to a satisfying climax...Silverman has given us another book where we can sit down and get our teeth into, and I look forward to the next in the series. Highly recommended."

– *Any Good Book*

"Fast paced and cleverly plotted, an edgy cozy with undertones of noir."

– Sue McGinty,
Author of the Bella Kowalski Central Coast Mysteries

SHADOW OF DOUBT (#1)

"Silverman provides us with inside look into the world of talk radio as Carol Childs, an investigative reporter, finds herself in the middle of a Hollywood murder mystery, uncovering evidence that may point to her best friend. A hunky FBI Agent and a wacky psychic will keep readers guessing from beginning to end."

– Annette Dashofy,
USA Today Bestselling Author of *Lost Legacy*

"Silverman creates a trip through Hollywood filled with aging hippies, greedy agents, and a deadly case of product tampering. Forget the shower scene in *Psycho*; *Shadow of Doubt* will make you scared to take a bath!"

– Diane Vallere,
Author of the Material Witness, Style & Error, and Madison Night Mystery Series

"A thoroughly satisfying crime novel with fascinating, authentic glimpses into the world of talk radio and some of its nastier stars... The writing is compelling and the settings ring true thanks to the author's background as a newscaster herself."

– Jill Amadio,
Author of *Digging Too Deep*

"Carol is a smart, savvy heroine that will appeal to readers. This is a cozy with a bite."

– *Books for Avid Readers*

"Absolutely engaging, I could barely put it down. The characters in the book were well-developed and the plot was chillingly genius."

– Lyn Faulkner,
NetGalley Reviewer

WITHOUT A DOUBT

Nancy Celest

WITHOUT A DOUBT
A Carol Childs Mystery
Part of the Henery Press Mystery Collection

First Edition | May 2016

Henery Press
www.henerypress.com

All rights reserved. No part of this book may be used or reproduced in any manner whatsoever, including Internet usage, without written permission from Henery Press, except in the case of brief quotations embodied in critical articles and reviews.

Copyright © 2016 by Nancy Cole Silverman
Cover art by Stephanie Chontos

This is a work of fiction. Any references to historical events, real people, or real locales are used fictitiously. Other names, characters, places, and incidents are the product of the author's imagination, and any resemblance to actual events or locales or persons, living or dead, is entirely coincidental.

Trade Paperback ISBN-13: 978-1-63511-025-8
Digital epub ISBN-13: 978-1-63511-026-5
Kindle ISBN-13: 978-1-63511-027-2
Hardcover Paperback ISBN-13: 978-1-63511-028-9

Printed in the United States of America

WITHOUT A DOUBT

A CAROL CHILDS MYSTERY

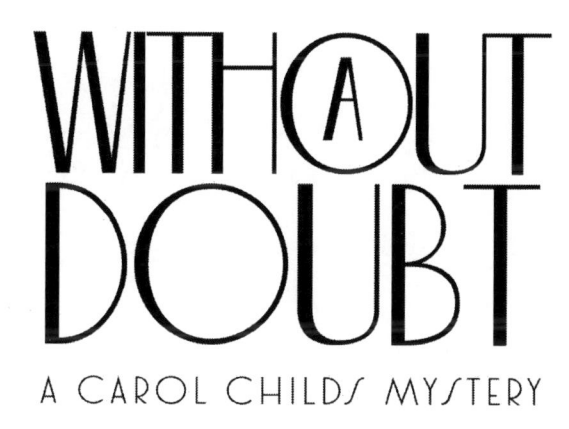

NANCY COLE SILVERMAN

HENERY PRESS

**The Carol Childs Mystery Series
by Nancy Cole Silverman**

SHADOW OF DOUBT (#1)
BEYOND A DOUBT (#2)
WITHOUT A DOUBT (#3)

To my family

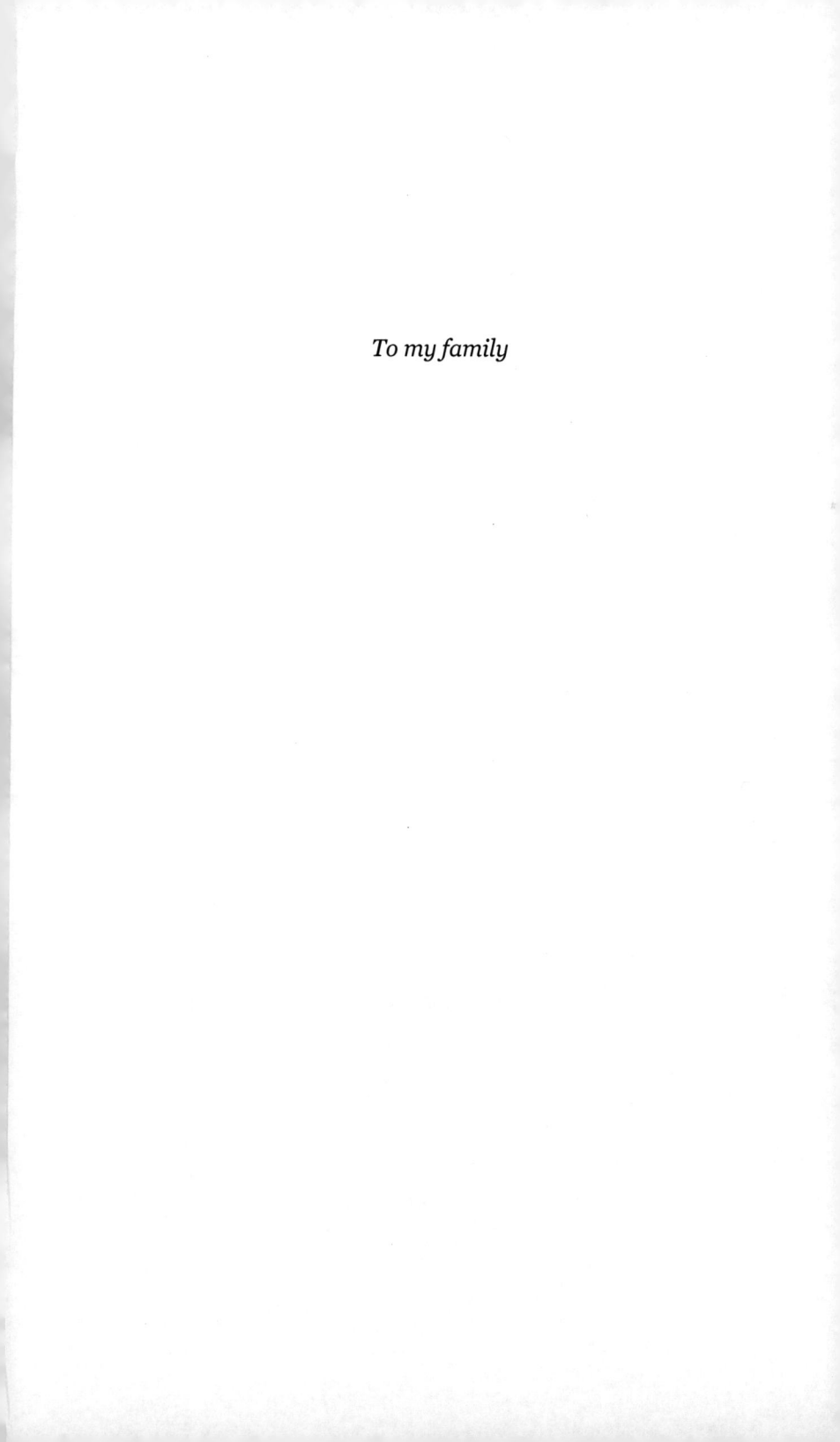

ACKNOWLEDGMENTS

I have to thank my good friend, hiking partner and first editor, Rhona Robbie, for helping me to find the opening scene in this book. It was at her suggestion we do the Beverly Hills chocolatiers' tour. Yes, folks, there really is such a thing, and during the holidays, if you're in L.A., it's a must. For us, the tour was not only fun, but we came away with such a chocolate high I was determined to use the scene in a book. It seemed natural for Carol and Sheri and a particularly tasty way to open *Without A Doubt*.

I also want to thank my publisher, Kendel Lynn, who has been a big support to me as the Carol Childs Mysteries have unfolded. My editors at Henery Press, Erin George and Anna Davis, are master craftswomen when it comes to refining story and I'm forever grateful for their keen eyes and understanding of story structure. Stephanie Chontos, who has done it again with another great cover and Art Molinares, who keeps the Hen House on an even keel.

And, finally to my family. Each and every one of you are what make my life wonderful.

CHAPTER 1

"Don't rush me. I need to savor this moment."

Sheri stood outside the Beverly Hills chocolatier and let the small square chocolate truffle liqueur melt in her mouth. Head turned up to the midmorning sun, she closed her eyes and, with a look of ecstasy on her face, sighed, almost orgasmically.

I grabbed her hand. I couldn't leave my best friend standing on the sidewalk with her eyes closed, looking flushed, like she'd just died and gone to heaven.

KCHC's new Chocolate Christmas Charity Campaign was dependent upon my roving report of the Beverly Hills chocolatiers. And no matter how tantalizing Sheri's descriptions for the competing makers of the sinfully sweet delicacies had been, we needed to move on.

"Carol? Are we ready?" Kari Rhodes's saccharine sweet voice boomed in my ear and out over the airwaves. "Or has our taster succumbed?"

"OD'ed might be a better description, Kari."

I explained that after visiting five different confectioners, Sheri was understandably lightheaded. We had begun the morning broadcast at Teuscher Chocolates on Brighton Way, sampling champagne truffles with buttery-sweet chocolate-filled liqueurs, and moved on to Vosges Haut-Chocolat on Beverly Drive. There we tasted their caramel marshmallows and later compared them to Madonna's favorite dark chocolate mallows from the Edelweiss on Canon. While Sheri sampled, I filled listeners in on the fact that

Edelweiss was the scene of the once-famous chocolate factory where Lucille Ball had gone to learn to wrap chocolates with Ethel. Off mic, I nudged Sheri and whispered, "One more, girlfriend. Hang in there."

Turning my attention back to Kari, I announced our next stop: Bouchon Bakery, famous for their French pastries, chocolate croissants, and small, intimate dining tables.

"Like an escape to Paris," I said.

"Oh, you must bring back samples, Carol. Some croissants and maybe the French press coffee? I can almost smell it."

I planned to get plenty of the coffee into Sheri, and quickly.

I described the bakery's best, *ooh là là*-ing over their tarts and cakes, their macarons, and their twice-baked chocolate croissants, then signed off. "This is Carol Childs with KCHC Talk Radio, hoping all our listeners will take our Chocolate Charity Challenge. Visit Beverly Hills and vote for your favorite chocolatier to help support St. Mark's."

A portion of all sales from participating merchants during the month of December would be donated to St. Mark's Children's Hospital and the chocolatier with the most donations would win a year's worth of free advertising. Tyler Hunt, KCHC's boy wonder, and my now-is-never-soon-enough boss, said it was a win-win for everyone. Especially since he demanded I return to the station with enough chocolate to replenish the candy stash hidden in the top drawer of his desk.

Finishing my coffee, I threw my mic in my purse and turned around to find Sheri outside the café. She was leaning up against one of the city's holiday garland-trimmed lampposts licking her fingers. In her hand were three more of the chocolate liqueurs she had been given as samples from Teuschers. I whisked them from her, pocketed two, and threw the third into my mouth. If it's possible to get drunk on chocolate liqueurs, Sheri was close to plastered.

Sheri looked down at her empty hand, furrowed her brow, then back at me. "So that's it? We're done?"

"For now." I glanced at my watch. I reminded her I needed to drive her home and that I had less than an hour to get back to the station for my afternoon shift. I turned and headed in the direction of the parking garage with Sheri close behind.

"I want my chocolates. I've been dieting all week for this, and I want them. I want them now." Sheri stopped behind me. I turned around to see her with her hands on her hips like a defiant child about to throw a tantrum. She was refusing to take another step. "They're mine."

"I know. Which is why I've put them away." I was about to remind Sheri she had made me promise I'd not let her overindulge when she grabbed my arm, the look in her eyes going from disappointment to shock.

"Oh my God, Carol. Don't look."

"What?" I couldn't imagine what it was Sheri didn't want me to see. Had we missed a new candy store she couldn't resist? I turned around, expecting to see some giant chocolate Santa, and froze in my tracks.

Less than a block up the street coming out of Henry Westin's, one of Beverly Hills' most exclusive jewelry stores, was Eric. My Eric. And tucked neatly under his arm was Carmen Montague, the soulless socialite. A dark, sultry, raven-haired beauty known for absolutely nothing, famous for being famous. That happens in Hollywood. With the right connections, showmanship trumps talent. In Carmen's case, she'd made that connection numerous times. She was famously divorced, filthy rich, and had been linked to a number of dubiously well-heeled international businessmen, actors, playboys, and the like. And now she was very definitely with the man I had rolled over next to in bed this morning.

I stood unable to move. My heart, like a rock in my chest, refused to beat.

Sheri leaned next to me. I could feel her breath on my shoulder. Eric, with his arm still about Carmen, dressed in a cashmere Burberry jacket and wearing glasses I didn't recognize, looked straight in our direction. Without so much as a nod, he ducked into a black stretch limo double parked in front of Henry Westin's and sped off.

"Was that...?" My mouth went dry. I couldn't finish the thought.

"No." Sheri looked at me, the dark curls against her head shaking as though she were trying to erase the picture. "Couldn't be."

Before I could make sense of what I'd just seen, an explosion far worse than what was going on inside my head rocked the ground beneath my feet.

From inside Henry Westin's, a thunder blast shook the street like an earthquake. The big gold double doors on the front of the building blew open. Alarms everywhere, up and down the street, began blaring. People screamed, panicked, and started running. It was chaos. From within the building, a white cloud of dust, like smoke, began to billow out the doors and settle in the now nearly empty street littered with shopping bags and orphaned shoes.

CHAPTER 2

It was a bomb.

Funny how instinct kicks in, even when there is no precedent to draw from. My chocolate high turned stone-cold sober. Ear-piercing white noise—surreal in its emptiness—caused a shrill ringing in my ears. Around me, things started to move in slow motion. Papers fluttered weightlessly in the air and people running by appeared to almost float in their haste to escape the scene. Time took on a wacky sense of proportion. Seconds stalled, stretching into minutes.

I yelled at Sheri, my ears still ringing, "Are you okay to get home?" Tipsy from the liqueurs, I worried she wasn't herself. But there was nothing I could do. I needed to stay. "Something's happened."

"What is it?" Sheri gripped my wrist, her brown eyes wide, riveted on mine.

"I don't know. I need to call the station and you need to get out of here. I'll call later."

I told Sheri to grab a cab and pointed toward Wilshire Boulevard where traffic was already starting to back up. In the distance, I could hear the warble of sirens echoing between buildings, coming in my direction. I reached into my bag for my phone and called the station.

Tyler answered on the first ring. "Carol, you still there?"

"There's been an explosion—"

"I know. I'm getting a report on the police scanner now."

"What's happening?" I felt vulnerable standing in the street as I waited for Tyler to answer. In the background, I could hear the squawking of the newsroom's small black police receiver and the clicking of computer keys. Tyler's fingers were already flying across the keyboard. I knew he'd be alerting Kari to the emergency. He yelled at me as he typed. "An employee inside Henry Westin's says there's been a robbery."

"Anyone hurt?" I looked down the street where minutes ago I'd seen Eric getting into a limousine in front of the jewelry store. Now all I could see were swarms of police cars. LAPD, Beverly Hills police, and emergency vehicles were parked outside the building. The gold double doors were still flung open. But no one was coming out.

"You tell me! You're the only one who's there. Go. Get the story, Carol. We need something. Now!"

Tyler slammed the phone down, the silence in my ear almost as deafening as the explosion.

I reached back into my bag for my mic and, finding it, began to run. Skirting abandoned shopping bags and businessmen in Armani suits, I dodged leggy supermodels in six-inch heels as moms pushing baby strollers rushed past me, away from the explosion. In the back of my mind, the memory of the Boston Marathon and the fear of another explosion pushed me forward. I had a story to cover. I needed to focus.

Ahead of me, more emergency vehicles had arrived, jamming the street in front of Henry Westin's. Their lights flashing and their doors flung open blocked my view of the entrance. Parked lopsided on the sidewalk was an LAPD black and white and double-parked on the street were an ambulance and a large black Bomb Squad truck.

Half a dozen uniformed cops had already begun to secure the scene with yellow crime scene tape. I stood behind it, my heart pounding. I had run only a hundred yards but with the bomb and the jolt of seeing Eric with Carmen, I felt as though I had run a marathon.

I leaned over the tape and yelled as an LAPD uniformed officer and a plainclothes detective came out of the building. A glint of light reflected off the detective's badge revealing his Sam Browne and shoulder holster. "Detective, can you talk? What happened? Was anyone hurt?"

"Stay behind the tape, ma'am." The detective, his face flushed with excitement, yelled back at me, pointing to the yellow tape between us.

"I'm with the press." I held my mic up in the air, hoping he'd see it and come closer. "Can you tell us what happened?"

He stopped momentarily. I noticed small beads of sweat had started to run down the side of his face. "Someone planted a bomb," he said tersely.

"Was it—"

"Terrorists? No." He shook his head. "This was a robbery. Third jewelry store this month." He started to move on.

Third? Robberies may have flown under my radar, particularly in a city the size of Los Angeles, but a bomb? I wouldn't have missed that. It may have the third robbery, but it had to be the first with a bomb.

"Anyone inside hurt?" I hollered back, my voice strained.

He stopped and came back to me. "What station you with, Miss?"

"KCHC."

He looked at the bright yellow station ID flag on my mic and smiled. "Chick Radio, huh? What are you doing here?"

I wasn't surprised by the question. KCHC wasn't exactly known for its news reporting. Robberies, homicides, and bombings weren't our thing. Instead of hard news, KCHC was entertainment-focused, light news and lots of talk. I introduced myself and I explained I'd been doing a holiday report in Beverly Hills when I heard the explosion and asked if I could get his name.

"Detective Lewis," he said. "My wife listens to KCHC. Calls it the good news station. She's a big fan." He shook his head again. "But I don't think your listeners are going to like this one."

"So someone *was* hurt?" I couldn't imagine being inside when the blast went off. Bells were still going off inside my head like a pinball machine and I'd been halfway down the block.

"Unfortunately, yes. Looks like an older woman, an assistant maybe, got hit with a piece of shredded glass from one of the display cases. Took a piece in the neck and bled out before paramedics could get to her."

"Anyone else?"

"Nope. Manager's okay. Little shook up. His name's Churchill. Stick around, you can ask him yourself. He'll be coming out in a minute."

"And the bomb, anything you can tell me about it?"

"Bomb Squad boys say it was a flash bomb, type of thing designed to create more of a diversion than do physical damage. Big sound, lots of smoke. Wasn't supposed to kill anybody."

I took notes quickly, my hands shaking as I scribbled onto my notepad. In the background, through my headset, I could hear Tyler talking to Kari, setting up my report. "Carol. Tell us what you know."

"I'm here on Rodeo Drive in front of Henry Westin's, where just moments ago a blast shook the street of this quiet shopping area, sending shoppers scrambling for cover. Police have confirmed one fatality."

"Do we have an ID?" Kari asked.

"Not yet. But police are telling me a woman inside the store appears to have been hit by a piece of flying glass. It's believed she bled out before the paramedics could arrive on the scene."

I watched as two EMTs emerged from within the building with an older gray-haired gentleman. This had to be the manager, Mr. Churchill. He looked to be somewhere in his seventies, his hair and clothes rumpled, a bit unsteady on his feet.

"Excuse me," I hollered across the yellow tape. "Mr. Churchill, can you talk to us?"

The old man stopped maybe twenty feet from me, and, noting the mic in my hand, patted the arm of one of the EMTs assisting him and walked towards me. From the dull expression on his pale creased face, it was evident he was still in shock.

"Sir, can you tell us what happened?"

Churchill reached for the mic, his thin hands trembling. I put my hand on top of his to steady them and nodded for him to go on. I detected a slight English accent as he spoke.

"All I can tell you, miss, is we'd just opened. Carmen Montague had come in early. She had a necklace she wanted to drop for repair and had just left when—*Boom!* There was an explosion. The building rocked. Everything went white, the store filled with smoke, and I was knocked off my feet."

"Was anyone else in the building with you? Any customers?"

"No." Churchill shook his head. He looked muddled, disoriented. "Only my assistant...I...I believe she's been badly hurt." He put his hand on his head and looked back over his shoulder as the EMTs rolled an empty stretcher from inside the building back toward the ambulance. I knew this wasn't a good sign. The body wouldn't be released until the crime scene had been completely investigated. He looked back at me, apparently confused. Why was the stretcher empty? I could see it hadn't hit him yet. His assistant was dead. "I'm sorry. Did you ask if anyone else was in the store?

"I don't believe so. Perhaps there was someone waiting. I'm not sure. You'd have to ask our security guard, Mr. Paley. He's speaking with the officers now." He pointed with a crooked index finger, his hand still shaking, in the direction of the patrol cars. An older beefy-looking guard was talking with two Beverly Hills cops.

I was about to ask Churchill if he had any idea what might have been stolen when he clutched his chest. He looked as though he were about to faint, his face even whiter than his collared shirt. I reached for his shoulder to steady him and told Kari to hold.

"Mr. Churchill, are you all right?"

"I...I don't think so." He looked as though he were about to collapse. "I need to sit down."

I shielded my mic to my shoulder and yelled to the EMTs, "I need help here."

The two EMTs who looked as though they were about to leave came running. I heard one say, as Churchill collapsed back into their arms, that he had refused to go to the hospital to be checked out, insisting he was okay. He wanted to stay to supervise the cleanup.

Within seconds, despite his objections, Churchill, looking deathly white, was put on a stretcher. An oxygen mask was placed on his face and he was hurriedly rushed back towards the ambulance.

With one hand to my ear to shield out the sound of the helicopters hovering overhead and the warbling sound of the ambulance sirens in the background, I pressed the earphone to my head and continued my report.

"Kari, as you can hear from the sounds of the sirens and helicopter above, this is still a very fluid situation. Earlier this morning this could have been a scene from a Hallmark card, the streets decorated for the holiday and bustling with shoppers. But right now it looks like a scene from a sci-fi movie. Westin's manager, Mr. Churchill, has just collapsed and been rushed to an ambulance, and there is no word yet on the cause of the explosion. However, if there is any good news concerning this attack, it's that the police do not believe this disturbance is terrorist-related. Instead, what I'm learning from police is that this was a flash bomb. A device designed to create a diversion for what investigators believe may have been an attempted robbery, possibly related to a recent rash of jewelry store robberies in the area. This is Carol Childs reporting for KCHC, live from Beverly Hills."

After wrapping up my report, in the absence of anything more pressing, I headed back to my Jeep. I had parked less than a block away, beneath Two Rodeo Drive, LA's answer to the Spanish Steps, a European-style shopping center complete with a cobblestone walkway, hanging flower baskets, and, best of all, two hours of free parking. I'd nearly reached the auto entrance when I came upon an old woman, hunched over and struggling to carry two handfuls of shopping bags. I felt compelled to stop.

"Are you okay?" I asked.

She looked severely shaken up.

"I'm...I'm fine, thank you." She sounded winded, and stopped and placed her hands over her heart as she caught her breath. She explained that she was on her way back to her car when the blast went off. She had huddled with her bags in front of the steps leading up to Two Rodeo Drive until all the hubbub had passed.

I could appreciate her concern, and when I realized we were parked in the same lot, I offered to carry her bags for her.

"So kind of you," she said. "People today are much too busy to stop and help an old lady. No such thing as a Good Samaritan these days."

I took her bags and helped her through the parking lot. When I turned, I noticed she had removed a small brooch from the lapel of her jacket. With gloved hands, she gently pressed it into mine.

"As a thank you," she said, "for rescuing me."

I glanced at the pin. It was a stunning work of art, a Phoenix rising from fire, with emeralds, rubies, and diamonds. I couldn't be sure if it were the real thing or some Beverly Hills knock-off, but either way, I couldn't possibly accept it. Listeners are always trying to give us things, but it's against policy. I attempted to hand it back.

"Really, you don't need to—"

"Please, you'll make an old lady happy." She stepped back, both hands up, refusing to take it back. "It's the least I can do."

Before I had a chance to argue about it, the valet pulled up with my embarrassingly dirty red Jeep. "Ma'am."

With the door wide open, the valet waved at me impatiently. I had overstayed my two-hour free parking limit and he expected to be paid. With the brooch in my hand, I scoured around in the bottom of my bag for change while explaining I was a reporter. I hoped upon hearing who I was, he might grant me a special dispensation for my role in covering the explosion, or perhaps even think kindly enough to extend my two-hour free parking privileges. But I was getting nowhere.

Finally finding a ten-dollar bill in the bottom of my bag, I handed it to him, expecting change. Instead, he snatched it from me and gave me the key to my car like he was handing off a dirty diaper. Next time, he suggested, I should consider the public lot down the street. By the time I got in the car and looked to see if the old lady was still there, she had vanished.

CHAPTER 3

When I got to the office, there was a message from Eric on my office voicemail.

"Carol, we need to talk. Call me when you get this."

Eric sounded stressed, like he was searching for the right words and having trouble finding them. The problem was, I wasn't quite sure how to respond.

My logical side knew better than to let my imagination run wild. FBI Special Agent Eric Langdon was a stand-up guy, thoughtful, considerate, and, because we'd both had enough life behind us to know better, a free agent. Albeit, romantically exclusive. And, up until this morning, at least as far as I knew, neither of us had even considered seeing anyone else. But still, Eric had clearly seen me as he exited Henry Westin's with Carmen on his arm. I couldn't imagine how he planned to explain that. How could he possibly have failed to tell me he had plans to be with Carmen Montague this morning? Just three hours earlier we had woken up together.

My only thought was it had to be work-related. I tried to dismiss the nagging thought of Eric with Carmen. I couldn't imagine a scenario where Eric was actually carrying on with a Hollywood socialite, and certainly not someone like Carmen Montague. But then there was that cashmere sports coat that looked so impossibly dashing on him, and Carmen with her long lashes and those milky white breasts of hers. They always seemed to enter a room five minutes ahead of her. And why were they at Henry Westin's? What were they doing? Shopping for rings? This entire scene was like a nightmare, the result of too many chocolate liqueurs and stress. I picked up the phone. I was determined to resolve my issues when Tyler buzzed me on the office line.

"Carol. I need to see you. Right away."

I took my finger off the speed dial, promised myself I'd call Eric back, and headed down the hallway to Tyler's office.

Tyler's first words, before I'd even cleared the door, were, "You bring the candy?"

I reached into my purse and took out a bag of assorted chocolates and caramels and placed them in front of him.

"Please tell me that's not why you insisted I see you."

He looked at the bag.

"You get the liqueurs?"

"Yes."

"The champagne gummy bears?"

"Absolutely."

"The chocolate bacon bar?"

"From Vosges Haut-Chocolat, with real bacon. Yeah, it's there."

He sighed, raised his eyebrows as though relief had just arrived in the form of a chocolate bar. Opening the bag, he put his head down close to the desk and took a big whiff.

"You okay?"

"No," he said. I could barely make out his muffled answer.

Closing his eyes, he leaned back in his chair, folded his skinny arms across his chest, and smiled. Smug, like he was happy I couldn't read his mind. I was at a loss.

"You called?" I prompted him. "You wanted to talk about the bombing? Or has that somehow slipped your mind?"

"Not at all." He shook his head and started rifling through the stack of sweets on the desk. "But as you're aware, with the directive from our new management, our focus at KCHC is now on softer news. Not robbery, murder, and mayhem, as you seem to have found yourself in the middle of this morning."

"Middle of?" I watched as Tyler unwrapped one of the

chocolate-covered pretzels and stuffed it in his mouth. "If I recall, just an hour ago you were yelling at me to get the story."

"I did. And between the two of us—you weren't half bad. Pretty good reporting, in fact." He spoke with his mouth full. "But unfortunately, I have been instructed, or perhaps I should say 'gently reminded,' that we need to leave the heavy news to the others in the marketplace."

"And what was I supposed to do? Pretend it didn't happen?"

Tyler ignored my protest and shook his head. I knew he wasn't any happier about this new directive than I was. Drowning himself in chocolate was only going to be a temporary fix.

"Seems Bunny Morganstern, the wife of our new president, is a former radio babe herself. And this new faster, friendlier, chick-lite format is none other than *her* idea." Tyler stared at me like I was the enemy. Guilty by association. At that moment, I thought he hated all women. "And right after she heard your report on the air, she called to say she'd like for us to...*try* a little harder. It seems while she liked your chocolatiers tour this morning and understands that you were, as you say, 'in the neighborhood' when the bombing went down, she didn't appreciate the gory details."

"What gory details?"

Tyler held his hand up, his meaning clear. Don't interrupt.

"She reminded me that when our listeners turn to KCHC, they want a safe, friendly place, entertainment, and feel-good stories. The fact you reported that the woman inside the jewelry store *bled out* upset her. So I was reminded that our mission is to package happy news. Things our listeners—and Bunny—would enjoy hearing about. The hard stuff she expects for us to leave to the heavy-hitters in town, the real news stations."

I considered telling him I had seen Eric coming out of Henry Westin's moments before the explosion. I was certain if he knew the FBI was involved, he'd think twice before telling me to table the story. I was about to say something when I heard Kari Rhodes, her shrill voice like that of a screeching eagle, entering the office from behind me.

"Tyler! You'll never believe who just called." She nudged her skinny body next to mine and stared down at the candy stash on Tyler's desk.

"Who?" I grabbed one of the champagne gummy bears off the desk and looked knowingly at Tyler. Kari's connections to Hollywood industry insiders never ceased to amaze me.

"Mimi," she said, her voice almost an octave lower.

"Carmen's sister?" I asked.

"Who else?"

I rolled my eyes.

"She heard about the bombing at Henry Westin's and she's worried. She's afraid E.T.'s diamond necklace—the one she's arranged to borrow for next week's awards show—might have been *lifted*."

"E.T.?" My eyes shifted to Tyler. In Hollywood, big stars' names, living or otherwise, were frequently abbreviated by those who thought their association should be on a need-to-know basis only. Tyler shook his head. He didn't know either.

"Do I have to spell it out for you?" Kari stared down at the pile of gummy bears on Tyler's desk and, selecting one, nibbled at it like a bird. "Oh, for heaven's sake, Carol. E.T., Elizabeth Taylor. Who do you think?"

"Oh. Of course. Elizabeth Taylor. Who else could it be?" I glanced back at Tyler. How could I be so out of it? "And was E.T.'s necklace stolen?" I asked.

"That's just it. She doesn't know. Not yet anyway. But after she heard your report, Carol, she called over to Henry Westin's and no one answered. Then, just a few minutes ago, she tried back and got a message saying the store was closed for the day. Evidently they're taking inventory. You ask me, Westin's got hit, and they don't want anybody to know what they've lost or just how much. Not with awards season coming up. Believe me, the Titanic sinking didn't ruffle as many feathers as a robbery at Westin's this time of year would."

I loved the way Kari's mind worked. As an entertainment

reporter, she always went for the dirt and frequently found it. This morning I couldn't disagree.

I tapped my finger on the desk in front of Tyler.

"Okay, so there it is. A star-studded diamond heist. How's that for your softer, more feminine approach to the news? Think Bunny might like that?"

Tyler swung his chair back to face his computer screen. He appeared to be scrolling through a list of police reports from Beverly Hills. "Carol, you said the cops think this morning's robbery might be related to several others in the area."

"Yes. That's what Detective Lewis said."

"And Henry Westin, he's the jeweler to the stars, correct? Supplies several of the pieces actors wear for these awards shows?"

"Absolutely," Kari said. "Every star in Hollywood knows Henry Westin. And if they were robbed and people had to go to an awards show without their jewels...Believe me, they'd rather walk naked down the red carpet than go without them. Can you imagine?"

I resisted the urge to smile.

"Kari has a point, Tyler. If this morning's robbery is related to any of the others in recent weeks, the timing's interesting. Wouldn't hurt to do a little snooping around, see if there is something more going on. Bunny may want us to avoid hard news, but when it comes to female listeners and awards shows, diamonds are—"

"A girl's best friend." Kari popped a gummy bear into her mouth and smiled like the Cheshire Cat.

Tyler shook his head then turned his attention back to his computer screen and quickly started typing as he spoke.

"Okay, so here's what we're going to do. Kari, you're going to be talking about awards shows this week anyway. Get Mimi to call in and talk about how devastated she is over the loss of her necklace. About how celebs and stars are frequently given the opportunity to borrow heirloom jewels for the shows and that kind of thing. And Carol, you can use that for a lead-in on these robberies. See if the police think there's a connection and build off that." He paused and looked up at me. "That good enough for you?"

I nodded.

"Good. Then you can go. Both of you. But remember, Carol, Bunny's going to be listening. Keep it—"

"I know, I know. Chick-lite."

I reached for one more of the chocolate liqueurs and was about to get up and leave the office when Renee Swell, KCHC's office manager, poked her head in the door. In her hand was a pink message slip.

"Carol, I'm sorry to interrupt. Your son's school called. Charlie's been in an accident."

CHAPTER 4

I glanced at the note in my hand and said a silent prayer as I put the key in the Jeep's ignition. *Please God, let him be okay.* Renee's hen-scratched message read that Charlie had been ambulanced to Cedars-Sinai with a broken wrist. I exhaled. I could live with that. I told myself as I whizzed between traffic up La Cienega toward the hospital that boys and broken bones are part of the program. Something to be expected. Especially when the boy in question is an overly ambitious teenager with his heart set on being an NFL quarterback. I think parents of young athletes know the risks. I tried to envision the circumstances as I arrived to find Charlie in the emergency room, his arm and wrist in a sling elevated above his head.

"Charlie?"

"Hey, Mom." He smiled uneasily.

"You okay?" I went to the side of the bed, kissed the top of his head, and tousled his sandy blonde hair. "You gave me quite a scare."

"The coach says I'm out for the season." He looked like an overgrown puppy, his eyes sad, pleading for me to say it wasn't so.

"Have they taken X-rays?"

"No, but the doc says it's busted. Two places."

Charlie explained that he and Clint, Sheri's son, had been horsing around between classes, tossing a book instead of a football over the heads of their classmates. Clint made a flying pass with their Modern History book, a book I seriously doubted either of them had ever cracked, and Charlie jumped for it, slipped, and fell.

He tried to break his fall with his hand and ended up snapping the ulna in his right arm. Ouch. Even hanging upwards in the sling it looked red and swollen. I could tell he was in a lot of pain but trying hard not to let on.

I suggested we not get too excited about football until we'd talked to the doctor, then reached into my bag and pulled out a small chocolate toffee from Edelweiss Chocolates, a mood enhancer for sure. Together we were enjoying the last of my candy stash when the doctor walked in. He apologized for the delay and explained they'd be taking Charlie down to X-ray and I should wait.

I returned to the waiting room, about to call Tyler and give him an update on Charlie when I remembered Churchill. He had to be in the same hospital. It was close to Beverly Hills, and since I was waiting around anyway, there was no harm in asking. If his condition wasn't serious, I just might get lucky and we could finish our interview. After all, if Mimi was right and a lot of Hollywood stars' jewelry had been stolen, it would be nice to have the inside scoop in time for my report on Kari's show. Plus, it made the uncertainty of sitting around and waiting for Charlie to return all the more bearable.

I went back to the lobby and approached the administrative desk. An older woman with a pleasant face and half-framed glasses sat behind the counter.

"Excuse me. I was hoping I could get a status report on Mr. Churchill. He was brought to the ER this morning."

She eyed me over the top of her half frames with suspicion. "I'm sorry, miss, but I can't give you a status report. You know that."

I leaned across the counter and whispered, "I'm his niece." I lied. I hoped she wouldn't recognize my faceless voice from the radio. "They called me from the ER. I rushed over as soon as I heard."

"His niece, huh?" Her eyebrows arched as she appraised me like she might a felon.

"I was hoping maybe you could tell me if he's been admitted."

She looked back at her computer monitor. "Mr. Edmond Churchill, age seventy-six?"

"That's him." I nodded nervously.

"He's in the south tower, fourth floor, room forty-eleven. Be sure to tell the charge nurse when you arrive."

On the fourth floor, I found the nursing station and asked if Mr. Churchill was allowed to have visitors. The nurse checked the roster, glanced up at me, and pointed towards the end of the hall.

"First door on the left. Visiting hours until nine p.m."

I took that to mean Mr. Churchill was not dying or in dire circumstances. I paused outside his door, peered into the room, and was surprised to see him sitting up in bed watching TV. He was dressed in a blue hospital gown and had on a small nasal oxygen tube. An IV and monitors were hooked up, blinking lights sending their readings back to the nurses' station.

"Mr. Churchill." I approached the foot of his bed and waited for him to acknowledge me. "I'm Carol Childs, from the radio station. We met this morning, after the—"

"The bombing. Yes, I remember." He adjusted his glasses, then smoothed the sheets about his slim body in an effort to make himself more presentable and patted the bed. "Please, come sit."

"No, I'm fine, thank you." I held my reporter's bag against my chest and stood rigid.

"I'm sorry to have frightened you. We were talking when I felt the palpitations. I get them from time to time. Bad ticker." He tapped his chest with his hand and smiled. "I suppose it goes with getting older. Hasn't killed me yet, but I'm here for observation, nothing more. What is it I can do for you?"

"I was hoping we might chat. I have some more questions about this morning, if you're able."

"I'm afraid my memory's a bit sketchy." He ran his long bony fingers through his thinning hair. "The explosion was quite unsettling, and the medication they gave me doesn't help."

"I wanted to ask you about Carmen Montague. You mentioned she was in the store before the explosion."

"Ah, Miss Montague. Yes. I'm afraid that's a bit of a thorny issue, miss. I shouldn't have mentioned her at all. You'll have to forgive me. I'm sure you understand. Our clients, their jewelry in particular, are a very private matter."

Even sedated, Churchill was taking the corporate line. If I wanted to know anything more about why Carmen Montague was there, and who she was with, I had to switch my approach.

"Actually, it was the gentleman Miss Montague was with. I was wondering if you'd ever seen him with her before?"

"The gentleman?" Churchill shook his head. "I wouldn't know one from the other. There's always someone. I think she called this one James or Jason. Something like that. I suppose whoever she has with her is as much a bodyguard as an escort. She'd need that with what she's carrying."

"Ca...carrying?" I nearly choked over the word. "What was she carrying?"

"Oh dear, I'm afraid I've said too much. It must be the sedative they gave me. Makes me quite chatty. Like a London Lassie on holiday."

"Would you prefer we talk off the record?"

"If you wouldn't mind. I really shouldn't have said anything at all, and now I've said too much. Promise me you'll not use my name."

I agreed.

Taking a glass of water from the table tray by his bed, Churchill took a long sip and started to explain the circumstances surrounding Carmen's visit to the store.

"Ms. Montague is a courier. It's not a secret. Her husband, or her ex, I'm never sure which, Señor Umberto Diaz de la Roca, dabbles in the trade of diamonds and one-of-a-kind heirloom jewelry. Most of what he brings to us comes from Europe, estate sales and the like. His connections are beyond reproach. I believe he's a member of the Spanish nobility. I don't follow such things, but from time to time he'll contact us with information concerning items we might find of interest. And when we do, we arrange to buy them. It's all a bit complicated, but I assure you, very above board. Although, as you might imagine, quite hush-hush."

Listening to Churchill, I suddenly had a much better idea of what Eric was involved in, and a sinking feeling it was going to come between us. With Eric working one side of a story and me investigating another, I knew it couldn't be good. Need-to-know versus right-to-know is a delicate balance when it comes to dating an agent. Already my stomach started to knot.

"And that's what she was doing this morning? Making a delivery?"

"Yes, but she was in a hurry. She had a lot of loose cut stones with her, diamonds mostly. Like she usually does. She hides them in a black eyeglass case. It's small enough to be discreet, and this morning she slid it across the counter and then produced a diamond necklace and earrings she wanted to have reset. I placed the case beneath the display case, looked at her necklace, and told her I'd have it ready for her in a couple of days."

"And she left right after?"

"Yes."

I thought about the positioning inside the showroom. "And where were you when the bomb went off?"

"I had left my jewelers' loupe in the office and I went to get it. The explosion threw me under my desk. I suppose it saved my life."

"And your assistant? Where was she when Carmen came in this morning?"

"Ms. Pero. She was in the back, getting something from the safe. But the police tell me her body was found next to one of the display counters in the front of the store. I just don't understand it. They told me she was hit with a piece of shredded glass and bled to death. Awful."

I sympathized with his loss, and then asked if he remembered anyone else in the store. "A customer, perhaps?"

"I think there might have been a woman. A redhead maybe. But I think she left. Went out the door right after Carmen. I'm sorry I sound so confused. I really don't remember. I suppose you could ask to see our security tape. Call Mr. Paley, our guard. Perhaps he could help." He nodded to the dresser by the bed and told me his wallet was in the drawer. "Mr. Paley's card is there."

"How much do think they got away with?"

"Off the record? You promised."

"Yes."

"Carmen's necklace and the earrings were worth about one point two million."

"And the diamonds in the eyeglass case?"

"Between you and me, close to fifteen," he said.

"Million?" I nearly choked.

Perhaps it was the excitement of the conversation, but for whatever reason, suddenly the heart monitor started to emit a pinging sound. Within seconds the nurse entered the room. She adjusted Churchill's IV, then turned and looked at me. The wallet was still in my hands. The look on her face and the tone of her voice were both annoyed.

"I'm afraid, miss, you'll have to leave. Mr. Churchill needs to rest, and unless you plan to take that wallet with you, I'd prefer you put it back where you found it. We don't need our patient to get overexcited."

I removed Mr. Paley's business card and waved it innocently above my head—proof I wasn't pilfering bills from Mr. Churchill's wallet—then returned the wallet to the dresser drawer. Churchill, his smile waning, fluttered the tips of his fingers and lay back on the bed.

I left him staring vacantly at a rerun of *Wheel of Fortune* and returned to the ER's waiting room. Charlie was still in X-ray. I took my phone out of my purse and called Eric while I waited.

"Hi, Jason?" I added a teasing lilt to my voice.

"Carol?"

"You were expecting Carmen, perhaps?"

"Look, I had no idea you'd be...why did you call me Jason?"

"I have my sources."

He laughed.

"Yes, you do," he said slowly. I sensed a little restrained flirtation. "Look, I couldn't—"

"I know," I said.

"I can't talk."

"Oh, I know that too. I figured you got called into something unexpected. I just wanted to call and say hello."

"Hello back," he said smoothly.

I paused.

"Charlie broke his wrist this morning." I explained that I was at the hospital waiting for the results, and it looked like he wasn't going to be playing football the rest of the season. Eric sympathized. He and Charlie had bonded over football. He knew this wouldn't be easy.

"Look, I can't promise, but I'll try to call you later. But you know—"

"Hey, I get it. You don't have to explain. We can talk later." I hung up. Eric didn't need to finish the sentence. I could have completed it without any effort. He was working a case. I was working a story. We understood the routine and that our respective roles—for the time being anyway—made for poor bedfellows and demanded a temporary hiatus to our romance.

"Ms. Childs?" I looked up to see the nurse standing in the doorway. She motioned for me to follow her.

I arrived back in the emergency room. Charlie was sitting on top of a bed in one of the privately screened sectioned-off areas that served as an exam room, his arm and wrist in a cast. He looked relieved to see me.

"I don't need surgery. The doctor said it's not so bad." He sounded hopeful the doctor would release him to play. I knew better but wasn't about to say.

CHAPTER 5

I called Tyler from the car. Charlie was riding shotgun. His right arm was in a sling, the expression on his face like a wounded warrior, his eyes cast downward. I explained to Tyler what had happened and that I was going home for the remainder of the day. He told me not to worry, that he'd fill in for my afternoon shift, and he wished Charlie well. He was about to hang up when I interrupted.

"You'll never guess who I ran into at the hospital."

"I don't have time for games, Carol. Who?"

So much for Tyler's bedside manner.

"Mr. Churchill."

"Talk to me."

"He was admitted to Cedars for observation and—"

"And what?"

I could hear the impatience in Tyler's voice.

"It wasn't *just* a robbery, Tyler. Churchill probably told me more than he should have. The medication he was on made him very talkative. He had me promise I'd leave his name off any report, but—get this—turns out Carmen Montague wasn't just there to drop off a necklace. She's a courier for her ex-husband, and she was there with—"

I stopped myself. I wasn't about to tell Tyler I'd seen Carmen with Eric. On more than one occasion, Tyler had made it clear he didn't think my relationship with an FBI Agent was wise and hoped it wouldn't influence my reporting. I didn't want him to think it would.

"With what, Carol?"

"Fifteen million dollars' worth of loose cut stones and diamonds. That's what," I said.

For a few seconds there was silence on Tyler's end, then the sounds of quick tapping across the keyboard. Tyler's mind was one step ahead of his fingers. Talking as he read the screen in front of him, he said, "The police report says this is still an open investigation. KNX is reporting the robbery was a failed attempt. That the store suffered minimal damage, and Westin's is claiming nothing was stolen. Where's that coming from if you're telling me Churchill said fifteen mil?"

"I don't know, unless Churchill issued a statement from his hospital bed after I left. Might be he thought he said too much and wanted to correct it."

"Let me get this straight. Let's say Mimi's right and Westin's took a hit—a big hit—and lost fifteen million dollars' worth of diamonds and stones. Stones the jeweler may have been planning to set into holiday pieces for the awards show next week, and—"

"And," I interrupted, "word gets out they were stolen. Not the type of news they want for business and certainly not right before a big awards show."

Tyler stopped typing. "That happens and suddenly we've got a lot of worried celebs thinking Westin's isn't safe. Maybe even wondering if what they're wearing on the red carpet isn't so real."

"So Westin's wants to make sure their clientele isn't upset and issues a statement via the news media saying everything's fine. That the robbery was a botched attempt and nothing was stolen."

"Sounds plausible," Tyler said.

"Except we know that's not the truth. Not if what Churchill told me is correct."

Even as I said it, I wondered if maybe the FBI had another reason for keeping things quiet. Something more. Something that might explain why Eric was with Carmen before the robbery and that could possibly be linked to the explosion.

I glanced over at Charlie. His eyelids were at half-mast; the painkillers had kicked in. I told Tyler I'd talk to him in the morning and hung up.

Soon as I heard the click, the phone rang again.

"What happened?" Sheri sounded impatient and I couldn't blame her. With all that had happened, I'd yet to get to her.

"It was a robbery," I said, "and—"

"No, not that." Now she sounded irritated.

"You mean Eric?"

"No!" she screamed into the phone. "Charlie. How is he?"

I didn't have time to ask how she knew; she was already explaining that Clint had called her from the school. Apparently while Charlie was being loaded into the ambulance, Clint was being escorted, none too ceremoniously, to the principal's office for disciplinary action. Mr. Walter, the headmaster, had placed the call to Sheri himself and suggested she come pick him up.

"Or bail him out," Sheri said. "I'm not sure which. All Walter would tell me was that he had spoken to the coach and that Clint was being benched for roughhousing."

I suggested they come over for dinner.

CHAPTER 6

Charlie spent the afternoon on the couch napping while I did as much follow-up on this morning's robbery as possible. I started by calling Henry Westin's and, like Mimi, got no answer. The call went immediately to voicemail, informing me they were closed temporarily and would open for business as usual tomorrow. I dialed the number on the card Churchill had given me for Westin's security guard, Mr. Paley. It too went to voicemail. I then tried the Beverly Hills police department and got nowhere. I spoke with a desk sergeant who told me this morning's robbery had been a failed attempt. Henry Westin's had sustained minor damage, and if I wanted more information, I needed to call the store directly. I was back where I started.

Then I remembered the detective I'd spoken to outside Westin's. Detective Lewis was not with the Beverly Hills Police Department, but with LAPD, and his wife was a fan of the station. I decided I'd try my luck. If LAPD had responded to the robbery, perhaps they had a different story to tell concerning this morning's incident. After all, Detective Lewis had said it was the third jewelry store robbery this month. There had to be something more he could add, if not about the robbery in Beverly Hills, then maybe the others. I called LAPD's robbery-homicide division and asked to leave a message. Detective Lewis returned my call within the hour.

"It's your lucky day, Ms. Childs. We were just about to issue an alert concerning a possible suspect when I got your message. I put your station at the top of the call list. Maybe because you were there this morning or KCHC is my wife's favorite radio station, either way I'll start with you."

I grabbed my notepad. "What have you got?"

"Understand, Ms. Childs, LAPD doesn't regularly get involved with things in Beverly Hills. But it just so happened I was following up on a previous incident in West LA when I caught a report on the scanner that there had been an explosion inside Henry Westin's. I raced over there, and I'm glad I did. Looks like we caught a break."

"Like what?"

"We got a picture of a possible suspect on videotape. Middle-aged. Well-dressed. With the exception of her hair color, she looks a lot like a woman we have on tape from some of the other robberies we've been following. We're calling her the Wigged Bandit."

"The redhead, right?"

Lewis paused. In the background, I could hear him shuffling through papers. "You know something?"

"Not enough," I said. I explained I'd spoken with Churchill at the hospital and that he had told me he thought his assistant, Ms. Pero, might have been waiting on a customer. "He described her as having red hair, and that she left immediately after Carmen Montague dropped off a necklace."

"Anything else?"

"I assume you know Carmen was a courier?"

"And did Churchill happen to tell you what it was Miss Montague was delivering?"

I was beginning to feel like I was on the wrong end of an interrogation, and I didn't like it. But I was willing to exchange information for anything I could use in my report.

"He mentioned an eyeglass case. But I assume you already know that."

I could hear the shuffling of papers again and figured Lewis was making as many notes of our conversation as I was.

I asked the next question. "Do you think Carmen might have been a target? That someone was trying to kidnap her, maybe hold her for ransom?"

"We're investigating a lot of different possibilities."

"But if someone wanted to rob the store and was following her, she could very likely be a target."

"I'm sorry, Ms. Childs, that's not something I can comment on. I did you a favor, calling you first, and now I've got a lot on my plate, so unless there's something else—"

"Wait, before you go. Maybe there's something I can do for you. Kind of as a thank you for putting KCHC at the top of your list. Doesn't have anything to do with the case, but sounds to me like you've been working hard and you've mentioned a couple times how your wife's a fan of the Kari Rhodes show. Any chance you might like a couple of free tickets for one of her Rhodes on the Road shows?"

It was a long shot, but I figured why not? If Lewis's wife was a fan and I could get him to continue to favor KCHC with police reports, it was worth a try. Once a month, Kari liked to get out of the studio for a remote broadcast. Usually it was from a coffee shop or some place of interest where she could meet up with her fans and dish the dirt on Hollywood celebrities in front of a live audience. The upcoming show had been a hastily scheduled affair. A recent burst of Santa Ana winds had damaged the Grove's Christmas tree, decapitating the top six feet like a giant sickle from the sky, leaving what remained of the tree to look like an overdecorated stump. Tree surgeons had been called in for reconstructive surgery, and Kari wanted to make certain she was on hand for the festivities. The event had been scheduled at the last minute, and show tickets were easy to guarantee.

"We've got one coming up the day after tomorrow, a special holiday promotion at The Grove on Fairfax."

"Free, huh?"

"Absolutely. We give them out on the air all the time. If you like, I can put a couple aside for you at our VIP table."

Lewis said he'd like that, talked for a moment about how much overtime he'd been working and how it would get him out of the doghouse. I hung up thinking I'd made a little headway. If not with the LAPD, at least I felt like I had everything I needed for Kari's show. She'd be salivating. The story had everything she could possibly want. A high-profile celebrity acting as a courier for her estranged husband. A bombing. A murder. A mysterious jewel thief the police were now calling the Wigged Bandit, and a missing little black case that might be worth millions.

At five o'clock my doorbell rang. Sheri and Clint were standing on my porch, their eyes barely visible above the grocery bags they held in their arms.

"I thought I was making dinner." I stood back and opened the door.

"Store-bought lasagna isn't my idea of cooking."

Sheri pushed past me and headed for the kitchen. She unloaded the bags and directed Clint to put the ice cream in the freezer. Looking over at Charlie on the couch, she announced she'd made her famous killer double chocolate chip brownies. Reaching into one of the bags, she produced a warm Saran-wrapped plate of freshly made gooey-in-the-center chocolate squares and passed it beneath Charlie's nose for approval.

"I would have thought after this morning you'd had enough chocolate."

"Carol," she looked at me sternly, "there is no world I ever want to be living in where there's too much chocolate." She returned the plate to the counter and reached for an empty wineglass. "Or wine, for that matter."

I filled her glass from an open bottle of red wine I had on the bar and sat down, while Sheri, in full chef-mode, grabbed an apron from the pantry and began prepping for dinner. Comfort food, she called it. One of my favorites: roasted rosemary chicken stuffed with onions and lemon with a side dish of small sea-salted potatoes with garlic.

"I've been thinking about this morning, Carol, and I have a theory."

"Really?" I took a sip of my wine and watched as she began

peeling the garlic, smashing it with the flat side of a big carving knife.

"Eric couldn't possibly be carrying on with Carmen. She's too..." Sheri stopped mid-sentence, raised her eyes to the ceiling as though she were looking for the right word, then said, "Hot. Oh, not that Eric's not hot. But think about it. Carmen's connected. Internationally. The only reason he'd be with her is because something's happened and he's working undercover."

She paused and looked at me.

I shrugged, lips tight. I wasn't about to say anything. I couldn't. But I knew given enough time Sheri would come to the only logical explanation available. The same conclusion I had.

"And for whatever reason, they just happened to be coming out of Henry Westin's just before the bomb went off. I don't know why, but I'd bet that plate of brownies you do."

I glanced over at the boys. They were watching TV.

I whispered, "The police think she might have been carrying diamonds for her ex."

"Her ex?" Sheri took a sip of wine, rolling it around in her mouth as though she were sampling it, then swallowed. "Of course. Umberto Diaz de la Roca." She let his name roll off her tongue like some verbal exercise.

I shook my head. I wasn't getting any mental pictures of the man.

"He goes by Diaz. He's the polo player, you remember him?"

I didn't follow the jet set, and beyond seeing Carmen's photo in the paper with a number of good-looking men, I had no idea which of the various international playboys Sheri was talking about.

She prompted me, "They used to, or maybe still do, own a big ranch out in Simi Valley. Los Caballos Grandes?"

She waited for some sign of recognition. I surrendered, hands up.

"It was in the news," she said. "Maybe ten years ago now. When they first got together, Carmen completely redid the place. Made it look like a Tuscan villa. It had an enormous barn for his horses. The barn alone had to be the size of Versailles, and the price tag was in the millions."

I vaguely remembered the story. It was long before I'd started working as a reporter.

"Then a couple years ago," Sheri said, "he skipped out on her with one of his horse trainers. Somebody he'd brought back from Europe with him. Certainly you remember? She looked exactly like Carmen, only younger, dark hair, big tits. You know the type, starlet wannabe. Anyway, Carmen and Diaz split and he went back to Europe, and the estate, for all I know, is empty. Used for Hollywood shoots and special events."

That story I did remember. It had run in the *LA Times* a little more than a year ago and been boiled down to a two-inch report. Los Caballos Grandes, estimated to be worth nearly forty-five million dollars, was for sale, and Carmen Montague was suing her husband for abandonment.

"But I'm not so sure they were ever divorced," Sheri said. "The story just kind of went away."

"Don't they all." I raised my wine glass in a mock toast.

"But if Carmen was at Henry Westin's *and* she was carrying diamonds, my bet is she's still in bed, so to speak, with her ex. Whether he's her ex or not. And *not* with Eric."

I smiled.

"Which is why," Sheri said, "Eric has to be working undercover."

I took a sip of my wine and considered what Sheri had said about Carmen. It was nice to know my best friend had come to the same conclusion I had about Eric. That he couldn't possibly be with Carmen. But after learning Carmen was a courier for her husband — or her ex—and a likely target by whoever had robbed Westin's, the woman was becoming infinitely more intriguing. I was becoming obsessed. Not only was she some pampered young Beverly Hills socialite, a predator in pursuit of wealth and social status, now she was a woman of international intrigue and mystery. She was a modern-day Scarlett O'Hara with an hourglass figure, raven-dark hair, piercing blue eyes, and dimpled cheeks, and, for the time being, on the arm of my boyfriend.

"I suppose Carmen's little delivery service might explain her very exorbitant lifestyle," I said. Even for a successful Hollywood star, Carmen's lifestyle was over the top. Her picture was frequently in the society section of the *Beverly Hills Courier* and she was always at fancy galas that must have cost a fortune to attend.

"It has to help," Sheri said. "There's no way someone like Carmen Montague lives like she does without somebody underwriting her celebrity status. It takes money, and lots of it, to do that." Sheri reached for her wine, leaned back up against the counter, and, holding the glass eye level, said, "I should know. I'm one of the lucky ones. I made mine the old-fashioned way. I inherited it and dammit, it's still not enough, not in this town."

I nearly laughed out loud. Sheri never took herself seriously. It was why I liked her. She was a member of the silver-spoon set but had no trouble telling people how fickle she felt the financial finger of fate could be.

CHAPTER 7

The next morning, I went directly to the news booth inside Studio A, where Kari Rhodes was in the middle of an interview with Mimi. With special guests, Kari enjoyed setting the stage, insisting tea or coffee be served. In truth, I think she liked the sound effects of the clinking cups while she visited with her guests, giving her broadcast a more intimate conversational tone. It was a little like eavesdropping on friends. This morning I noticed Kari had chosen a holiday red china pattern and ordered up a plate full of cranberry scones, which she picked at in her traditional bird-like manner.

I slipped quietly into the news booth, a small closet-sized room separated from the studio by a large plate glass window, and listened. With my headphones on I could hear the broadcast as Mimi, looking like a young Elizabeth Taylor, talked casually about what she planned to wear for the upcoming awards show. She described her gown, a one-of-a-kind vintage emerald green silk chiffon affair, designed by Pierre Cardin.

"Of course, the pièce de résistance is the necklace Henry Westin's agreed to loan me for the event. It goes perfectly with my gown."

With long manicured fingers, Mimi played with a simple strand of pearls that hung around her neck as she described the necklace, called La Peregrina. It was no wonder Westin's had agreed to loan it to her. Mimi's resemblance to the iconic star, with her dark hair and piercing violet eyes, contacts or otherwise—was remarkable. Mimi and La Peregrina together would no doubt result in a good photo op that would appear the following day in papers all around the world.

"Of course, it's not the famous Taylor-Burton diamond. But I think it's equally as stunning. Richard bought it for Liz's birthday when they were filming *Cleopatra*. It's a pear-shaped pearl, maybe the biggest in the world. It belonged to the King of Spain and was worn by Queens Margarita and Isabel. Liz later had Cartier set it with diamonds and rubies and wore it for a publicity shot for *Anne of Thousand Days*, a role she never played. The director thought she was too old. Can you believe that? But she later wore it when she filmed *A Little Night Music*."

"Well, I do hope you have a chance to wear it, Mimi. Have you heard anything from Westin's about the robbery? Do we know if it was stolen?" Kari picked up her cup. The sound of fine china tinkled in the background.

"I don't know. I haven't heard a thing."

Kari turned to me, her cup still in her hand. This was my cue. "Carol, have you heard anything? Do we know any more than we did yesterday?"

"It's still not clear exactly what or how much may have been stolen. The Beverly Hills Police Department is reporting yesterday's robbery was a failed attempt. However, a source close to the investigation, who asked not to be identified, has told me the robber made off with several million dollars' worth of loose cut stones and diamonds."

"Well, that is a big difference." Kari's green eyes loomed like saucers behind her round eyeglasses.

"Oh, I do hope Liz's necklace wasn't one of them," Mimi whined like a spoiled child. "It would be such a loss. Please tell me that's not the case."

"If it was stolen, Mimi, I'm sure Henry Westin's will issue a revised statement very soon. But there is some good news. The police tell me they believe yesterday's robbery was not an isolated incident, but part of a series of robberies they've been following over the last six weeks. In fact, they suspect they're looking for a serial thief. A woman they've nicknamed the Wigged Bandit."

"A woman?" Kari laughed, the trill of her laughter like that of an ascending scale. "Isn't that unusual?"

"The police have pictures of her as a blond, a brunette, and a redhead. But they haven't been able to get a shot of her face. She's always wearing glasses or hats and appears to know where the cameras are. What they do know is that whoever she is, she's a master of disguise."

"Well, I should hope so," Kari said. "If it's a woman who's got to compete in a man's game of robbing jewelry stores, there's no excuse for not having style. She's certainly got to up her game."

I let Kari's sarcastic remark pass and wondered if she was spiking her tea with something other than the stacks of sugar substitutes lined on the console in front of her.

"But there is more," I said. "Mimi, I apologize if you're hearing this for the first time, but the police believe your sister, Carmen Montague, was in the store just prior to the explosion and may have been—"

"Wait a minute." Mimi adjusted her headphones and glared at me through the glass separating the studio from the news booth. If looks could kill, she was sending daggers. "I hope you're not saying that you think my sister Carmen had something to do with this."

"On the contrary. The police believe Carmen may have been working for her ex-husband Umberto—"

"Ex-husband?" Mimi said flatly. "Umberto Diaz de la Roca is her husband. Not her ex. And I know where you're going with this. You're about to say Carmen was making a delivery, dropping off jewelry for him. It's a side business, all very legit and—"

"I'm sorry," Kari interrupted, her hands waved wildly above her head. "I'm missing something. I thought Carmen and Diaz were separated. He's a polo player, right? And now you're telling us he's in the diamond trade business?"

"Oh, for heaven's sakes, Kari." Mimi narrowed her eyes and shook her head. "You think there's money in playing polo? With his lifestyle?"

Kari glanced over at me, her eyes squinted. I could see she wasn't quite following. I explained that in addition to his polo ponies, Diaz had a reputation as a high-end trader of gems and jewelry, most of it coming from liquidation sales in Europe where he would collect rare one-of-a-kind items and stones and bring them back to the U.S. to sell.

Kari jumped in, "So then, Mimi, do you think your sister was doing a favor for Diaz and—"

"What I *think* is that places like Henry Westin's don't expect their priceless heirlooms and jewels to arrive via UPS. Trusted sources—like my brother-in-law—make deliveries. It's not exactly common knowledge, but if Westin's was robbed, it's probably because my sister was carrying a package to the store for him. Diaz is in the country for a polo match, and no doubt someone was following Carmen. In my opinion, she's just lucky she wasn't killed, and I can only hope the police are really looking into this."

Kari looked stunned. Not only had Mimi surprised her with knowledge of Carmen's work as a courier, but the fact that she thought her sister might also have been a target opened up a whole new discussion neither of us had expected. Kari smiled at me and grabbed the mic. "Mimi, that's a stunning accusation, and I'm sure our listeners would like to know more. In fact, I can see from our call-in line that we have several calls waiting. Shall we take a few?"

The first caller wanted to pass on her condolences to Carmen, and Mimi promised she would. The second caller was Tim from Sherman Oaks. He was a photographer who said he just happened to be in Beverly Hills and taken a picture of Carmen with an unknown male escort coming out of Henry Westin's just before the explosion. I had seen the picture in the paper that morning. A handsome couple ducking into a limo. With his hair slicked back, wearing glasses and face unshaven, nobody—except Sheri and me—would have known the man with Carmen was Eric. Mimi said she hadn't seen the paper, and Tim said he was glad Carmen had escaped unscathed. Then ending the call exactly like the first caller had, Tim asked Mimi to convey his best wishes to her sister.

But it was the third caller that made me think our casual, chatty conversation concerning the robbery was being monitored by someone other than KCHC fans.

Kari welcomed the caller. "Good morning. This is Kari Rhodes. You're on the air. May I ask your name?"

"Tomi, with an i," she said softly.

The voice was mid-range, youthful, and quick-speaking. Not too dissimilar from a lot of KCHC callers.

"Welcome to the show, Tomi-with-an-i. And may I ask where you're calling from?"

"Beverly Hills, or maybe I should say Beverly Hills adjacent. Does it matter?" A light, nervous chuckle followed.

"No, not at all, Tomi." Kari sounded reassuring. "And what can I do for you today?"

"I was hoping to talk with Carol Childs." My ears perked up. Working for the station, I must have heard close to twenty to thirty different voices a day, but this one sounded oddly familiar, although I couldn't place it. "I wanted to call and say what a good job Carol did the other day. I was there when the bomb went off."

Kari's eyes shot in my direction, her brow furrowed. It was one thing for me to be in the field and to dig up news to share on the air. She loved the talking points I provided for her show, but she wasn't used to having fans call in and ask to talk to me. Her pencil-thin brows raised begrudgingly in my direction.

"Well, Carol, it appears you have a fan." Kari sat back and crossed her arms.

I picked up the conversation before Kari could say anything more.

"Thank you, Tomi. May I ask where you were when the bomb exploded?"

"Running for cover." She laughed again. "Like everyone else."

"Yes. It was manic out there. People were very frightened." I covered my earphones with my hands, pressing them close to my head. I wanted to concentrate on the voice.

"But not you, Carol. No, you ran towards the scene."

I still couldn't place the voice.

"I'll never forget it. But the police...they got it all screwed up. They're such pigs—"

Kari nearly fell off the stool as she hit the seven-second delay button. I could tell she was about to signal Matt, our producer, to dump the call. But I put my hand up against the glass between our two studios and shook my head. I wanted to talk to this caller. If Tomi knew or had seen something, perhaps it could be helpful.

"Tomi, what is it you think the police got wrong?"

"The murder." The voice sounded like a hatchet hitting a wood block. There was a finality about its tone and delivery.

Kari grabbed her mic and shook her head at me. We were close to commercial break. She wasn't about to let my conversation go on longer than necessary.

"The old lady wasn't supposed to die! Nobody was supposed to. That's not the way it works."

"Tomi." I pushed the palm of my hand harder up against the glass. *Please, Kari, don't drop the call.* "Do you know something about the robbery? Did you see something?"

There was no answer. Only silence.

Kari, Mimi, and I stared through the glass into the production studio at Matt. I pointed to the phone and mouthed, "Could we trace the number?" Matt gestured back at us, his hands up. The line had gone dead, and the sound escaping out over the airwaves droned in my ear.

Kari was first to jump back in, filling the void. "Well now. That was a surprising note to end today's show on. But unfortunately, folks, we're out of time. You've been listening—"

The musical sting announcing my top of the hour newscast began to play, drowning out Kari's sign-off. I pulled up a list of chick-lite news stories, my stomach turning, and began my report.

"Spice the missing Pomeranian has returned home. The lost pooch, who last week was believed to have been kidnapped from his backyard, was found on the doorstep of his home in Woodland Hills early this morning. In other news..."

CHAPTER 8

Whoever Tomi, my mystery caller, was, she didn't call back. Nor did she make any attempt to leave another message. Often times the station gets a crazy, someone who calls in for no other reason than to spook the host and rile the audience. With close to half a million listeners it's not unusual and with no way to trace the call, I gave up worrying about it. I figured next time I talked with Detective Lewis I'd mention it. I knew the cops had their fair share of the same. People who'd confess to crimes they didn't commit or call to offer false leads. I filed the idea of Tomi in the back of my mind. If she called back, I'd worry about it then, but for now, I needed to focus my attention on finding Carmen.

Nobody had seen or heard from Carmen since she was last seen on video inside of Henry Westin's three days ago. As far as I knew, the last person to see her as she hurriedly left the store with Eric in a stretch limo, was me—and of course, Sheri.

The only thing I could figure was that if Mimi believed someone had been following Carmen and had spilled the beans on the air, then Carmen must need protection. And, after seeing Eric with her, I figured the FBI had been called in to do the job undercover. Added to that fact was Detective Lewis, who said he was investigating a recent rash of robberies in the Beverly Hills area. And since jewelry store robberies are one of the FBI's specialties, it wasn't a big stretch to imagine they might be working together as a joint task force. In my mind, LAPD had to be working the robberies from their side, while the FBI protected Carmen and perhaps investigated Diaz, or maybe both of them. I didn't know if Carmen was a potential target or part of some international jewelry theft ring, but I was going to find out. Bombings and robberies in Beverly Hills were one thing, but a socialite predator on the arm of my boyfriend was another, and I wasn't about to let it go.

I picked up the phone and called Carmen's agent. I needed to find her. Despite the fact that Carmen wasn't an actress, she retained a high-profile public relations agency to handle all her appearances. Their job was to quietly cue the paparazzi whenever needed. Carmen went shopping, they were there. Carmen went to the theater, and she was surrounded by fans. Carmen went out to dinner, more paparazzi. Her publicist, Penny Salvatti, answered the phone.

Penny's answer to my question concerning Carmen's health and whereabouts felt over-rehearsed. I was certain she was telling me exactly what she told every other reporter in town. "Miss Montague was greatly disturbed by the events of this week's bombing and is taking some much-needed time for herself. I'm sure you understand how deeply distressing something like this can be. I'll be certain to relay your message, and when she wishes to speak to the press, I'll see she has your name. Now if you'll excuse—"

"Can you tell me where she is?" I blurted into the phone before she could brush me off.

"I'm afraid I'm not at liberty to say. Goodbye."

I felt as though I'd just been tossed a bone by a dismissive master and locked outside in the doggie run with all the other media people. I was at a dead end. But unlike any other reporter in town, I, at least, knew Carmen was last seen with Eric. Which meant one of three things: A, Carmen was at home, hidden behind the twelve-foot walls that surrounded her Bel Air Estate. B, Carmen was with Diaz at their former ranch in Simi Valley, preparing for an upcoming polo match. Or C, after the bombing, the FBI had decided Carmen's life really was in danger and she had been whisked away and was maybe onboard Eric's yacht in the marina. That thought, like the vision of Eric with his arm around Carmen, was a bit unsettling. Quarters aboard the *Sea Mistress* were tight, with little room for privacy.

I decided to call Eric. Not that we could talk about Carmen or what was going on. That was strictly taboo. Open communication concerning the case, particularly between Eric and me, was verboten. I knew it. He knew it. But aside from the case, there was no reason we couldn't have an idle conversation, something that might give me a hint as to where he was.

"Hi. It's me."

"Hey, me." Eric's voice was hushed, almost whisper-like.

"So..." I stammered, trying to think of what I could say, my mind frozen on what I couldn't. After all, I wasn't supposed to really know what Eric was doing. Although we both knew I did.

Eric filled in, his cool demeanor setting the tone. "So how's Charlie?"

"Good. Doing better, in fact. Back at school." My response felt forced and stilted.

"Anything else?"

"No. Just wanted to say hello."

"Hello back," he said.

There was an awkward silence. I wanted him to take the conversation in a different direction. I'd hoped he'd volunteer something, anything, that might hint at what was going on with Carmen, but clearly that wasn't going to happen. Frustrated, we agreed we'd catch up later. I hung up, knowing later would only be another dead-end conversation.

I glanced at the clock. I didn't have time to think about it. Kari's remote broadcast was scheduled at The Grove, a good fifteen minutes away, traffic permitting. I grabbed my reporter's bag and filed my concerns about Eric in the back of my mind.

The Grove, designed to look like a quaint European shopping quarter, was a bustling promenade of trendy stores, hip restaurants, and a theater. Located adjacent to the old Farmers Market just south of Beverly off Fairfax, there was never a time of day when it wasn't crowded with locals and tourists.

For the holidays, The Grove's cobblestoned Main Street, with its trolley car and lampposts, was dressed with Christmas garlands and tiny white lights. Christmas wreaths adorned every shop door, and a Santa's village, complete with a sixty-foot white fir Christmas tree, stood on a small knoll behind an enormous musical water fountain.

KCHC's street team had set up a broadcast table at La Piazza, one of several restaurants facing an open air courtyard. Despite the view of The Grove's maimed Christmas tree with its decapitated top and today's warm southern California temperatures, it looked like a winter wonderland.

Kari arrived dressed in a red fringed caftan and strappy gold gladiator sandals that wrapped halfway up her skinny white calves. The shoes looked impossible to walk in. She entered the restaurant in her usual huff, talking as she approached the table, and ordered a large glass of ice water with lemon wedges on the side. Then, noticing me standing by the table, she asked if I'd seen Bunny.

"Bunny?" I hadn't heard anything about the new owner's wife attending today's broadcast. My heart sank. Were our plans derailed? How could we chat casually about the robberies with Bunny here after her firm dictate about chick-lite news? "Why? Did you invite her?"

Kari looked at me like that was an absurd question. Tossing her head back and rolling her eyes upward, she crossed her arms across her skinny flat chest. "It just so happens, Carol, that *she* told me she planned to be here today. Turns out she's not only a fan of my show but also of Michael Bolton, and when she learned he was going to be a guest with us today, she insisted on coming. What would you have me do? Say no?"

I wanted to groan. Our proposed agenda to continue our discussion about the robbery had already hit its first snag.

"However," Kari continued, "I wouldn't worry. Mimi's promised to call in. She says she has big news. She wouldn't tell me what, but I see no reason for you to be concerned. Perhaps you might use whatever she's calling about as a lead-in about the robbery. I know you want to, and if Bunny's upset, it's going to be with you, not me."

Before I could think of an appropriate response, a small white hand, fingers wiggling frantically from within the crowd of shoppers, interrupted me. "Kari!" I turned to see Bunny, her dark curly hair piled atop her head along with her designer glasses, barging through the crowd like a force of nature. She was dressed in a ruby red blazer, black tuxedo pants, and red stiletto heels, a short, tight-bodied cougar with her skin smooth and botoxed like she'd just come from the tanning salon.

Kari tapped the white linen tablecloth in front of her and looked at me. "You don't mind, do you? I'd like Bunny to sit next to me. You could take a seat at the end of the table, or perhaps over there." She pointed to a smaller café table where her producer Matt was setting up.

I stepped aside as Bunny wiggled into the seat between us, asking the waiter to bring her a glass of champagne. I took the chair at the end of the table and listened as Kari described today's lineup. Michael Bolton was here to sing "White Christmas." A group of Hollywood Rockettes would perform a brief dance number. Santa would stop by and say a few words, and—"Oh, by the way, you know Carol, our news gal?"

Bunny flashed a curt smile in my direction and turned her attention back to Kari. I was about to start reviewing my notes concerning the robbery when I noticed Detective Lewis. He was seated at the station's VIP guest table directly across the room, wearing one of the station's Santa hats. Next to him, dressed in a matching red cardigan, was a woman I assumed to be his wife. With his arm around her and a glass of champagne in his hand, he looked very relaxed. I waved a welcome and he nodded, whispered something in his wife's ear, then waved back. I took that to be a good sign and made a mental note to do a shout-out to him during the broadcast. Another opportunity to slip in something about the robbery.

Halfway through the show, after Kari had completed the

rededication of the Grove's maimed Christmas tree and Michael Bolton had finished singing, Kari's on-air producer announced he had an excited caller on line one.

Kari shot me a quick look. We both knew the caller was Mimi, my lead-in to our discussion concerning the robberies.

I glanced over at Bunny. By now she'd had at least three glasses of champagne and had switched to white wine. The woman was feeling no pain. Michael Bolton had thoroughly charmed her with his stories and kissed her goodbye. The woman was too starstruck to object to much of anything.

"Mimi!" Kari said. "How nice of you to call in. Merry Christmas, my dear. And why are you not here with us today?"

"I would be, Kari, but I've been so busy. Getting ready for the holidays and upcoming awards shows. But the big news...you won't believe it. I just received a call from Henry Westin's. They found my necklace. It wasn't stolen in the robbery after all."

I looked over at Lewis. He was staring at his cell phone, his Santa hat on the table beside him. I wondered if he was getting the same news concerning Westin's robbery as Mimi had just reported. I hadn't heard a thing regarding any of the missing jewels, much less Miss Taylor's necklace. Since sobering up in the hospital, Churchill had become very tight-lipped and had offered nothing more concerning his knowledge of what had been stolen. I raised my hand and wiggled my index finger in his direction, hoping I might get his attention. *Could we talk?*

Lewis shot me a quick look and nodded. I reached for the mic, and with Mimi still talking in the background, I interrupted.

"Mimi, this is Carol Childs. I was at Henry Westin's the day of the robbery. I'm happy to hear your news, and—"

"It's wonderful, isn't it?" Mimi chattered on. "A real Christmas miracle. It would have been such a loss if—"

"In fact," I said, talking over her, "with us in the audience today is one of LAPD's robbery-homicide detectives, Detective Lewis. He was there the day of the robbery. And if I might, Kari, I'd like to ask Detective Lewis to join us. Perhaps he might be able to shed some light on your good news." I paused, nodded towards his table and gestured to an empty seat between myself and Bunny. When Lewis sat down, I handed him an extra set of earphones.

Bunny glanced over at me. The look on her face said it all. *Happy news, Carol.* Her eyes narrowed. I shrugged. I wasn't about to let the opportunity pass. Mimi had opened the door and it was better news than either Kari or I could have planned. The necklace was found. I couldn't just leave it at that. This was Liz Taylor's La Peregrina, estimated to be worth eleven million dollars. It didn't get bigger than that, not in LA, and not on an entertainment-based radio station.

Bunny bristled beside me, readjusting herself in her seat as I recapped the activities of the robbery, careful to leave out the gory details of Ms. Pero's death, and quickly introduced Lewis. I explained the detective was a member of LAPD's robbery-homicide division and had been in the area the morning of the bombing. He was following up on another recent burglary when he heard the alarm and raced to the scene.

My first question concerned the necklace.

"This is stunning news Mimi's reporting. She's obviously extremely excited, but I have to ask—Westin's still has yet to issue a list of the stolen items, and I'm curious: did you know the necklace had been found?"

"To be honest, I'm as surprised as you and anxious to get the details." Lewis explained that he was here today because he and his wife were celebrating their anniversary. But he was sure his team would be filling him in shortly.

"Detective, I know you can't talk specifically about the case, but the police have issued a description and a photo of a possible suspect. Is there anything you can add?"

"Carol, I'm not going to give details on an open investigation. However, I will say, it's no secret there's been an increase in the number of jewelry store robberies in the Beverly Hills area, and, despite all our due diligence, we weren't surprised Westin's was hit."

"Not surprised?" Bunny leaned closer to Lewis and, grabbing the mic in front of him, shot me a look. *I'll take this.* "Are you saying the police knew Westin's was going to be robbed?"

Lewis smiled at me. I could see he appreciated my attempts to interview him had been compromised by Bunny hijacking the mic between them.

"Ever hear of a group called the Pink Panthers?" Lewis asked.

"Like in the Peter Sellers movies?" Bunny put her elbows on the table and leaned closer to Lewis. "I love Peter Sellers."

Lewis answered, "They were named after the series. Partly because their crimes were so cinematic and, for lack of a better word, spectacular. The group's believed to be behind some of the largest diamond heists of the century. Several years ago, I was assigned to join a special task force to study some of what was happening in Europe. At the time the Pink Panthers had just hit Henry Westin's in Paris. It was very similar to the hit here. It occurred right before Christmas. Only in Paris it was four men, all dressed as women, with wigs and makeup. They entered the store brandishing handguns, threatening customers and frightening employees. They demanded the safe be unlocked and then made off with one hundred and seven million dollars in heirloom jewelry and diamonds. The only reason they didn't get away with more was because a lot of Westin's more exotic pieces were already here in Beverly Hills. They'd been sent ahead for the awards season."

"And you think this Wigged Bandit Carol's reporting on is related to the robbery in Paris?"

"There are elements of that case we find interesting. As for the Wigged Bandit, all I can tell you at this point is she's a person of interest we'd very much like to talk to."

"And what about the jewels? Were they ever found?" Bunny asked.

"For all we know, they could be in a jewelry store window in Beverly Hills right now. They may have been sold, resold, and remounted, or they could just as easily be buried somewhere where nobody can find them."

"And you think these people are here in Beverly Hills now to pick up what they missed in Paris? You make it sound like whoever's behind this came with a shopping list."

"If there's anything I've learned about jewel thieves, it's that they take their time plotting their hits and that the jewels themselves are almost never found. As for the thieves, the good ones anyway, they frequently get away with it. The masterminds behind the Pink Panthers remain at large. They consider themselves above the law. For them, it's more of a sport than a crime. A lot of them are in it more for the bragging rights than the actual jewels. It's a game for them."

I jumped in. I couldn't let Bunny, owner's wife or not, run away with the interview. This was my story. "Given what you know about these types of robberies, Detective, and the fact that Miss Taylor's necklace appears not to have been stolen after all, is there any chance LAPD might be luckier here than the investigators were in Europe?"

"We certainly hope so, Carol."

Matt signaled Kari he had a caller on the line and shoved a small white erasable board beneath her nose. Lewis shifted his eyes to the board and smiled. *Carmen, line two.*

I locked eyes with Kari. She thanked Lewis and then announced we had a surprise caller on the line.

In a soft voice, not much louder than that of a purring kitten, Carmen came on the air.

"I want to thank everyone who called my agent expressing their concern for my well-being. While I was shaken up by the events at Henry Westin's, I assure you all I'm just fine."

"Carmen, dear," Kari jumped in before I had a chance. "Can you explain to us what happened?"

"As you all know by now, I'd gone by Henry Westin's to drop off a diamond necklace and earrings. They needed to be cleaned and I wanted the mountings checked. Like my sister, I planned to wear them for next week's awards show. It's my understanding that after I had left, there was an explosion and my necklace was stolen.

I know Mimi thinks this must have something to do with my husband's activities, but, honestly, much as I love you, Mim, you do tend to be a little dramatic. I'm afraid there's really nothing to this. I was simply in the wrong place at the wrong time and, fortunately, everything is fine. I'd like to say thank you to my fans, the Beverly Hills police, and the LAPD for all they're doing to recover any lost jewels."

Kari wrapped the show, and I glanced down at the pre-approved news reports Tyler had selected for my portion of the show. I wanted to trash the stories. News of Carmen's reappearance and Lewis' statement on the recent rash of robberies, how they appeared to be related and perhaps even connected to an international jewel ring, seemed far more important. Certainly more substantial than the chick-lite features I was required to read. But with Bunny sitting next to me, I didn't dare. I was forced to stick with the script.

"Looks like Santa Claus might have to give two young boys a black mark against their names this Christmas. The two dialed 911 in an attempt to reach Santa and ended up sending emergency response units to their home. The boys' mother said she had no idea what the boys had done until a fireman showed up on her doorstep and asked if there was a problem."

CHAPTER 9

I hadn't planned on going to the polo matches in Santa Barbara on Saturday, but by Friday, Monday's robbery was old news. There was little happening with the investigation, the Wigged Bandit was still at large, and I hadn't received any other mysterious calls to make me think "Tomi-with-an-i" was anything but a prank. Whoever the Wigged Bandit was, she had gone dark, and with no further robberies to report on, I'd hit a dead end in my investigation. The police department had nothing new, and I hadn't heard a thing from Eric.

Meanwhile, Tyler had assigned me to produce KCHC's annual Christmas Wish Campaign, which had me reading through stacks of listener letters, most of them hard-luck stories, and selecting one that KCHC's Christmas Santa could answer. Every day I produced a sixty-second vignette, selecting bits and pieces from the letter I'd read over holiday music. Something that KCHC's Christmas Santa could easily fix, either with a few hundred dollars from the station's Christmas Fund or in the form of gift certificates from some of our advertisers. It made for a very poignant feel-good moment, but by Friday my Christmas wish was to get away from the station. I needed a break.

Sheri suggested we check out the polo matches in Santa Barbara. Charlie was going off to his dad's for the weekend and had asked Clint to go with him, so why not? Sheri didn't want to miss an opportunity to see Umberto Diaz de la Roca up close, and since I'd never seen a polo match, I thought it might be fun.

The drive up to Santa Barbara was postcard perfect. Just past

Ventura, the 101 narrows and hugs the coastline. On one side, the Pacific's sparkling blue waters were dotted with surfers in black wetsuits, straddling their boards and waiting for waves, while on the other, the green rolling hills were bunched with bungalows nestled among wine vineyards, avocado trees, and citrus orchards. It was exactly what I needed; even the air was intoxicating.

As Sheri drove, I pulled up as much information as I could from my iPhone about polo. Teams were made up of four players, who may ride as many as four or five horses per game. Games were one and a half hours long. Periods were called chukkers. And polo ponies weren't ponies at all, but actually horses known for their agility, not because of their size or breed. "And get this; it's one of the few sports where you can't be left-handed. It'd be like driving on the wrong side of the road."

Sheri wasn't listening. Her mind was elsewhere. With no comment concerning my research, she started talking about Diaz: his aristocratic roots, his business holdings, and his many extramarital affairs. According to Sheri, Diaz had as many ex-lovers in his stable of stars as he did polo ponies in the barn, and he liked to travel with many of them. It was no wonder Carmen had left him. What I didn't understand was why someone like Carmen would remain so closely involved in her husband's affairs.

The minute we pulled into the parking lot of the Santa Barbara Polo and Racquet Club, I felt like we'd entered another world. A valet took Sheri's car and directed us to one of the four polo fields, where white hospitality tents with red-vested attendants had been set up for the event. Inside the main hospitality tent, celebrities and fans intermingled, all casually dressed in their sporting best and drinking champagne from Waterford crystal goblets and eating caviar off silver trays. A server offered Sheri and me glasses of Dom Pérignon, and we wandered outside to the field, where the scene was only slightly less ostentatious. In the warm sunshine, guests stood idly checking on the string of polo ponies, talking casually with more Hollywood stars, trainers, and grooms, while riders, dressed in their breeches and boots, milled about. It was no wonder polo was called the sport of kings. I felt as though we'd been invited to the court and were rubbing shoulders with Hollywood royalty.

We hadn't been outside but a moment when Sheri poked me in the ribs and nodded to the string of polo ponies. Following her gaze, I noticed Mimi standing with Diaz and another young woman who appeared to be grooming one of the horses.

I'd never seen Diaz in person, only in small black and white headshots in the newspaper. Most of them were old, perhaps taken ten years ago when he and Carmen were in the midst of their never-finalized divorce. But with his dark curly hair, deep tan, and white jodhpurs that left little to the imagination, Diaz could have been a stand-in for Michelangelo's *David*.

"You see that remarkable creature over there?"

"The horse?" I joked.

"No." Sheri laughed. "That girl."

I glanced back at the young dark-haired woman grooming one of the polo ponies. Even with her back to us, it was easy to see she was attractive. With long wavy hair hanging loosely over her shoulders and dressed in riding breeches and tall black riding boots, she was a knockout.

"That's Donatella. The young trainer Diaz left Carmen for. Like I said, he never leaves them behind on a trip, and judging by way Mimi's standing next to him, she's here to protect her interest."

"In Diaz? I thought Mimi said he was—"

"Was what? Married to her sister?" Sheri gave me a look that told me I was beyond all hope. "Don't you *ever* read the tabloids? Mimi's had her eye on Diaz since the day they met."

I was about to go on about how silly I thought tabloid journalism was when I noticed a red convertible Maserati approaching the end of the field. Sitting in the passenger seat with a silk scarf about her head was Carmen Montague and driving, wearing a sports coat and cap I'd never seen before, was Eric.

Sheri turned to me. "I get that we're not supposed to be talking about it, but did you know Eric would be here?"

"No," I said sternly. "I certainly did not."

"Well, then this *is* going to be interesting." Sheri stepped back and said she was going to check out the polo ponies, leaving me on my own.

I had no idea exactly how I was going to handle meeting Eric socially, particularly with Carmen on his arm. I didn't want to make the situation uncomfortable. I realized this was accidental, but there was little I could do. The two of them were approaching the front entrance of the hospitality tent. Carmen's arm was linked loosely in the crook of Eric's elbow. My feet refused to move. I had to think fast.

"Carmen?" I extended my hand and ignored Eric's gaze. "I'm Carol Childs, with KCHC talk radio. I've been trying to reach you."

"The reporter?" She stopped and adjusted her dark glasses. I thought for a moment she might be about to shake my hand, but instead she squeezed Eric's elbow tighter, pulling his arm closer beneath her breast. I wanted to kill her.

I smiled through my teeth. "Yes, I was—"

"I apologize," she said. "I'm afraid I can't talk to you now. My publicist is around here somewhere; perhaps you could chat with her." Carmen looked over her shoulder, spotting Diaz and Mimi, and turned to Eric. "James, could you help find Penny and introduce her to Carol? I need to talk with my sister."

I watched as Carmen unleashed herself from Eric's supporting arm and sashayed off in the direction of her sister and Diaz.

"Is it James or Jason? I'm having trouble keeping up." I smiled disingenuously, enjoying the moment, and waited for Eric's response.

Eric glanced back in Carmen's direction, then put his hand gently on my elbow, leading me towards the front of the tent. "What are you doing here, Carol?"

"Sheri invited me. She thought it might be fun. Besides, I needed a break from the day to day. You know, burglaries, robberies. That kind of thing. They can be such a bore."

Eric shook his head. "I get it, Carol. I know—"

"Believe me," I interrupted. I knew Eric couldn't explain his situation, but I could at least justify my own. "I had no idea you'd be here. But since you are, would you mind introducing me to Carmen's publicist?"

Eric nodded in the direction of the parking lot where a twenty-something woman was getting out of a convertible Volkswagen. "Her name's Penny Salvatti. But I assume you already know that."

I smiled.

Carmen's publicist was maybe six feet—taller than me—and thin, with a mass of red hair she wore in a ponytail beneath a baseball cap low on her brow. Getting out of the car, she spotted Eric and waved, then, clutching a clipboard, came running like a gawky young Army recruit.

"Miss Salvatti, this is Carol Childs with KCHC Talk Radio. Miss Montague suggested you talk."

Penny glanced at the clipboard then back at me. "Yes, KCHC radio. We've actually spoken."

"I was hoping I might be able to talk to Carmen about her experience. Where she's been. These last couple of days, it's like she just vanished," I said.

Eric stepped back slightly, a thin smile on his lips as he crossed his arms and waited. I could read his mind. No way was I going to get the real story.

"It's not something she wants to talk about. But if you like, I know Mr. Paley, the security guard from Westin's, is here. Miss Montague insisted I send over tickets to both Mr. Churchill and Mr. Paley as a thank you. I'm sure I could find him for you and you could discuss whatever you like about the robbery with him."

I glanced back at Eric. He shrugged his shoulders and winked. I felt a spark in the pit of my stomach and had to bite back a nervous laugh. Pretending I wasn't involved with Eric, particularly in front of strangers, had a sense of intrigue about it. My eyes followed him as he excused himself and disappeared into the tent.

Despite my awkward encounter with Eric, I enjoyed the first half of the game. It was fast, furious, and muddy. It had rained the night before. Not enough to drown out the game, but enough to soften the field and make for a lot of muddy divots that needed to be stomped back into place for the game to safely continue. Sheri told me halftime was traditionally when the grooms and their families used to go out onto the field and do the dirty work. Today, it was like a seventh-inning stretch. Fans were invited to the field, drinks were refreshed, and the divots, muddy or otherwise, were replaced by patrons who under other circumstances would never get their hands dirty.

During halftime, I pulled Sheri with me out to the midfield where I did my best to navigate us inconspicuously close to Eric and Carmen. I was hoping to catch bits and pieces of their conversation. Perhaps Carmen might drop some hint about the robbery or, equally as interesting to me, some clue about how things were heating up between the two of them. After all, far as I knew, Eric had spent the last four days in her company. As her "escort."

I was standing with my back to Carmen, miming a conversation with Sheri when I heard Mimi.

"You need to back off." The voice was high-pitched and threatening.

I turned around to see Mimi with a muddy divot in her hand, facing off with her sister.

"Oh yeah? What are you going to do about it? Are you threatening me?" Carmen, half a head taller than her sister, took a step closer to her, another muddy divot in her hand.

"He doesn't love you. You're never going to get him back. He's just using you." Mimi's face was red with rage.

"Well, that's my problem, isn't it? He's my husband, and I can do whatever I like." With that, Carmen stuffed the muddy divot down her sister's snowy white cashmere sweater, then smeared the palm of her hand against Mimi's chest.

"You bitch!"

Mimi grabbed what remained of the grassy, muddy divot from between her breasts and, making a fist, started to pound on Carmen's shoulders. Eric grabbed Carmen by the hand and pulled her away. Leaving Mimi like a spoiled child, a fashionista in breeches and riding boots with tears streaming down her face.

"You'll be sorry," Mimi yelled. "He never wanted you."

I stood in the center of the field trying to take in everything I had just seen when my thoughts were interrupted. Penny Salvatti came running in my direction.

"Miss Childs. I found Mr. Paley for you, like Carmen asked. He's in the barn, but he suggested you could call him later. He's looking at a horse."

CHAPTER 10

Tyler called while Sheri and I were in the car driving home from the polo match. Kari Rhodes had phoned him in a hissy fit. She'd come down with the chicken pox. The outbreak was blamed on a small but growing group of Californians Against Vaccinations that was causing an increase in the number of childhood diseases, like measles and chicken pox, that were once considered nearly obliterated. Unfortunately, as a child Kari never had the pox, and now she had been exposed. Her temperature had spiked to one hundred and two, and her doctor had forbidden her to go out in public. According to Tyler she was a mass of itchy hives, which she was treating with a yellow cream she said made her look like a melted wax figure. Knowing Kari, I was certain she had tried everything to cover the spots, but unable to do anything about the itching, had finally relented, calling Tyler at the last minute.

"I need you, Carol, to cover the American Music Awards tomorrow night."

"The Music Awards? But I—"

What I wanted to say was that reporting on Justin Bieber's various bad boy antics was the extent of my music knowledge. Beyond that, I had a tin ear.

"I don't have a choice, Carol. I need you to take it." Tyler said he would email me Kari's notes along with Mimi's number. "She says you need to call her. The two of them were planning to go together and..." He paused. I knew I wasn't going to like what followed. "She's arranged for an escort for you."

"An escort? Why would I need—"

Sheri looked over at me. She had been catching one side of the conversation, and when she heard the word "escort" raised a brow in my direction and mouthed, "Eric?"

I tried to protest, but it was no use. Tyler insisted; if I had a problem, I should call Mimi. I hung up and looked over at Sheri.

"It appears I'm going to the American Music Awards tomorrow night."

"That's great news." I could see from the needle rising on the speedometer Sheri was excited. "So what are we going to wear?"

"We? Sorry, girlfriend, *we* aren't wearing anything. I'd love to have you go with me, but this is work. I'm going alone, or rather, with an assigned escort." I explained Mimi had hired one for the evening, and that I'd be wearing my little black dress.

I had splurged three hundred dollars on a classic Donna Karan, and I'd barely taken the tags off yet, wearing it only once. My cost per wear, my personal barometer for figuring the cost of the dress divided by the number of times I'd worn it, was still into the triple digits.

Sheri looked disappointed. My thoughts, however, were more panicked. While I had spent my career in radio, most of it was on the AM side, focused on news and talk. Music wasn't my strong suit. I would have to spend the night studying *Billboard* magazines and other top industry rags just to be ready for tomorrow's show. My second thought was even scarier. How was I going to avoid looking like I wasn't stalking Eric, particularly after today? I was certain he would be there with Carmen. I really wasn't looking forward to another awkward run-in.

Once home, I reviewed Kari's notes for the show. Thankfully, she'd forwarded a detailed list of the nominees. Most of the names on the list were barely recognizable, and I realized I had my work cut out for me. I skimmed through the rest of the notes, then picked up the phone and called Mimi. I began by apologizing, saying that since I'd be working the event we couldn't possibly go together. I'd be way too busy, and, by the way, I really didn't need an escort. They'd only be in the way.

"Nonsense," she said. "I can understand you'll be preoccupied, filling in for Kari with all those stars. But there's no reason you can't attend my after-party, and for that you'll need an escort. Don't argue, it's already arranged. There's nothing you can do about it."

"Yes, but—"

"Listen to me, Carol. My sister and I go to these things all the time. We're not actors or musicians, but everybody expects us to be there. And nobody hits the red carpet at one of these affairs without a walker."

"A walker?"

"Good-looking young model types, each more delicious than the last. It's their job to escort the nominees up in front of the cameras, that's all it is."

"But I'm not going to be in front of the cameras."

"But you're with me, and the cameras will be following me. They always do, and when I show up with a good-looking man on my arm it keeps everybody talking. Besides, these walkers aren't just to make me look good, they're also along to make certain my Liz Taylor necklace and I get home safe and sound. Never hurts to have a little hot muscle with you."

I continued to protest, but I was overruled.

"It's too late, Carol. Kari knew I'd have an escort and insisted she have one too. She thought it'd be fun. You know Kari. What could I do, refuse? So I ordered one up and now he's all yours."

She said it as though she had called for a pizza delivery. But my curiosity was piqued. If Eric was there with Carmen and working undercover, how many other FBI agents would also be there? Knowing Mimi was wearing Liz Taylor's necklace made me think her escort had to be FBI. I couldn't help but wonder if my assigned walker might also be one of Eric's team. I cringed at the thought.

CHAPTER 11

The red carpet was out in full force by the time I arrived for the American Music Awards. The event was scheduled at L.A. Live, Hollywood's answer to New York's Times Square with its big-screen TVs and LED billboards. Located directly across the street from the Staples Center, the forty-thousand-square-foot plaza was crowded with fans, movers and shakers, and paparazzi who would sell their mother for a position close enough to the action. Together they were all standing like sheep, huddled shoulder to shoulder behind the red velvet ropes, hoping to get a photo or at least a glimpse of the arriving stars. All day long crews had been setting up lights and cameras and rolling out the red carpet, and now, with the arrival of the nominees, it was all about the action.

Kari's notes warned me to expect the unexpected. I had heard horror stories about stars falling on the red carpet, wardrobe malfunctions, and worse, things like catfights between rivals and ex-lovers being hustled ahead in line to avoid an embarrassing encounter. But I was ready. Armed with my mic and dressed conservatively in my little black dress, I was poised for the unexpected and ready for the predictable, if ever there was such a thing in Hollywood.

My job was simply to mix with as many celebs as possible before the event and to report back to the station with mini updates. What Tyler wanted was my take on the crowd, the excitement and, of course, a detailed description of what everybody was wearing. The type of thing Bunny Morganstern would love.

Snippets of interviews with nominees that KCHC's evening host, Cupid, could use with his entertainment report. It was a three-part assignment. Interview as many nominees and celebs as possible before the event. Stick around for the show and take notes and names of the winners. And finally, prepare a glowing report in time for the eleven o'clock news.

Aside from the names of the winners and the designer gowns they were wearing, I could have written my report blind, without even attending the event. Due to the size of the crowd and the rush, there was no time to ask any in-depth questions. It just wasn't possible. The nominees were ushered like cattle. After walking the red carpet and having their pictures taken, they were waved into the arms of waiting reporters, who all asked the same questions, congratulated them, and then pushed them onto the next. By the time I got to them, most were anxious to enter the theater where they could relax their plastic smiles and disappear from cameras and the frenzy of welcoming fans.

I was happy by the time the evening ended. I had filed the last of my live updates and I was looking for a way to cut the evening short. I was hoping I might be able to skip out on Mimi's after-party at the Ritz Carlton when I received a text: "Looking forward to seeing you. We're at Wolfy's on the twenty-fourth floor. Don't disappoint."

Wolfy's was short for Wolfgang Puck's restaurant, Nest, where views of the city were only outdone by the food. Mimi had reserved several tables. With a demand for my presence and the fact Mimi was so close to Kari, I had to show. I told myself I'd stop by for a single glass of wine, nothing more. But when I walked into the restaurant, I realized this wasn't going to be a quick and easy meet.

The lounge area was crowded and the dim blue mood lighting made it difficult to see over the shoulders of those waiting for a table in front of me. I stood up on my tiptoes. Where was Mimi? There was a buzz of excitement in the room. The clinking of crystal champagne glasses interspersed with whispered conversations and bursts of laughter, like sudden little whirlpools of energy coming from within the crowd, drowning out any opportunity of actually being heard.

Servers with silver trays above their heads wandered through the crowd, offering champagne and hors d'oeuvres. It was impossible to see through the groups of people huddled so close together. Even in heels, Mimi was maybe five foot four. She was easily dwarfed by those taller. I couldn't see her anywhere, and I was about to give up when I heard my name from within the din.

"Carol, over here."

I looked in the direction of the voice and spotted a tall, buff-looking gentleman in a black tux. One of Mimi's escorts? He pointed to the corner of the room where Mimi was seated on a sofa in front of a large floor-to-ceiling window overlooking the LA skyline. With her was a small group of people, all with drinks in hand. She waved to get my attention. "Carol, come join us."

A roomful of eyes flipped in my direction, then back to Mimi. A murmur echoed through the room. Word that Mimi was wearing Liz Taylor's famed million-dollar necklace spread through the crowd like a wild game of gossip. "Isn't that Mimi?" "Is that the necklace? I thought it had been stolen."

Then, as though Moses had parted the waters, the crowd stepped aside, and Mimi stood up. She was dressed exactly as she had told Kari she planned to be, in a vintage green silk gown that fit her like a glove. And around her neck, hanging delicately above her full breasts, was the most spectacular pearl and diamond necklace I had ever seen. The pear-shaped pearl dangled beneath a diamond and ruby-encrusted festoon. It was almost too big to be believed. Even in the dim lighting the pearl had a luminescence that radiated an almost iridescent glow. Like a model about to take her first steps on the runway, Mimi shyly handed her drink to her escort, lowered her sable lashes so as to avoid the gaze of those around her, and cat-walked directly across the room toward me.

With a sly smile, Mimi grabbed my hand. I followed her back to where she had reserved a secluded section of the restaurant for her private party. Seated on one of the long low leather wrap-around couches, facing a dramatic view of the city with thousands of twinkling lights below, was a group of about twenty people. All of them were absorbed in tight little conversations, their heads together while discreetly scanning the crowd LA-style, their eyes darting over the shoulders of those closest to them, hoping to spot the next big name walk in the room. One of the men, who I assumed to be Mimi's escort, stood up as we approached. He offered me a seat, and I declined.

"But you can't leave. Not yet. I have someone here for you." Mimi turned and gestured to a handsome young man.

I shook my head, more anxious than ever to be on my way. "I'm sorry, I really have to be going—"

"Nonsense. Stay." From within the group on the couch, I heard Bunny's voice. She stood up, barefoot, having kicked her shoes off, and, with a glass of champagne in her hand, approached me. She was wobbly on her feet, her eyes glassy. "Perhaps if you do, dear, your Wigged Bandit will show up. Now wouldn't that be an exciting story? I'll bet you'd love that."

If Bunny hadn't been so drunk I never would have replied, but I was growing tired of her Pollyanna approach to news and the leash I felt she had tied around my neck, restricting my reports. "If the Wigged Bandit is here, Bunny, I'm sure you'd beat me to the punch." I smiled sweetly.

"Ladies." From behind me, I felt a hand on my shoulder. I turned to see Churchill, drink in hand and as far gone as Bunny, if not more. He reeked of whiskey. "I don't think we need to worry about the Wigged Bandit. At least not tonight. Westin's has enough security here that nobody would dare bother us."

He gestured wildly with a wave of his hand. I feared he was about to topple over and put my hand on his arm to steady him. I wondered if Churchill was talking about Westin's own private security. Something he had hired to assure the safety of the La Peregrina necklace, or was he aware of the FBI's undercover operation? I couldn't be sure.

Mimi laughed and fingered the large pearl necklace around

her neck. "He's so right, Carol. I may not be safe, but with my friends here, if nothing else, they'll make certain these jewels get back to Henry Westin's, with or without me." She patted the chest of her escort, her fingers running suggestively down the lapel of his black tux.

I turned my attention back to Churchill. The old jeweler looked a little too sauced to have anything to do with security. I wondered how wise it was for a man with a heart condition to be drinking.

"It's nice to see you're feeling well enough to be out and about," I said.

"Wouldn't miss it. Big night for the jewels, you know."

"It certainly is," I said.

I was about to make another attempt to leave when I notice Carmen approaching from across the room. She'd changed from the black lace gown she had worn earlier in the evening for the awards show to a very revealing red cocktail dress. It showed off her flawless figure and an even more spectacular diamond ruby necklace. But what caught my eye was Eric walking behind her, looking like he'd just stepped off the cover of *GQ*.

I knew it wasn't unusual for celebrities attending events like tonight's awards show to book a suite of rooms in the hotel. Many did so, planning on numerous changes so they might appear fresh and comfortable for the after-parties. However, I wasn't expecting to see Carmen at her sister's party. Not after yesterday's mudslinging affair, and certainly not with Eric.

"Mims." Carmen reached her hands out, diamond bracelets up and down her wrists, and beckoned her sister to come to her. Mimi responded in like fashion. The two embraced with light Hollywood air-kisses on each side of their faces. If I hadn't seen yesterday's angry exchange on the polo field, I wouldn't have believed it. It was like they'd never argued a day in their lives.

Carmen placed one hand on Mimi's shoulder and, pulling her closer, gently lifted the diamond necklace about her sister's neck, examining it carefully.

"So this is it then? The famous La Peregrina."

Mimi nodded, the look on her face as though she'd one-upped her sister.

Carmen glanced over at Churchill. "Next time, Edmond, I hope you'll remember me with something so quaint."

Churchill nodded. I could see he wasn't about to get into a bidding war between the two.

Turning away and looking as though this was the first time she'd ever seen me, Carmen's eyes scanned my person head to toe. "And…just what is this?" Her eyes came to rest on the brooch I was wearing.

"Oh, this?" My hand went to the pin on my shoulder. As I left the house, I'd taken one final look in the mirror by the front door and at the last minute decided my little black dress needed a little sparkle. I remembered the Phoenix brooch the old woman in Beverly Hills had given me the morning of the explosion. I returned to my bedroom, found it in the bottom of my jewelry box where I'd nearly forgotten about it, and hastily pinned it on.

"Yes." Carmen stepped forward, eyes and fingers to my brooch. Directing Churchill to take a look, she said, "It's very unusual, isn't it, Edmond? I don't think I've ever seen anything so vibrant or original. Where on earth did you find such a gem?"

Eric looked at me. I could see he had the same thought.

"Do you have any idea what it might be worth?" Carmen looked curiously at Churchill.

The old jeweler took his glasses from his breast pocket and placing them on his face, asked if he might examine the pin. I nodded. He leaned closer to my shoulder, his arthritic fingers shaking as he carefully traced the shape of the bird's fiery wings.

"Well, if I didn't know better, I'd say it was a copy from the private collection of the late Huguette Clark. The Phoenix Rising. It would have been one of her favorites. Are you familiar with her?" He looked at me, his eyes questioning mine.

"No," I said.

"She was an heiress. Her father made a fortune in mining,

banking, and railroads. She had an estate in Santa Barbara until a couple years ago. Beautiful place. Right on the water. Died a total recluse."

I put my hand back on top of the brooch to cover it. My heart was pounding. In my mind, I retraced my steps the day of the robbery. I could see the old woman struggling with her bags and remembered how I had stopped to help. Had she stolen the brooch? She had seemed so helpless. And I'd carried her bags for her all the way back to my Jeep. Please, God, tell me I didn't help the Wigged Bandit escape.

I managed to muster a reply. "I'm flattered, but the lighting's poor in here, and, like you said, Mr. Churchill, it's probably just a copy. One of many, I'm sure."

Churchill put his hand on my shoulder then whispered in my ear, the smell of whiskey overpowering, "Like I said, Ms. Childs, *if* I didn't know better. But in your case, I'd get an appraisal." He patted me lightly on the back and then turned his attention back to Carmen. "Did you bring the ring?"

Carmen looked distraught. A frown crossed her brow, then she turned and looked at Eric. "Do you mind, James? I forgot my bag. I have something in it I need to give to Edmond. It's in the room. Would you be a love and fetch it for me? I'm sure Mimi's friend here won't mind filling in for you and watching over me while you're away. And Mimi, you won't care, will you, darling?" She glanced hungrily at Mimi's escort, like she planned to eat him for dessert, then back to me. "And while you're at it, James, why don't you take Ms. Childs with you? She's been making eyes at you from the moment we walked in. Perhaps she'll be luckier with you than I've been."

CHAPTER 12

I would have done anything to get away from Mimi's after-party, but being dismissed by Carmen and leaving with Eric felt wrong, even awkward. The fact Eric was working undercover and I wasn't supposed to know but clearly did only added to the problem. And then there was this new issue concerning the brooch. I had an uncomfortable feeling it was somehow connected to the robberies and that maybe Eric thought so as well. Added to the mix was the overwhelming thought of being alone with Eric, particularly in Carmen's private suite. After our self-imposed hiatus, the idea had me feeling like I was sixteen again.

Eric had to be feeling the same thing. He stood behind me in the elevator, and as the doors closed, he rested his hands lightly on my shoulders. With his lips pressed ever so softly against my ear, he whispered, "You again."

"Yes, me," I said. I leaned back against him. Thoughts of anything else, the brooch, his work, my job, melted from my mind. His gentle touch sent small electric charges up and down my body as he wrapped his arms around me.

"You shouldn't be here, Carol."

"I know." I closed my eyes and leaned back against his chest. I felt myself growing warm, my temperature rising as the elevator took us up to the penthouse. When the doors opened, Eric took my hand and led the way down the hall, past several more plainclothed security guards who appeared to ignore our passing.

"Welcome to Carmen's retreat." Eric stepped ahead of me into the room and gestured to the surrounding opulence. "Three thousand square feet of sky-high luxury, for one night only."

Inside was the most luxurious suite I'd ever seen. It was hard to believe anyone would lavish such extravagance upon themselves, particularly when they lived in the same city and only planned to use this as a changing room. But obviously money wasn't an issue. Fresh floral arrangements were everywhere. A masseuse's table had been set up in the center of the great room. Gowns, shoes, and garments were hung on a porter's gold clothing rack. Changes for Carmen's walk down the red carpet, the awards show, something for the after-party, and a negligee. On the sofa, I noticed the small clutch Carmen had sent Eric to fetch. He picked it up.

"We need to talk, Carol."

Behind him, thousands of tiny white lights from the windows overlooking the city blinked back at me. I stepped closer and laced my fingers flirtatiously around his neck.

"You don't need to rush back to Carmen?" I was enjoying this little seductive moment, payback for time with Carmen, and hoping if he had any thoughts of discussing the brooch she had noticed, I could divert his attention.

He put his hands on top of mine, Carmen's small white bag still between his fingers, and smiled into my eyes. "Carmen's fine, Carol. There's enough security in this hotel to guard Fort Knox."

"And you don't think she'll be waiting for you to bring her bag? That she won't be concerned about the ring or Mr. Churchill?"

"It's the same ring she had on the morning of the robbery," Eric said.

"Could I see it?"

"The ring?"

"Yes. If it was important enough for her to send you up here to get, it must be fabulous. Do you mind?"

Eric stepped back from me, opened the small white clutch, and took out the largest diamond ring I'd ever seen. He held it between us, like a forbidden fruit, and together we stared at it, my hands on top of his. It was spectacular. A huge square cut stone, so big it didn't look real.

"I can't believe she forgot that."

"Carmen was supposed to give it to Churchill the day of the robbery. She says it slipped her mind, that she was so busy with her necklace and earrings that she forgot to take it off and leave it with him. But the ring's not why we need to talk, Carol."

I felt my stomach turn. We were back to the brooch. There was no getting around it. Eric hadn't forgotten, and I could think of a thousand other things I wanted to talk about. Things that wouldn't make it look like I'd stepped into the middle of a case he was working and maybe even helped a suspect to escape.

"Maybe we better hurry back," I said. "Carmen must be getting worried."

"I don't think a little longer will hurt. But you, on the other hand, you look like something might be bothering you." He put Carmen's ring back in the bag and put his hand back on mine. "Is there something you want to tell me?"

Something I wanted to tell him? I pulled my hand away. What about what I wanted him to tell me? I had so many questions. About him. About Carmen. About the diamonds. About what he knew.

I touched the pin above my pounding heart. "You mean about this brooch?" I fessed up. There was no point in avoiding the obvious.

"Yes, Carol, the brooch. Where did you get it?" Eric took my fingers in his hand and waited for me to reply.

I explained how after my broadcast on the day of the robbery that I was coming back to my car when I stopped and helped an old lady. "An old *gray*-haired lady," I said. The way I said it made me wonder, was I trying to justify it to myself or convince Eric the woman I stopped to help couldn't possibly be the redheaded bandit everyone was looking for?

"And you didn't think there was anything suspicious about that?"

"No. Not at the time." I knew I sounded defensive. My voice had a shrill ring to it. I took a deep breath and concentrated on sounding more controlled. "Look, she was an old lady, and I had just witnessed an explosion and *you* coming out of Westin's with Carmen on your arm. I wasn't exactly thinking clearly."

Eric stared into my eyes, the look on his face dumbstruck. I wasn't sure if he was feeling sorry for me or couldn't believe what I was telling him.

"Besides, you know how I am. I rescue lost dogs and talk to old people." If there was one problem Eric and I had, it was that he thought I was too trusting. Maybe I was.

"Okay," he said. It appeared he was putting things in perspective and working very hard to understand how I came be in such a predicament. And, I thought, maybe he understood how it was partially his fault I had been so sidetracked. "This old woman, Carol, could you describe her any better than that? How tall she was, size, weight?"

"Old. Bent-over. Like I said, *gray* hair, and she was carrying several large shopping bags."

"Go on. What else did you notice about her?"

"The bags were full. Overloaded, in fact. I think she had a coat or something covering one of them, and she was wearing gloves. I remember the gloves. They were long and white. Out of season, come to think of it."

"That's good." Eric smiled and squeezed my hand. "What happened next?"

"She looked like she might have been struggling with the bags, and I offered to carry some for her. She seemed appreciative, and when we got to the garage, she gave me the brooch as a thank you for helping her. I tried to tell her I couldn't possibly accept it, but the valet interrupted me. By the time I found my wallet she had disappeared. To be honest, I totally forgot about it until this afternoon when I was looking for something to dress up my outfit for tonight's show. I had no idea if it was real. I thought it was just some fancy piece of costume jewelry the old woman had on her jacket."

"Do you mind?" Eric carefully unpinned the brooch from my

dress and looked closely at the workmanship. "I'm no jeweler, but this does look real."

"I know. Churchill told me as much a few minutes ago. And now I think the woman who gave it to me may very well be the Wigged Bandit, and maybe I helped her escape."

I could see Eric was making a mental note of everything I told him. He asked me to recount the events of the morning of the bombing and everything that had happened since then. I began with telling him what he already knew. How Sheri and I had seen him on the street with Carmen just moments before the doors on Henry Westin's blew open. How I'd interviewed Detective Lewis and knew Westin's wasn't the only robbery LAPD was concerned about, and how Mr. Churchill had confided in me about Carmen being a courier for her husband. That she had used a black eyeglass case to deliver loose cut stones and gems to Henry Westin's the morning of the explosion. And that I suspected the FBI was involved and knew Eric had to be working undercover.

"And since the bombing, anything else happen you think might be related?"

"Not that I can think of, why?"

"I'll explain later, but right now, I need you to think. Has anyone contacted you or sent you anything you found strange since the robbery?"

I started to shake my head, and then I remembered the crazy caller, Tomi, who had called the station the morning after the bombing. I explained to Eric what had happened.

"She kept going on about how Ms. Pero wasn't supposed to die. That it was an accident. She started to get upset, and Kari wanted to dump the call, but I stopped her and I asked Matt if he could trace it. But he said he couldn't. And then the line went dead. After a while I dismissed it. The station always gets a few crazies after a big story." I told him I had mentioned the call to Detective Lewis, but that he didn't think much about it. Said unless she called back, not to worry. "Why, you think it's connected?"

"Let's just say it wouldn't be out of character."

"Really? You think Tomi might have something to do with the robbery? That maybe she's the Wigged Bandit?"

"I don't know. But what I can tell you—off the record—is that the police reported finding several abandoned shopping bags just around the corner from the parking garage where you were the morning of the bombing. And guess what was in them?"

"I don't need to guess. A red wig."

"Among other things we believe our Wigged Bandit may have used to disguise herself for the robbery."

Dammit. I put my hand back over my heart, just below where the pin had been. It was beating even harder than it was before. I could kick myself.

"So I'm involved."

"Looks like it," Eric said.

"Okay, then suppose I ask you a few questions."

"I'll answer what I can."

"Does Carmen know who you really are? Or Churchill? Do they know the FBI's involved?"

Eric shook his head. "Not at all. And as far as Carmen's concerned, she thinks we're all professional escorts. Nothing more."

"All of you?"

Eric ignored my obvious implication and answered, "We've infiltrated Carmen's network of escorts. She hires them regularly. She doesn't like to go places alone, and it was an easy cover."

"I'll bet." I raised an eyebrow a bit sarcastically and smiled.

"Nobody knows, Carol."

"Not even Mimi? She mentioned something downstairs about security. She said they'd make sure her necklace made it back to Westin's, even if she didn't. You're telling me she doesn't know?"

"No, and we need to keep it that way. I need you to agree to leave certain facts concerning the FBI's involvement with Carmen out of your broadcast. You may be a material witness, and as such, may be useful in helping us to apprehend whoever is behind these robberies. If you agree to help, I may be able to help you fill in some information down the line. But not until then. Agreed?"

"And in the meantime?"

"Oh, I'm pretty sure between the two of us, we can come up with something." Eric looked towards the bedroom, then back at me, and winked. "Kind of a shame to let a beautiful room like this go to waste."

"I couldn't agree more." I grabbed his hand and led him into the bedroom. Between my house and Eric's boat, this was probably one of the nicest rooms we'd ever been in. What harm could it be? A little romantic rendezvous between lovers.

It wasn't until Eric's cell phone buzzed an hour later that I knew we weren't just hunting for a diamond thief anymore. He took the call and I watched as the color drained from his face.

He hung up and looked at me. "Carmen's dead."

CHAPTER 13

Eric walked ahead of me into the restaurant and disappeared. The room, which only a short while ago had been crowded with guests happily toasting one another, now looked deathly still. A low murmur encircled the room like fog. I pushed through the crowd toward the area where Mimi and her entourage had been partying.

"What happened?"

There was no answer. In the dim blue light, people stood like cardboard cutouts, their arms wrapped tightly around themselves, staring blankly at one another, uncertain what to say.

From behind Mimi and Bunny, I got my first glimpse of Carmen's body. It was spread ungracefully across the end of the couch, her arms thrust outward, her legs crumpled beneath her as though she had suddenly fallen backward. Her head was cocked against the back of the sofa at an awkward angle, her mouth open like a fish gasping for air. I noticed Mr. Churchill next to her, adjusting her skirt. It had slipped above her pale white thighs, exposing a garter belt and lacy panties. Even in death, Churchill was doing what he could to protect his client.

I turned to Mimi and asked again, "What happened? I thought your escort was watching over her."

Mimi shook her head, her mouth trying to form words, but there was no sound.

Bunny grabbed her arm. "It's okay, dear, let me explain." Bunny looked at me like she expected me to take notes. "We were talking and having drinks. Carmen had a question about tonight's show and sent him away to find a program."

"The server," Mimi interrupted, her voice nearly cracking. Standing on her tiptoes she pointed towards the kitchen as though she were looking for someone. "He had just refreshed her drink. Then Carmen started to—"

"Choke," Bunny said. She continued to hold Mimi's hand while she described the scene. "Carmen grabbed her throat. It looked like she had swallowed the wrong way, like she was going to be sick. She started to wheeze and then cough all at the same time, like she couldn't catch her breath. Finally, she just doubled over and fell back on the couch. Like she is now."

"Mr. Churchill called 911, but I think it's too late." Mimi looked at me like she expected me to dispute the obvious.

I hadn't seen many dead bodies in my career, but I had no doubt looking at Carmen she was gone. Her eyes had rolled back into her head, her face was slack and colorless, and her hands hung limply by her sides.

"And what about Carmen's glass?" I asked. I looked around the floor beside the couch. If Carmen had been drinking champagne, there was no flute to be seen. Mimi and Bunny were still holding theirs. What happened to Carmen's?

Both women looked at me and shook their heads.

"Who ordered the champagne?" I asked.

"I did," Mimi answered. "We were all having such a good time, I ordered another round for the group. The server brought a tray and handed a glass to Carmen. You don't suppose it was poison, do you?"

This was the second time Mimi mentioned the server. Her response seemed almost too convenient, and the fact she had mentioned poison even more so. I wouldn't have put it past her to put something into Carmen's drink. From what I knew about Mimi's relationship with her sister, she certainly may have had cause. But for the moment, her grief and surprise looked as real as the tears in her eyes.

I scanned the room for Eric. I needed to report this story, but before I did, I wanted one last word with him. I was about to leave when I saw him talking with a uniformed LAPD officer. I figured there must have been some need-to-know exchange between the two, because moments later, the officer blocked the front door and told us all we were on lockdown.

"I'm sorry, folks, we need to secure the area. Until we've had a chance to talk to everybody, nobody leaves."

As the officer continued to explain LAPD plans for evacuation, Eric pulled me aside.

"I know you're going to want to file a report with the radio station, but—"

"I know. There's a lot I can't mention. Starting with the fact the FBI was here tonight."

"As far as anyone needs to know, the plainclothes guards here tonight were simply security, hired to make certain nobody made off with any of Henry Westin's jewels."

"I guess they did that much for sure."

I pointed back at the body and then at Churchill. He was standing next to it like a sentry. Whoever had murdered Carmen hadn't done it for her jewelry. Around her neck was the necklace she'd worn to the awards show earlier that evening, a stunning diamond ruby choker I estimated to be worth be several hundred thousand dollars.

Eric didn't answer. Instead, he said we'd talk later. I watched him disappear back into the crowd and found an empty space in front one of the big plate glass windows overlooking the city. I took out my phone and called Tyler. If I hurried, I could call in the news of Carmen's death before the station went dark for the evening. If I missed, I'd have to wait until morning to break the story. I didn't want to do that. Even though the restaurant was on lockdown and nobody could leave until after police had spoken to them, everybody had cell phones. I didn't want to risk news of Carmen's death escaping the room before I had a chance to report it. I knew once news hit the street, it'd spread like a California wildfire.

CHAPTER 14

Tyler answered on the first ring.

"Carmen's dead," I blurted out before Tyler had a chance to say hello or tell me I'd reached KCHC's newsroom. "Someone or something killed her, just a few minutes ago."

"What?" The surprise in his voice was quick and cutting like a knife. "What do you mean dead? Where? How?"

I described the scene. The restaurant on the twenty-fourth floor of the Ritz Carlton. Carmen's body slumped lifelessly on the couch. A crowd of friends and fans, all helplessly staring at the body. The paramedics had arrived—too late—and were wrapping up their emergency equipment. The police were cordoning off the area, and onlookers were being questioned. The medical examiner had been called to the scene.

"All I can say, Tyler, is that between you and me, it looks suspicious. Not like a robbery gone bad. Whoever did this wanted Carmen dead. She's still wearing the ruby diamond necklace she wore to the awards show."

I could hear the clicking of computer keys in the background. Tyler had already begun to type up the story. In a few minutes, he'd interrupt KCHC's final broadcast for the night and we'd be live on air with breaking news.

"I need you to stay where you are. I want you to fill in the facts, talk to the crowd and get their reaction. I'll pull up Carmen's obit file. We'll double-team this with you there and me here in the studio."

I stayed on the air with Tyler until well after midnight,

postponing the station's overnight broadcast of popular old mystery theater plays. I wondered how many of the station's listeners tuning in and hearing "socialite drops dead at awards show" might think this was a joke, a modern-day mystery theater like that of H.G. Wells' *War of the Worlds*, before they realized it was an actual news event.

Tyler pulled up Carmen's obit file, a digital history including pictures and news stories the station kept on high-profile personalities. Information we could use at the last minute to cobble together a story in the event of an untimely death.

The file indicated Carmen and her sisters had grown up the privileged daughters of a wealthy west-side investment banker. Carmen's mother had died when she was still in college—barely eighteen—while her globe-trotting father gambled away his grief and lost much of the family fortune. Ultimately, he committed suicide while on vacation in the Bahamas, although the circumstances of his death were never confirmed. To Carmen's credit, she kept the family together, parlaying family connections into marriages of convenience for both herself and her sisters. While none of the unions had proved to be the match made in heaven she had tried to present publicly, each had secured their financial status. Listening to Tyler had me feeling almost sympathetic to her circumstances.

I filled in Tyler's report with comments from Mimi, Mr. Churchill, and a few fans who were willing to make a statement. It was well past two a.m. by the time I closed out my report and headed home.

On the drive home, I scanned the radio dial. I was curious to hear if any other news stations had picked up the story of Carmen's death and how they were reporting it. Instead, I got news of another robbery. This time at the house of Marty Montana, a popular country singer who had co-hosted the Awards Show tonight with his wife, Jennifer. The story was several hours old and I was catching an edited version from an early televised broadcast, but it caught my attention. It seemed that Montana and his wife had returned home after the awards show to find their garage door standing wide open and the back door leading to the house unlocked. I doubted anyone would have tied the news of the break-in to that of the Beverly Hills robberies, and I might not have either, until I heard Montana talking about what it was the burglar had taken.

I could picture the scene. The reporter explained he was standing outside Montana's home off Fryman Canyon in Studio City. I knew a lot of stars had second homes in the area. Studio City was considered the Valley's Beverly Hills. It was close to the studios, backed up to the Santa Monica Mountains, and was popular with hiking enthusiasts. It was also less than a mile from two local television news stations, and when something happened in trendy Studio City, it frequently made the news. It didn't take much to imagine that when the police scanner indicated there was a possible robbery in the star-studded area the TV vans had likely rolled in right behind the cops.

Montana explained that he and his wife had been picked up for the preshow around four p.m., and they remembered seeing a hiker coming out of the park, but that they didn't think it was unusual.

"There's always a steady stream of walkers coming out of the park at that hour."

I knew it wouldn't take a lot of homework for a thief to figure out who lives where in the city. Star-sighting maps were for sale on nearly every corner in Hollywood, making it easy for a fan to zero in on their favorite star's home. Some of the homes were protected behind tall walls or hedges and guarded, but a lot in the Studio City area weren't. Just nice, quiet residences along tree-lined streets. It wasn't a big stretch to think someone plotting a robbery might stake out their favorite celeb, watch their comings and goings and target the residence; particularly on a night like tonight, knowing no one would be home. All they would have to do is look like one of the hikers coming out of the park and blend in. With no one guarding the home, it'd be easy for a professional thief to break in, take what they wanted, then walk out and join the rest of the hikers. In LA, where neighbors seldom know one another, nobody would notice anything.

The reporter asked, "What did they get?"

Montana replied, "Whoever it was seemed to know what they wanted. Took a couple of watches, Rolexes, and most importantly, a diamond tennis bracelet I'd given my wife as an anniversary present. It had once belonged to Elizabeth Taylor."

I turned up the volume. Jennifer was describing the bracelet. Fourteen karat gold with white and canary diamonds. I couldn't believe it. A bracelet belonging to Liz Taylor? Was Bunny right? Did the Wigged Bandit really have a shopping list? And had she targeted the Montana's home because she knew exactly where the bracelet was and when they'd be out of the house? I was probably the only reporter in town who thought there might be a connection.

CHAPTER 15

Five and a half hours after wrapping up my report on Carmen's death, I was back in the studio preparing to deliver my top of the hour newscast when Tyler walked in. I was sleep deprived and operating on nothing but caffeine and the type of adrenaline that comes from seeing dead bodies every time I closed my eyes. No matter how much I tried to erase the vision, I couldn't get the picture of Carmen's body, lying spread eagle on the couch, out of my mind. It was haunting me.

I looked up from the stack of news stories in front of me. "Tyler, you can't possibly expect me to lead with another light-hearted story about a lost puppy or a bear in somebody's pool in Pasadena. Not after last night."

Before Tyler could answer, my cell phone buzzed. Eric. I lunged for it and held the phone to my chest. "Excuse me, it's Eric. I need to take this, it's about the case. Can you give me a minute?"

Tyler narrowed his eyes, a look he reserved for when he was about to launch into a lecture about why reporters and law enforcement were a bad match; then, shaking his head, he walked out of the studio.

I whispered into the phone, "Is everything okay?"

Despite Tyler's retreat, I didn't trust I couldn't be heard. I'd spent the night blaming myself because Eric hadn't been in the restaurant when Carmen's killer struck. Perhaps if we hadn't been fooling around in Carmen's suite, things might have been different. Eric prided himself on his job. I worried his absence might have compromised his position with the investigation and gotten him in trouble.

"Everything's fine, Carol," he answered almost too quickly.

"It's just—"

"I called to let you know the brooch you turned over to me last night is real. Churchill was right. Our investigators matched it up with a piece missing from Huguette Clark's estate. It's worth about fifty thousand dollars."

"Wow. So that's good news, right?" I was hoping to hear relief in Eric's voice. I didn't.

Instead, his voice sounded flat, void of any emotion, and professional. A tone I'd only heard him use when talking with other agents on the phone, never with me.

"And I want to thank you for turning it over to us and for the tip you gave us concerning the mystery caller." It sounded like he was reading from a script. Either that or the call was being monitored.

I stumbled in my reply. "I...I'm glad to hear that. I only hope I didn't interfere in any way with the investigation." It was a half-hearted attempt on my part to open the door and discuss what had happened last night, but with no success. Eric switched the subject instantly.

"Carol, nothing you did was a problem. In fact, everything's fine. But going forward, I've been asked to remind you this is a very sensitive investigation. The FBI and LAPD have put in a lot of time and energy, and anything you say or report, particularly with respect to the brooch or what you know about our undercover operation, could damage the work we've done. I have to ask that you not include anything about it in your news reports."

Now I was certain the call was being monitored. Eric would never talk to me in such a stilted manner. With the exception of verifying the brooch was real, he was repeating everything he had told me last night. I decided to play along and responded in like manner.

"I understand, Agent Langdon. Is there anything else I can do?"

"No. Not at the moment. But we'll be in touch."

I hung up the phone. I had a cold sinking feeling in my stomach. I hadn't eaten, but I knew food wasn't going to fill the emptiness I felt growing there.

I tapped on the door, certain Tyler was standing just outside.

He stepped back into the news booth.

"You wanted to talk?" I asked.

"Why don't you start by telling me exactly what's going on? Beginning with that call and what happened last night."

I exhaled deeply. Tyler wasn't going to like it, but what could I do? "The FBI's involved in the investigation of the Beverly Hills robberies." I figured that was no big revelation on my part. The FBI was always called in on jewelry heists and I knew Tyler knew that much. "And they were at the awards show last night—off the record—to keep an eye on Carmen and the jewels."

"Do they think Carmen's death is related to the robberies?"

"I don't know. It wasn't a robbery, that's for sure. Carmen died with the ruby necklace she wore to the show still on and Mimi went home with Liz Taylor's La Peregrina. But that wasn't why Eric called."

"Then what was it?"

I paused. I wasn't certain how I was going to tell Tyler about the Wigged Bandit.

"You're not going to like it, but I seem to have somehow become a material witness for the FBI."

"What?" Tyler looked at me, his red-freckled complexion paling as he leaned against the wall.

"The FBI believes I may have met the Wigged Bandit as I left Beverly Hills the day of the robbery. And that I may have *accidentally* helped her with bags she was carrying as I walked with her back to my car."

"Accidentally? Carol, how does one accidentally escort a thief from the scene of a crime?"

"You have to understand. I didn't know who she was. Not at the time. I thought she was just a sweet little old lady, confused by the explosion. That is, until last night, when Eric informed me the

FBI believes the Wigged Bandit and my little old lady are one and the same."

"You and Eric?" Tyler asked. "You're working together?"

"Not exactly. Like I said, I'm a material witness and he's been working undercover."

"I'm not even going to ask."

"Good," I said, "because I'm really not at liberty to say a whole lot about it. But I can tell you this: the FBI thinks the Wigged Bandit may have fixated on me."

"Fixated on you?" Tyler laughed. "Exactly what does that mean, Carol?"

"After I met her the day of the robbery, I think she called the station."

"You never said anything."

"I wasn't sure, but after talking with Eric last night he thinks this might be a good thing."

"A good thing? How is any of this a good thing?"

"Well, for one, I'm a material witness, and if she's fixated on me for whatever reason, I'd be privy to—"

"To absolutely nothing, Carol." Tyler ran his hands through his hair. "Don't you get it? You can't be both a reporter *and* a material witness for the FBI. You're one side or the other, not both. They'll pressure you for any information you've got. They can even threaten to put you in jail if you don't reveal it. And if they don't do that, they'll tie your hands with what you can and can't say because it might interfere with their investigation."

"That's not going to happen, Tyler. Besides, it's not like I was able to say a whole lot more under Bunny's chick-lite, good news restrictions anyway." I grabbed a bunch of printed news stories from the in-basket on my desk and stacked them, tapping the bottom edges together on the desk. "You don't really expect me to deliver all this chick-lite news, do you? Not after last night and Carmen's death?"

Tyler shook his head. "I didn't come in here to talk to you about Bunny. I came to tell you Kari Rhodes heard your broadcast last night. She's rallied. She called and said although she's still quarantined with the chicken pox and not well enough to come into the studio, she'll do her show live from the bedroom of her home. She's going to have both Mimi and Diaz on the air with her via phone patches. And I'm one hundred percent certain Carmen's sudden death at the awards show is bound to come up. So go ahead and do whatever you like with your report, but remember, Bunny's listening. No gory details."

Tyler walked out of the news booth, leaving me with visions of Kari sitting on top of a satin brocade comforter, her face spotted with anti-itch cream, while I sat alone in a darkened studio.

If it wasn't for his heavy Castilian accent, I would not have recognized who Kari was speaking with on the air. Umberto Diaz de la Roca sounded like a broken man. Between his voice cracking with emotion, the sobbing, and the going back and forth between Spanish and English, it was difficult to understand what the man was saying. On more than one occasion during the interview, he referred to Carmen as his wife, the woman of his dreams, and his ex. It was obvious the man was overcome with grief. More than I would have expected from someone who has been officially separated from his wife for a number of years and was known to travel the world with as many lovers as he did polo ponies.

Halfway through a nearly incomprehensible interview with Diaz, Kari suggested he hang on and brought Mimi on the air. Mimi sounded much more in control. She said she was with Diaz at his ranch, consoling him in his time of need. Mimi and Kari talked for a few minutes, and then Kari asked me if I had news to add to the events of last night.

"Carol, do the police have any idea what happened?"

"At this point the police haven't ruled on the cause of Carmen's death. They are looking at any number of possible circumstances, including natural. The only thing we do know for certain right now is that if this was a homicide, the motive does not appear to have been robbery. Carmen died with the same ruby necklace she wore to the awards show last night."

"Yes," Mimi said, "it was a gift from Diaz. He had given it to her for her birthday last year."

"It was an heirloom," Diaz said. "I picked up for her in Spain. Carmen adored rubies. I knew she'd love it."

"Any word, Carol, on how long it will be before the coroner has a cause of death?"

"Please," Diaz interrupted. "I know your listeners want to know what happened to my Carmen. She was a beautiful woman, but I can't listen to this. What I wanted to do today, Kari, was to come on your show and talk about happier times. To share my Carmen's light and to let those who loved her know what her sister Mimi and I have planned to celebrate her life. On Wednesday, I will be opening our home, Los Caballos Grandes, for a memorial service. Carmen and I loved this ranch. We had many beautiful days here. She will always remain a part of it. I would hope since I can't invite all who loved her to come to the ranch, that you will come, Kari, and broadcast the celebration of her life so that everyone who hears it might remember her as I do."

"I would be honored, but under the circumstances, Diaz, I'm homebound until the doctor releases me. Until then, I can't be out in public. But Carol, our reporter, can. I'll send her in my stead."

CHAPTER 16

I had never been to Los Caballos Grandes before, but Sheri had. Her father, a former big-time movie producer, had used the ranch numerous times for location shoots, and Sheri had frequently accompanied him. She said she knew Los Caballos better than her own backyard and insisted she come along as my guide. She promised she'd provide me with little-known inside information, the type of thing I hoped to drop into my report if things got dull and I had a lot of time to fill.

On the drive out, Sheri filled me in on everything she knew about the ranch and even more about Carmen and her strained relationship with her sisters. Diaz still used Los Caballos Grandes when he was in town, and when he wasn't, the six-hundred-acre estate nestled in the foothills of the Santa Monica Mountains was frequently leased out for movie shoots and special events. With its elegant Mediterranean buildings surrounded by rock-studded hills, the property could be made up to look like a Tuscan village in the south of Italy or exactly what it was, the wealthy estate of an international playboy. As for Carmen, even the station's very thorough obit file couldn't touch what Sheri knew. When it came to celebrity gossip, Sheri was like a walking Wikipedia.

Carmen was the oldest of her sisters. I knew next to nothing about Nina, only that she was the youngest and several years ago had distanced herself, at least publicly, from both Carmen and Mimi. Any news on how Carmen and Nina got on was simply nonexistent. I couldn't find anything besides old family photos of the three girls together from much younger days. As for Carmen and Mimi, their rivalry dated back to childhood, according to Sheri.

Mimi and Carmen were close in age, Nina much younger. Growing up, the two older girls had been dressed alike and comparisons were inevitably made. After their mother died and their father committed suicide, it was Carmen who kept the family together. Ultimately, as I knew, she'd played matchmaker, setting her sisters up with wealthy men. Diaz, Sheri said, was supposed to be Mimi's beau, but when Carmen met him for the first time, she shoved her sister aside and took Diaz for herself. Something Sheri thought Mimi had never gotten over. The relationship between the sisters would have been destroyed were it not for Diaz's money, and the fact that Carmen made certain both Mimi and Nina were well taken care of financially.

Carmen's publicist, Penny Salvatti, was standing at the entrance to Los Caballos Grandes in front of a large ornate iron gate ensconced with images of horses. In her hand, she held a clipboard with a list of invited guests. Her eyes narrowed as I pulled forward and flashed my station ID. She peered into my red Jeep, her gaze settling on Sheri.

"I'm sorry, Ms. Childs. I'm afraid it's invite only."

I smiled back confidently and lied through my teeth. "I guess you didn't get my message. This is my assistant, Sheri Billings. Her name should have been added to the list. There's no way I can cover this event alone. Too many stars, and we wouldn't want to leave anyone out. I'm sure her name's there somewhere."

Behind me, someone in a black Bentley honked impatiently. The line of the cars was beginning to back up to the freeway exit.

"Look, I'm sure there's been a mix-up. She won't be a problem, I promise."

Penny's cheeks began to flush. Another honk and she looked anxiously back at me. I shrugged innocently. Penny waved us through like she was batting a fly, anxious to have us move on.

Once beyond the gate, we were directed by men in golf carts toward a large green equestrian field—a Grand Prix arena—behind the stables. Inside, hundreds of white folding chairs had been set up. On the seat of each was a single long-stem white lily. In front of the chairs, a makeshift podium stood next to a large color photo of Carmen and an even larger bouquet of white roses. The crowd was somber, dressed in black mourning attire; the weather, by contrast, was a balmy seventy-five with clear skies and a soft breeze that belied the seriousness of the gathering.

Sheri and I made our way toward the podium. I wanted to have a good view of the crowd from the front. As we approached, I noticed a group of men standing in front of the first row of chairs, like groomsmen dressed in dark suits at a wedding, and huddled in small groups with their backs to us. I was almost to the first row when one of the men turned. Our eyes met like magnets.

It was Eric. My heart beat a little faster. I whispered to Sheri that I'd catch up and strode forward. Coming to stand next to him, I smiled silently. Without a word, I did an abrupt about-face, and standing shoulder to shoulder with the man I loved, stared out at the crowd. There was an awkward silence between us, like a brick wall. We hadn't spoken since Eric had called the station after Carmen's death and said we'd be in touch. But clearly we weren't.

I can take a lot of things, but being ignored isn't one of them. I whispered under my breath, hoping a little humor might melt the ice between us, "Just so you know, I'm not stalking you."

"I get that." Eric continued to look forward, like a wooden soldier, his hands neatly folded in front of him, his face expressionless.

"And I know we can't be talking about *things*."

"That's right."

More silence passed between us. I watched as people walked past us in various states of mourning, men and women in black, some with hats, some not, all politely avoiding eye contact, looking downward.

Finally, frustrated with his short answers, I joked softly, "So...do you think the killer's here? I've heard murderers like to show up at memorial services."

Eric's eyes slid sideways then snapped forward. I caught a slight twitch in his jaw, a partial grin he quickly wiped from his face. In a voice barely above a whisper, he said, "This is a group of Hollywood actors and agents, Carol. What do you think?"

I bit back a smile. We were still in sync. I noticed his focus on the far end of the field. My eyes followed his gaze.

Beyond the back row of white chairs, Mimi stood with Diaz, and next to him was another woman I didn't know. This had to be Nina. She was slightly built and much less stylish than either of her sisters, but the family resemblance was undeniable. She had the same raven-dark hair, pale skin, and delicate features. She was dressed in a simple black sheath, her hair in a neat little bun secured at the nape of her neck. She held a large black hat and sunglasses.

By contrast, Mimi was clad from head to toe in white. She was wearing a shiny pearl white jacket, a knee-length chiffon skirt, and white ballet flats so that she might walk on the grass without a problem. She looked as though she'd just stepped off a cloud. On her head, she wore a large dramatic sequined hat that shaded her face. I watched as the three advanced in unison, like a bridal party, with Diaz in the middle and a sister on either arm. Together they walked smoothly down the center aisle atop a white satin runner toward the podium.

As Mimi approached, a shimmer of light caught my attention. Beneath the shadow of her hat and the open collar of her suit jacket, a red ruby diamond necklace reflected a rainbow of colors. Carmen's necklace? Her sister's body was barely cold and already she was wearing it. I felt my throat tighten and watched as Diaz offered Mimi his hand as she placed one dainty foot on the podium. I looked down at the ground. I didn't want the shock of what I was thinking about Mimi to play out on my face.

Moments later, a portly man with thin red hair, dressed in a long black robe with a clerical collar, approached the podium. He looked like he had come directly from central casting, a Hollywood priest for hire. Someone, perhaps Mimi, may have plucked from the internet for the occasion. He stood before the crowd and, raising his hands above his head, asked for a moment of silence.

Clearly this priest hadn't known Carmen, and he admitted as much in the eulogy. He said in talking with her family and friends about her good works he took great comfort and hoped to offer us all the same as we gathered to remember her. He praised her for community involvement and her various charitable projects, which, far as I knew, were in name only. The type of events Hollywood socialites were paid to endorse, where they show up, smile at the camera, and sign autographs before making a quick escape. Not exactly philanthropic. He ended with a touching reminder of how when death had taken Carmen's parents at a very early age, she had stepped up to take care of those closest to her and shouldered the responsibility of holding the family together. "While her life, like her parents', was short, her gift of kindness, love, and the importance of family will be remembered by many."

I wondered just how true that might be. As the priest completed the service, I took my mic from my bag and found a quiet corner where I could broadcast an account of the event. Tyler would retrieve bits and pieces of my report and include them in Kari's show as needed. In hushed tones, I recapped the scene. The lush green equine training field. The rocky biscuit-colored hillside. The palatial Tuscan mansion with its fountains and Spanish-tiled courtyards. The crowd in their funeral black—with the exception of Mimi in white—tight-faced and somber. When the last amen was uttered, I went into the crowd to solicit comments. I waited until Diaz, Mimi, and Nina had bid goodbye to the hired priest then watched as they descended from the podium. They looked like a family bound together by grief, their arms about one another, their heads bowed, eyes moist with tears. I approached Diaz and asked if he had anything he wanted to say.

He took the mic softly from my hand and delivered the equivalent of another long eulogy. I thanked him, told him I was sorry for his loss, and turned to Mimi. Did she have anything she'd like to add?

"Only..." Mimi appeared to be choking back tears. "...that there was no one like my sister. I may have two sisters, but Carmen was an original. There will never be another like her."

I was tempted to ask about the necklace Mimi was wearing, then sensed Nina was about to pull away and turned to her. Nina shook her head and backed away from me, her eyes searching for a quick retreat. It was obvious she didn't want to talk. Diaz put his arm around her and pulled her closer to him, then together with Mimi, exactly like they had entered, the three started in the direction of the hospitality tent. Halfway there I noticed Nina slip from beneath Diaz's shoulder and separate from the two, heading off in the direction of the barn. Curious, I followed.

CHAPTER 17

"Excuse me, Nina." I quickened my step to catch up. "Could we talk?"

Nina stopped and stared at me. She looked irritated, her lips pinched together as though she was holding back something she might regret saying.

"I know this must be difficult for you, but I was in Beverly Hills the morning of the bombing, and I was hoping I could talk to you about your brother-in-law."

"You mean do I think he did it?" She laughed a little and shook her head. "Or maybe just caused it to happen?"

I hoped my shock wasn't registered on my face. I took a deep breath and stepped closer to her.

"I don't know, you tell me. Did he?"

"How would I know? Carmen and I weren't exactly close." She turned her back and stomped ahead of me.

"But you did talk?" I was glad I'd thought to wear flats. Heels on grass would have made it impossible to keep up with her.

Nina entered the barn ahead of me, a huge Mediterranean-style structure with a rounded two-story entrance that looked more like the gateway to a castle than a barn. I followed her inside and stood in the foyer. This was unlike any barn I had ever been in. A twelve-foot crystal chandelier hung from the dome above my head, while imported carpets lined the entry. On either side of me were two identical stable wings, each easily the length of a football field, home to two dozen horses. There wasn't a fly or a stray piece of hay anywhere.

"I wouldn't exactly call it talking. But since you're a reporter and I know you're going to snoop around, I will tell you we saw each other regularly."

Nina stopped at one of the stalls. A beautiful bay with a brass nameplate that read "Chino" hung his head out over the yoked door. He nuzzled her as she ran her fingers through his short mane.

I placed my hand on the other side of the horse's neck and slowly stroked him. "So if you didn't talk, what did you and Carmen do?"

Nina picked up a groom's brush from a bucket outside the stall door and began brushing the big bay's neck. "Carmen was a control freak. You must know that. She was driven. Status. Money. Fame." The pacing of her words matched the long strokes of the brush.

"I suppose she did what she thought she had to do. From what I understand, your father left things in a bad way financially," I said.

"Yeah, he gambled our fortune away, and Carmen arranged for my sister and me to marry wealthy businessmen. She used us. I was barely eighteen when she married me off for the first time. And when my first marriage didn't work out, she arranged for my second. But after that ended, I'd had enough. That's when I settled up with Carmen, gave her half of everything I had and started over. Told her I didn't want to be part of her little Hollywood celebrity act and went back to school." Nina stopped brushing the horse and put her hand on his neck. "I got a job and bought a small place for myself out here in Simi Valley. I work in a bank now. Carmen would come by once a month. Not to visit me, mind you, but to visit her safe deposit box. So you see, we didn't exactly spend quality time together."

Nina sounded angry. I couldn't blame her if she hated her sister, but what I didn't get was how at home she seemed in the barn. From the way she handled herself around the horse and appeared to know where things were, she'd obviously been here before.

"And you kept in touch with Diaz? Even though you and your sister were estranged?"

"Why not? He's always been good to me. I probably spend more time here visiting with the horses than I ever did with Carmen. Diaz knows I love them. I come and go as I please."

I wondered if Nina really suspected her brother-in-law, or if she was still reeling from the sudden death of her sister and just lashing out. People said odd things when a loved one died suddenly, out of fear or anger. Either way, her relationship with Diaz struck me as odd.

"Did you know your sister was a courier for Diaz, and that she was making a delivery the morning of the bombing?"

"So? She had a business arrangement with Diaz, what of it?"

"A moment ago you seemed to question his involvement in her death. Maybe Carmen did something that angered Diaz, and he killed her."

Nina turned her back to me and began brushing the horse again, her strokes longer and harder than before. It was obvious she didn't like my question.

"Do you think Carmen might have been skimming off the top?" I asked.

Nina stopped abruptly and looked at me.

"I wouldn't put it past her."

"And do you think Diaz knew?" I kept thinking about the ring Carmen had sent Eric to get from her room the night she died. She was supposed to have given it to Churchill the day of the robbery, but she had apparently forgotten to bring it with her. Maybe that wasn't an accident.

"Perhaps. I don't know for sure. They had a kind of mutual respect for one another. Things happened long ago, and they were there for each other. I don't know if he would have killed her if she cheated him or not, but I doubt he would have had to. There were a lot of women who didn't like my sister."

Nina glanced down at the end of the aisle where a horse in crossties stood surrounded by a group of men and an attractive-looking young woman in riding breeches, the same woman I'd seen at the polo matches. From the look of disgust on Nina's face, I felt certain the woman was Donatella, the trainer. The fact that she hadn't attended the memorial didn't surprise me. I couldn't imagine that Diaz would show up at his wife's memorial service with his girlfriend on his arm.

But what did surprise me was one of the men in the group. He was clearly one of the mourners, dressed in a black suit and looking very out of place among a group of grooms. He was standing very close to Donatella. The two appeared to be studying the horse's hoof and whispering. I looked closer and realized the man in question was Paley, the gray-haired security guard from Henry Westin's.

"What's that all about?" I nodded in the direction of the horse.

"That's Six Pence. He's Diaz's favorite, but he's got a problem with one of his hooves. They're working on him now. I'm afraid it's not good."

I knew a little about horses. Growing up, I'd ridden at the local stable. Like most young girls, I had dreamed of one day owning a horse of my own. I'd spent my summers with trainers, mucking stalls, carrying feed and water. And I knew hoof and leg problems, if not properly cared for, could spell big troubles for a horse.

"And that's Donatella with them, right? His trainer?"

"Trainer?" Nina laughed. "I suppose you could call her that. In my book, she's simply some little gypsy-trick Diaz picked up in Spain."

I glanced back again in the direction of the horse. "That's a little harsh, don't you think?"

"Hardly harsh enough. She's Euro-trash. Just some little wannabe actress he brought back from Europe. But the only role she's been auditioning for is that of Diaz's wife."

"You think she could have killed your sister?"

"I don't have any proof. Sometimes I think it was Donatella, but it just as easily could have been Mimi. There wasn't much love lost between my sisters. I don't like that I think that, but the truth is, both Mimi and Donatella have been after Diaz and his money for a long time."

"Is that what you meant when you said Diaz might have caused it?"

"Diaz is a womanizer. He can't help himself. Women flock to men like that. Carmen understood it. As for Donatella and Mimi, I think he drove them crazy. And with Carmen out of the picture, they each think he'd be free to marry again."

"And you think he might?"

"I don't know. I hope not. I didn't have a lot of respect for Carmen, Carol, but she was my sister. And much as I didn't like what she did, she didn't deserve to die. I want whoever killed her to pay for it."

"You realize, of course, the coroner has yet to rule on a cause of death. It may very well be she died of—"

"What? Natural causes? Don't kid yourself, Carol. My sister was in great shape. She didn't have any allergies or heart problems. I hardly think she died of natural causes at thirty-two. Somebody killed her, and if you want to talk to me, I want you to find out who it was. Promise me you'll find out who killed my sister." She put the horse's brush down and reached into a small shoulder clutch for a business card and handed it to me. "Call me when you know something."

CHAPTER 18

On our way home from the memorial, I caught Sheri up with what I'd learned.

"It's odd," I said. "Nina blames Diaz, but not directly. She's convinced it was either Donatella or Mimi who killed Carmen, for the oldest reason in the book."

"Money," Sheri said. "They're each after Diaz for everything he's got. Always a great motivator."

"Maybe. But until I have a coroner's report, we can't be certain Carmen's death was a murder. What if it wasn't?"

"What?" Sheri looked over at me in disbelief, her hands in the air. "Then explain to me why Eric's been working undercover. He was shadowing Carmen everywhere she went. Why would the FBI be involved if there wasn't something sinister going on? Either he was protecting her or they thought she was in on it. After all, you did tell me even Carmen didn't know who he really was."

"That's just it. I don't know. I keep coming back to that very thought. I mean, Carmen's death could have been anything. But if her death is connected to the jewelry heists, and if Mimi or Donatella murdered her—why? I could see wanting Carmen out of the way, but stealing the jewels? It doesn't make any sense. Half the jewels stolen were ones Carmen was carrying for Diaz. They'd be ripping off a fortune from the very man they hoped to marry."

"You're assuming the robberies and Carmen's death are connected, Carol. It could be a coincidence. Like you said, maybe Carmen's death was an accident, and she had a reaction to something or a heart attack. Things like that do happen."

"Maybe. But when I was in the barn with Nina, Mr. Paley, the security guard from Westin's, was there too. I would have sworn Paley wasn't involved, but after seeing him in the barn, I'm not so sure."

"Did you ever consider maybe Paley just likes horses?"

"I don't know, Sheri, something just doesn't feel right." I was thinking aloud. Paley had been helpful after the robbery. He was the one who called 911 and had secured the store until help arrived. "I wouldn't have figured him to be involved. But after seeing him with Donatella this afternoon—the way she was standing next to him and the two of them whispering, all quiet-like—it's just a hunch, but there was definitely something going on between them."

"I'm not surprised. Seeing any man with that little vixen would certainly pique my interest."

I kept playing the scene from the barn over in my head. Donatella and Paley had appeared unusually friendly. My mind was working overtime.

"What if Paley's involved? Maybe he was the inside contact and helped the Wigged Bandit get in and out of the store. Churchill did say Paley had gone outside for a smoke when the bomb went off. If you ask me, that's a bit convenient. Plus, he hasn't returned any of my calls, and he didn't want to see me at the polo match in Santa Barbara even after Carmen's assistant went searching for him and told him I wanted to talk. Maybe he's not so innocent and was worried Carmen knew something. Maybe she was supposed to die in the explosion instead of Ms. Pero, and when she didn't, Paley sent Donatella to do the job."

"And just how would he do that?"

"Donatella's an actress. There isn't an actor working in LA who hasn't at one time or another waited tables. Maybe she passed herself off as one of the waitstaff, poisoned Carmen's drink, and got out of there before anyone knew what happened."

"Okay, forgetting Paley for the moment, how is it nobody noticed her?"

"I don't know. The room was dark, crowded. People don't look at who serves them. At a party like that, they just accept what's given to them and keep talking. Maybe she wore a disguise or—"

"Or maybe she disguised herself, snuck in as a guest, and managed to get close enough to the group to switch out the drinks when the server arrived. Trust me, I've been to enough of those parties to know, people are too plastered to know who they're talking to or standing next to. It would have been easy enough to do."

I considered what Sheri had said. She was right, the room was dark and either scenario was a possibility. But so was Mimi. She was with her sister when she died, and according to her, she'd ordered the drinks.

"I still don't think we can rule Mimi out. She just as easily could have slipped something in Carmen's drink. She certainly wanted her sister's husband, and after seeing her this afternoon with Diaz and wearing Carmen's necklace, I'd say she's well on her way to securing that relationship."

Sheri glanced over at me. "Then if I were Donatella, I'd be looking over my shoulder, worried Mimi might be coming after me next."

Later that night as I was getting ready for bed, the house phone rang. It was almost eleven thirty, and I was surprised to hear Eric's voice. I hadn't expected him to call, particularly after today's memorial service. Since Carmen's death, the magic between us was beginning to feel strained. I was starting to fear our relationship would become a casualty of the investigation.

"Sorry to call so late, Carol. We need to see you tomorrow."

"We?" I sat down on the edge of the bed, cradling the earpiece beneath my chin. The tone of his voice wasn't what I would have preferred at this late hour. I felt my throat growing tight.

"The FBI. We'd like you to come down tomorrow and look through some pictures. See if you recognize anyone."

"Really?" I looked up at the ceiling, fighting back the tears behind my eyes. I hated the formality in his voice. I tried to cover the disappointment in my voice. "This isn't a social call then? You didn't just call to wish me good night?"

"Carol, I—"

"I get it. You can't talk." I wondered if the call was being monitored. I was getting tired of this. I sat up straight and played with the phone cord. By now I was certain our little romantic rendezvous back in Carmen's hotel room had resulted in some form of disciplinary action that made Eric have to be careful. What else could it be? I knew he would never tell me if he had gotten in trouble, and whatever hot water he might be in, he would keep it to himself. My eyes darted across the room at a picture of Eric and me aboard *The Sea Mistress*. Happier times. "But does that mean you can't listen?"

He laughed softly, and I felt as though someone had just plunged a knife into my heart. I closed my eyes and wished I could have felt Eric's warm breath against my ear. I missed him more than I wanted to admit to myself.

"I'm listening," he said. "What is it you want to say?"

Dammit. I was doing exactly what Tyler said. Giving the FBI information and getting nothing in return. But this was Eric. What did Tyler know about love?

"Well, here's what I've worked out so far. Some of it you no doubt know, but hear me out."

"Go on."

I told him my theory about the FBI watching Carmen and her courier activities and recounted the details of my conversation with Nina, that she thought either Donatella or Mimi might have killed Carmen, and waited for him to respond. When he said nothing, I filled in the silence. "What do you think?"

"You know I can't comment."

"Damn. I hate the strong, silent type. You know that, right?"

"Carol—"

"Okay. Then consider this. Nina told me Carmen would visit her at the bank regularly. Actually, she said Carmen made regular visits to her bank deposit box. Nina thinks Carmen might have been stealing from Diaz and hiding whatever it was she took from him in her safe deposit box."

Eric's voice deepened. "How often did she say she'd visit?"

"Monthly. She said Carmen never missed a visit. She'd come to the bank, wave hello, and then go directly her safe deposit box. She spent more time *visiting* with whatever it was she was keeping in that box than she ever did with her sister. I'm thinking she found a place to hide the jewels she was skimming from Diaz."

"It'd be easy enough to check out."

"And if I'm right and Carmen was skimming off the top, that gives Diaz motive. Maybe he even persuaded Donatella to do it because he couldn't or thought he might be caught if he did. He might have even promised Donatella he'd marry her if she did. Goodness knows, the girl wants that."

Eric was quiet. There was another long awkward silence. I knew he was weighing the information I'd given him against what the FBI already had on file. I stood up, paced the room, and picked up the photo of Eric and me.

"Eric?"

"I'll see you tomorrow. Our offices on Wilshire. One o'clock work for you?"

CHAPTER 19

The next morning, I found a box of chocolate truffles on my desk. Edelweiss Chocolates had been thrilled with the response from KCHC listeners for our Holiday Chocolatiers' Contest and had sent over a large box as a thank you. A note attached from Tyler asked me to put together a short report congratulating them as our winner and announcing our combined monetary gift to St. Mark's.

I opened the box to see someone had already helped themselves to a number of truffles. I took one for myself then walked the box back to the newsroom.

"I see you got my note." Tyler glanced up at me as I entered.

With the sweet taste of a chocolate raspberry liqueur still in my mouth, I smiled and sat down. I was about to share with him some of my thoughts concerning Carmen's murder when he said he needed me in the studio that afternoon.

"Kari's not expected back 'til next Monday, and until then I could use you as a temporary host. Margo Thompson will be here from St. Mark's to collect the check from our chocolatiers' drive, and I can't have her sitting in the studio by herself with only a phone patch in to Kari. So I'm going to need you. Plus, Bunny's here."

"Bunny?" I asked.

Tyler popped one of the chocolates into his mouth, and with his mouth full, said, "The Chocolatiers' Tour was her idea. She suggested St. Mark's and she expected to be on hand when Kari presented the check to Margo. So now you get to handle it. She'll be joining you in the studio."

"Where is she?" I looked over my shoulder, expecting to see Bunny lurking, sifting through Tyler's in-basket, double-checking the newswire for soft news. I didn't see her anywhere.

"She'll be around. Right now she's out wandering the halls, making herself indispensable."

I could tell by the snide way Tyler had said it, he wished Bunny's husband might feel the same way about having his wife at home. Instead, our new owner was making a habit of dropping his wife off at the station while he disappeared, returning each afternoon tanned and relaxed, looking like he'd been chasing a few of Santa Monica's beach bunnies.

"How much longer are they in town?" I asked.

"Only through the holidays."

I cleared my throat, registering my disdain, and stood up. Tyler stared, his eyes focused on the door behind me. I knew from the look in his eye that Bunny had entered the room. I grabbed the box of chocolates off Tyler's desk and swung around to greet her.

"Would you like one? I understand we're going to be working together today. We might as well start off on a sweet note."

Bunny looked longingly at the chocolates. Her hand hovered over the box, her fingers twitching anxiously. "Yes, I think I will. I'm still having nightmares after Carmen's death. I really don't know how you do it, Carol. Aren't you glad we're not focused on such things here?"

I glanced over at Tyler. Bunny's eyes were still on the box of chocolates, debating which of the sinful treats she wanted. He circled his finger around his ear and mouthed, "She's nuts."

I didn't think Bunny was nuts. She was maybe only ten years older than me, but generationally she was in a different world. I knew she'd been at the top of her game in radio when she met her husband. I imagined at the time Mr. Morganstern had been a real catch, a hot, handsome, successful entrepreneur with a little flash and a lot of money. He probably persuaded her to trade it all in for a Mrs. title and a trophy-wife status, which included ownership of not only the radio station where she had worked but a growing group of stations, worth ten times more than anything she possibly could have imagined. In her mind, Bunny Morganstern had traded up.

Unfortunately, as I watched Bunny down the chocolates like Xanax, I could tell things hadn't worked out quite as nicely as she'd hoped. While her husband may have been a mover and shaker in the boardroom, I got the feeling that, where Bunny was concerned, Howard Morganstern wasn't such a mover and shaker at home anymore. Perhaps this explained Bunny's sudden interest in KCHC's new softer, friendlier chick-lite format. She needed something of her own.

My first clue that today's show wasn't going to go as planned came when I walked into the studio an hour later. Bunny was seated behind the console with an empty stool next to her and an even emptier box of chocolates in front of her. Matt announced that Kari wouldn't be with us today, not even by phone patch. Her fever had spiked, and the doctor had insisted she stay in bed, close the curtains, and rest. No excitement. My second clue came in the form of a traffic report immediately preceding the show. The 405 was backed up. A police pursuit had shut down the northbound freeway and commuters were being rerouted off at Santa Monica. Somewhere in that sea of cars was Kari's guest, Margo Thompson. She called in to say she was doing the best she could to cut through traffic, but it didn't look good. Matt suggested we patch her in via her cell phone. I was on my own. Or more accurately, I was alone in the studio with Bunny.

I opened the show, explaining that Kari was still home, under the weather, and that our special guest, Margo Thompson, was stuck in traffic. "But, good news, I have Bunny Morganstern with us this morning. She's..." I stumbled for a moment. How could I best describe Bunny? The wife of our CEO? A former radio exec? Nothing seemed to fit, and then it came to me. "The creator of KCHC's new fresher, friendlier chick-lite format."

Bunny seemed awed; she smiled and put her hand over her heart, as though to say she was flattered at the recognition.

I continued, adding it was Bunny who'd introduced KCHC to St. Mark's. That she had suggested the Beverly Hills Chocolatiers' Tour as a holiday promotion, and how appropriate it was that she was here with us today to present the check to Margo Thompson.

Matt patched Margo in, and suddenly, through the magic of radio, the three of us sounded like we were all together in a small cafe, having coffee and chatting. I recapped KCHC's Beverly Hills Chocolatiers' Tour, making sure to mention all of the participating merchants and crediting Sheri for her discriminating taste. Matt pulled up a digital recording of my report and we laughed over portions of Sheri's almost slap-happy descriptions of the chocolate liqueurs. Some of them sounded like a sommelier describing a fine wine. I thanked our listeners for their generous support and was about to suggest Bunny present—or at least announce—the amount of the check the station had ready to give to St. Mark's when Matt interrupted.

"Excuse me, Carol, we have a caller on line one. I think you're going to want to take this. It sounds important."

I furrowed my brow. I wasn't expecting calls during this part of the show. "Who?" I mouthed. Matt shrugged and held up a white eraser card with a large dollar sign drawn on it. I took the call.

"Good morning. Welcome to the Kari Rhodes Show. This is Carol, how may I help you?"

"Actually, I think I'm the one who can help you." The caller paused and I put my hands on my headset, straining to identify the voice. Usually I was pretty good, particularly if it was a regular caller. "I'd like to make a donation."

My eyes snapped back to Matt. He was giving me a big thumbs-up.

"That's very generous of you," I said. I looked over at Bunny. This was highly irregular. The promotion had ended and the station had already cut the check. Bunny signaled with her hand as though she was writing a check and smiled. We could always use more.

"I'd like to double the amount of the donation your station is willing to make," the caller said. "Up to fifty thousand dollars."

Through my headset, I heard Margo gasp. "Fifty thousand?"

Bunny and I exchanged a look. Was this for real? The station's goal had only been twenty thousand. This was more than twice that.

Bunny grabbed the mic in front of her. "That's extremely kind of you. You realize, of course, that would be almost thirty thousand dollars?"

"That won't be a problem. It's a worthy cause. And I can assure you, I'm more than good for it."

I placed my hand on Bunny's shoulder. Before she could go on about how wonderful the gift was, I needed more information.

"I'm sorry," I said. "I didn't get your name. Can you tell us who you are?"

"Oh, now, that would take all the fun out it, wouldn't it? I'd much prefer to remain anonymous."

Anonymous? I grabbed a blank piece of paper, scrawled out the words "Caller ID," and held it up so Matt could see. He responded with a shake of his head. The number was blocked.

"Well, if you won't give us your name, perhaps you might tell us a little about yourself." I tried to sound friendly and casual, but I had a gnawing feeling in the pit of my stomach that I knew this caller. The tone sounded vaguely familiar, the voice slightly raspy and quick. "I'm sure Ms. Thompson would like to know something—"

"I'm a fan." The voice came back quickly, cutting me off before I could finish. "And I enjoy helping others. Like you did, Ms. Childs, the day of the explosion in Beverly Hills."

"Tomi?"

"And I like chocolate," the voice interrupted again. "Almost as much as your friend Sheri does."

Was that a veiled threat? The synapses of my mind were firing off like firecrackers. I had to find a way to keep the conversation going, anything that might give me some hint as to the caller's identity. Was it the same gray-haired lady I had walked to the car?

The Wigged Bandit? I wanted some clue, some indication from where she was calling.

"Have we met?" I asked.

"That's not important, Ms. Childs. I'll deliver the money tomorrow morning. Until then, I'll be listening."

The line went dead, exactly like it did when Tomi had called the first time. I wrapped the segment with a thank you to Bunny and Margo Thompson, and to our very generous mystery caller and all of KCHC's listeners and merchants who had participated in the station's promotion. I then signaled Matt to go to a commercial break. I needed a moment.

I raced back to my office. I had less than five minutes before I needed to be back on the air. I wanted to be alone when I called Eric. I prayed he would answer. I was in luck.

"She called." The words escaped my lips before I could I even say hello.

"Who—"

"Tomi, the Wigged Bandit. She called a few a minutes ago. While I was on the air. She spoke to me." I leaned against my desk, my heart pounding.

"You're certain?"

"It had to be her. The voice, it was raspy and high-pitched and she mentioned she liked to help people. Like I did the day of the bombing. I think she's sending a message; she knows I know who she is."

"Carol, listen to me. This is important. Can you get your producer to email me a digital file of the show? Right away. I need to hear that tape."

"Yes, but Eric, she's planning to be here tomorrow."

"What?"

"The reason she called. She's making a donation to the St. Mark's Fund. She said she was bringing it to the station tomorrow morning." I glanced at the clock. I had less than sixty seconds to get back to the studio and another fifteen minutes of Kari's show to go before I could sign off. "Look, I've got to go, I'm due back on the air. I'll meet you at your office after the show."

I hung up and raced back towards the studio, detouring through the newsroom where I grabbed a pile of pre-approved news stories. I needed filler news for the last segment, something light to end the show on. I had no intention of continuing the conversation concerning our anonymous donor or the chocolatiers' tour, and I knew there was no way Margo Thompson was going to arrive before the end of the hour. Traffic was still snarled on the west side.

I took a deep breath as I grabbed the studio door and entered, smiling, as though nothing unusual had happened.

Bunny looked at me curiously.

I glanced down at the stack of news stories in my hand and found one I knew Bunny would like.

"Perhaps a change of pace? A little something fun to end the show on?" I smiled and handed the top story to Bunny. "Why don't you take it?"

"Missing White Cobra Found Alive and Well in Thousand Oaks." Bunny was delighted.

CHAPTER 20

I left Bunny in the studio, looking pleased with herself. She had handled the last part of the broadcast surprisingly well, laughing with callers and joking about the escaped Cobra. "Just how might one go about capturing it? Answer: Carefully. Caller, what did the cobra say to the flute player? Charmed to meet you." For her first time behind the mic alone, she wasn't bad. I knew Tyler would say the callers had carried the show with their suggestions and one-liners, but Bunny was happy and my mind was elsewhere. I was anxious about meeting with Eric. Even without traffic it would take me a good forty minutes to cut across town. Instead of hanging around and bonding over snake jokes with Bunny, I grabbed my cell phone. My eyes skimming my inbox for messages, I started walking back toward my office. I was halfway down the hall when I heard my name.

I looked up to see Tyler directly in front of me. Another five feet and I would have knocked him over. "My office, right away."

Tyler did an abrupt about-face, and I followed him back to the newsroom, my eyes continuing to scan my phone for messages.

Without a word he entered his office and pointed to the chair in front of his desk—the hot seat—then sat down and stared at me like I'd done something awful.

"Mr. Morganstern called this morning." Nobody called the new owner by his first name. Howard Morganstern had made it very clear after buying the station that he preferred to be called Mr. Morganstern, or Mr. M. for short. Tyler paused, as though he was waiting for a response from me.

I sat quietly, my arms and legs crossed, and continued to clutch my cell in my hand. I had no idea why Tyler was telling me Mr. M had called, but I knew it wasn't going to be good. I could only wish he'd hurry up and get it over with. I was anxious about meeting with Eric. My stomach was doing all kinds of flip-flops, and the clock was ticking.

"He was listening to the show this morning. To be exact, he was listening to his wife." Tyler rolled his eyes up to the ceiling. "Why on earth you allowed her to do more than sit in and answer a few questions about the St. Mark's campaign, I'll never know. But because you did, he now thinks it'd be a good idea if she filled in for Kari until she's ready to come back to work."

I put my phone down and stared back at Tyler. "Bunny fill in? You've got to be kidding. She wasn't that good." Damn that Cobra story. I should have given her something more mundane.

"It doesn't matter if she was good. She's the owner's wife and now I'm going to want you to sit in with her every day. No way I'm leaving her in the studio alone."

"What? You want me to babysit? She's the owner's wife."

"Call it whatever you like, but she doesn't go near a mic unless you're there. We've got enough trouble keeping listeners without Bunny putting them to sleep with her goody-two-shoes approach to news."

There it was. Remaining in the studio, particularly with Bunny, meant I wasn't going to have time to research the jewelry store robberies or to find out what really happened to Carmen. I was about to protest when my phone buzzed. I glanced down at the screen. "Results in on Carmen's death. Call me. DG."

I stood up. "The coroner's report for Carmen's in. You'll have to excuse me." I knew no matter how frustrated Tyler was with Bunny and Morganstern, the results of Carmen's autopsy trumped it. Tyler would want to be first on the air with the cause of Carmen's death no matter Bunny's dictate.

"Go." Tyler waved his hand dismissively at me. "But tomorrow, you're back in the studio with Bunny. No excuses."

I didn't argue. I got up from the chair, returned to my office, and called Dr. Gabor, DG for short. Eric would have to wait.

I was one of the few reporters in town who had Dr. Gabor's personal inside line. Before Bunny's chick-lite format, if I was working on a story, Dr. Gabor would text me first before releasing the results to the media. I'd become his favorite newsperson, if for no other reason than I had survived his orientation requiring all new reporters wanting access to his reports to attend an autopsy. The fact I hadn't fainted or refused to come back appeared to have earned his respect. Of course, it didn't hurt that I also plied him from time to time with free tickets to Disney Hall.

"Got your text, Doc. What do you know about Carmen?"

"I can tell you someone definitely tried to poison her."

"Tried?"

"She aspirated, choked on her on own vomit. Someone spiked her drink with copper sulfate. Stuff wouldn't have killed her by itself, but either way she died, and as a result, the cops look at that as a homicide."

I scribbled "copper sulfate" on my notepad and Googled the name.

"It's a crystal or powder, also known as bluestone or blue vitriol. I'm afraid it took us a while to get the results back. Always does with poisons. Can't say it killed her all by itself, but it certainly contributed. Stuff's wicked. The effects would have had a burning sensation in her chest. She probably felt hot, sweaty, disoriented, and then started vomiting. Convulsions. I'm afraid that's what killed her. She choked to death. I'm surprised nobody tried to help or clear her throat. But then with that crowd, people were probably too drunk to realize what was happening or didn't want to get their hands dirty."

My Google search listed copper sulfate as an herbicide used for the treatment of fungal infections. Also commonly used in veterinary medicine. My eyes stopped. Veterinary medicine? The article, written by a farrier, suggested the use of copper sulfate mixed with Venice Turpentine and polypropylene was excellent for the treatment of horses' hooves. But hardly something someone would mix with champagne.

I knew of three people close enough to Carmen who would have known about copper sulfate and its uses. And two of them had been in the barn the day of Carmen's memorial.

I hung up the phone and made notes from my conversation with Dr. Gabor. I included information concerning the effects and uses of copper sulfate and my suspicions that Donatella, Paley, and Diaz—either together or separately—might have used it to poison Carmen. I filed it on my computer under "Wigged Bandit Investigation" and then sent a note to our promotions department to reserve a set of tickets for Dr. Gabor for the next Christmas Concert at Disney Hall.

CHAPTER 21

Before I left the station, I wrote out a quick thirty-second news report announcing the LA Coroner's findings on Carmen's death and emailed it to Tyler.

The LA Coroner has ruled Carmen Montague's recent death a homicide. Sources close to the investigation, who asked not to be identified, believe Ms. Montague's death may be related to a recent string of jewelry store robberies in the Beverly Hills area. No further information is available at this point.

Brief as it was, I knew Tyler would want to use it in the upcoming news segment, and sandwiched between enough chick-lite news stories, Bunny couldn't complain. After all, Carmen was a celebrity, and we could hardly ignore it. I followed up with a quick email telling Tyler I'd be out of the office for the next couple of hours.

On the drive over to Eric's office, I kept thinking about what the FBI knew about Carmen and the robberies and wondering how well it matched up with what I knew. I was growing frustrated. I felt certain Carmen's death was related to the robberies and that an international jewelry ring was operating in Beverly Hills. But as much as I wanted to break details about it, I couldn't. My hands were tied by what little I could report per the FBI, and what I couldn't get on the air per Bunny.

I pulled into the parking lot behind the FBI's Los Angeles office on Wilshire and glanced up at the tall white building. It took up most of the lot between Veteran and Sepulveda and stood like a giant monolith overlooking the busy 405 freeway. The façade of the building reminded me of an old-fashioned computer keypunch card, the windows with their dark recessed portals looking like punched chads.

Eric's office was on the seventeenth floor. My palms began to sweat as I parked my Jeep. I had been to Eric's office exactly once, and that was before I started working as a reporter. Now I felt like I was entering enemy territory, that anything I said could and would be used against me. I knew my imagination was getting the best of me, but I'd never been a government witness. I had no idea what to expect. I straightened my skirt, ran my fingers through my hair, and took a deep cleansing breath. I hoped it would strengthen my confidence.

I entered through a set of bulletproof glass double doors and was immediately greeted by a middle-aged uniformed guard. The man's muscles bulged beneath his shirt.

"Take your shoes off and place your purse on the counter. Keys, belts, and jewelry in the basket. If you have firearms on you, take 'em out as well." Muscle-man shoved a basket across the counter and waited for me to comply.

"Don't carry a gun, but I've got a mic. That count?" I smiled and reached into my bag for my microphone.

He ignored my weak attempt at humor and glanced inside my purse. Seeing nothing suspicious, he nodded me through the metal detector and told me to sign in. I was given a guest ID and pointed in the general direction of the elevators. I guess they didn't think me much of a threat. I was on my own up to the seventeenth floor.

When the elevator doors opened, Eric was standing in the hallway. Our eyes locked. There was a moment of hesitation on both our parts. I stood rigid, unsure what to do. He looked at me, his eyes scanning my body from head to toe, then indicated I should follow. I trailed behind him down a long hallway covered with pictures of agents and awards until we came to a set of double doors, the entrance to a large formal conference room.

Inside the room, half a dozen agents, all dressed in blue business suits, white shirts, and ties, were seated around a long oak table. They stood as I entered. An unexpected but polite action I assumed was an attempt to make me feel at ease. It had the exact opposite effect. I began to sweat. My head started to feel warm and the palms of my hands were even wetter than they were on the drive over. Eric introduced me as KCHC's reporter. He made no mention of our personal relationship, but did say I was a possible material witness to the robbery in Beverly Hills. I recognized a few faces as we sat down, undercover agents I'd seen as escorts the night of the awards ceremony.

At the head of the table was Special Agent Douglas Donner. I had heard Eric speak of him. Agent Donner was a short bookish-looking man. Not someone I would have pegged as an FBI agent. Slightly overweight and balding, he didn't fit the mold. But Eric had said the man had the mind of Stephen Hawking and the instincts of a well-trained pit bull, a deadly combination for anyone on the wrong side of the law.

Donner was the last to sit down and the first to speak. "Ms. Childs, I understand you're the reporter who appears to have *accidently* inserted herself into our investigation. And that you may be able to help us identify the Wigged Bandit."

"I think so," I said. In hindsight, I wasn't so sure. I had only met her once, and so much had happened since then. I hoped I could remember enough to make some type of ID.

"Ms. Childs, am I correct in understanding that you believe you walked the Wigged Bandit to your car the day of the robbery?"

"Not my car. She was headed in the direction of the parking lot where I was parked, and I offered to help her with her things." This sounded worse than it was. I was making myself out to be an accomplice. I pushed several strands of loose hair behind my ear and smiled nervously.

"And she gave you a gold brooch."

I nodded nervously. "And I gave it to Agent Langdon, once I was aware what it was."

"You realize, of course, Ms. Childs, we don't typically run into situations like this, particularly with the media. Ever."

"No, sir. I wouldn't think so. It's highly unusual, and it certainly wasn't planned."

Donner shot Eric a look and there was an uncomfortable pause as Donner shuffled through some papers and Eric filled a water glass in front of me. I took a long sip, placed it back on the table, and waited for his next question.

"And prior to walking this Wigged Bandit back to your car—let me rephrase—prior to the explosion, did you identify Agent Langdon as he was leaving Henry Westin's with Miss Montague?"

"Yes, sir, I did. But not on the air. I had just finished my report when my friend Sheri saw Agent Langdon with Miss Montague."

"Sheri Billings, correct?" Donner pulled one of the pages from the pile of papers in front of him and stared at it. I could see he had a picture of Sheri and some scribbled notes.

"That's right."

"And why was she with you?"

"I'd asked Sheri to join me. The station had been doing a Chocolate Charity Campaign to benefit St. Mark's. A kind of Beverly Hills chocolatiers taste-off, and her chocolate palate is much better than mine. My expertise extends about as far as a Three Musketeers bar from the nearest vending machine."

There was a snicker around the table. Donner leveled his eyes at me like a battering ram.

"Miss Childs, much as I appreciate your need to insert some levity into the situation, I hope I don't need to remind you this is a serious matter."

"No, sir, not at all. I just meant I wasn't on the air when I saw Agent Langdon. Nor did I mention his presence or that of the FBI in any of my reports concerning the robberies. I put two and two together pretty quickly and realized after the bombing and spotting Eric that he had to be working undercover. My spotting him was an accident."

Donner put the papers down in front of him and stared at me, his eyes boring into my own. "That's a smart assumption on your part, Ms. Childs, and try as we do to keep our agents' identities a secret when they're in the field, we can't always guarantee that. In fact, Agent Langdon was a last-minute replacement. We hadn't expected to have him in the field for this operation at all. We thought he was too old for Carmen."

I choked back a nervous laugh and glanced at Eric. "I'd have to agree."

Eric raised an eyebrow. I could see the fact Donner no longer considered him a young stud was mildly annoying to him. I smiled.

"One of our other agents had a family emergency. His wife went into labor early, so Eric stepped in."

Donner reached across the table for a pitcher of water and poured himself a glass. "Ms. Childs, did it ever occur to you that the old lady you helped may have had something to do with the robbery?"

I paused. It was definitely getting hotter in the room. Either somebody had turned up the heat or I was having a hot flash.

"In hindsight, I suppose it should have. But you have to understand I was in a hurry to get back to the station. I had just seen my—" I stopped myself. I was about to say "boyfriend," but that seemed like a ludicrous term to put upon ourselves, particularly now.

"I had just seen Eric with Carmen Montague and witnessed an explosion. I don't believe I was thinking all that clearly. And later when I got home, I tossed the brooch in my jewelry box. I never thought it was real. A lot of women, particularly in Beverly Hills, have copies made of their more expensive pieces. The real ones stay home in the safe while they wear paste, you know, imitation stones that look real but aren't. I figured she was just some sweet old lady. Maybe some former Hollywood star who didn't get out much. I thought I was just being nice when I offered to help. I didn't think about the brooch again until the night Carmen died."

Donner cleared his throat. "I appreciate your efforts, Ms. Childs, to keep this investigation under wraps. If any word were to leak out, all the work we've done would be worthless. The case would be blown."

I told Agent Donner I appreciated the delicacy of the situation. "In fact, as a result, Agent Langdon and I have been very careful not to mix our personal affairs with that of the investigation. I suppose you could say we've even tabled our relationship—temporarily—at least until this investigation is over."

Donner's eyes tracked between Eric and me, his face not giving me a clue as to what he was thinking. But I had no doubt in my mind he knew exactly how successful we'd been at *curtailing* our relationship, particularly the night of Carmen's murder. But with half a dozen agents in the room, I figured he wasn't about to say anything.

"Ms. Childs, I'm not here to critique your personal relationship with one of my agents or to dash any future hopes of romance. But I would like to ask a favor."

"Anything," I said. Anything? I couldn't believe the words coming out of my mouth. What kind of reporter was I? I should be asking more questions, not agreeing to anything. Tyler was going to kill me.

"Agent Langdon tells me you believe this Wigged Bandit has been calling your radio station."

"I do."

"And he tells me you've provided us with an audio tape with what you think may be this mystery caller's voice."

"I'm convinced it's her," I said. "She's called the station several times. I'm pretty good with voices and hers is distinct. It's a little raspy and midrange. My bet is she's probably a smoker, or has been. I think I'd recognize it anywhere now. She calls herself Tomi."

"We've been running the digital recording through some voice recognition software and with a little luck we may get a match. But right now, we have some photos we'd like you to look through. See if you can identify any of them as the person you saw the day of the bombing."

The person? I thought it odd he referred to the Wigged Bandit as the person. "You mean the woman?"

Eric reached for a remote clicker on the center of the table and pointed it in the direction of a large screen on the wall. A group of nine photos, mug shots, three across and three down, appeared instantly on the monitor.

I glanced at the screen and looked back at Eric.

"There must be some mistake. I thought you wanted me to identify a woman. These are all photos of men."

"Exactly," Donner said. "We think the person we're looking for, this Tomi, a.k.a. the Wigged Bandit, you met outside of Henry Westin's the day of the robbery, is using a disguise."

"And you think the Wigged Bandit is a man?"

Eric nodded. "Take a close look, Carol. Do any of these men look familiar?"

I stared at the screen. I didn't know any of them. But there was a similarity about them. They were all white, clean-shaven, and middle-aged. Maybe thirty-five to forty years old. I couldn't imagine any of them as women. I squinted at the screen and tried to imagine if makeup and a wig might make one of them look like my Wigged Bandit.

"Look at the eyes, Carol. The chin. The nose. See if you see anything that makes you think one of the men in these photos might be the woman you met the day of the robbery."

"Maybe number three." I pointed to the photo of the man on the end of the first row. "Something about the mouth, thin lips, cheekbones maybe."

"Anyone else?"

"I don't think so." I shook my head and stared back at the screen. Was the face I was looking at the face of a robber or murderer or maybe both? "You think there's a connection between the robberies and whoever killed Carmen?"

Eric and Donner exchanged a look. An answer to my question required another level of approval. Donner nodded for Eric to speak. It was obvious from their exchange I was being given privileged information.

"We believe Carmen's death was an accident. That whoever murdered her didn't intend to kill her, but to scare her."

"So you know about the copper sulfate? You've seen the coroner's report?"

Eric nodded. "We suspect Carmen was being blackmailed. We think she may have known who was behind the robberies and threatened to go to Diaz and expose the operation, but couldn't."

"Why not?"

"Because whoever killed Carmen knew she was skimming off the top of her husband's jewels, and may have threatened to expose her first."

Donner stood up and walked over to the monitor and pointed to the picture of the man I had identified. "There's no honor among thieves, Carol. But if the Wigged Bandit is who we think...murder's not usually part of his MO. Somebody wanted to frighten her, remind her to stay quiet. Master thieves like these pride themselves on their skills, and violence is seldom one of them. They consider what they do an art. The bigger the haul and smaller the collateral damage, the happier they are."

I studied the photo on the screen again. Eric had enlarged it. The man's features were delicate, almost feminine, his nose small, the eyes nicely shaped, deep set with thin brows. With the proper makeup and skills he might be made up to look like a woman.

"How tall is he?"

"About five-five. Slight build. Maybe a hundred and forty-five pounds."

I considered his height and that *she* had been bent over, carrying shopping bags. The jacket he was wearing might have given the appearance of a hunchback or the frail shoulders of an elderly woman, making her even smaller than five-five.

"If it is him, when he called the station the first time, he said exactly what you said a few minutes ago." I looked at Donner. "That nobody was supposed to die. She or he said that it was an accident, and the police had it all wrong. And then he hung up."

Donner came back to the table and spread out pictures of some of the stolen items and Liz Taylor's famous necklace, La Peregrina.

"We think Ms. Pero may have taken the pearl necklace Mimi was planning to wear to the awards show from the vault before the bomb went off and hidden it inside her jacket. That's the reason Westin's took so long to notify Mimi that they had Miss Taylor's necklace. It was missing, for a while anyway. And Westin's was hesitant to report it. That is, until the coroner found it on Ms. Pero's body. Mr. Churchill says she had taken the necklace out of the vault to show Carmen. But when Carmen arrived and was in such a hurry, there wasn't time for her to see it. Then Carmen left and suddenly there's this big explosion. We suspect the Wigged Bandit, or the mysterious redheaded woman, was in the store before the explosion and stepped outside. Right behind Carmen, just before the bomb went off, then raced back inside. Covered by all the smoke, it would have been easy for her to take the necklace where Ms. Pero would have left it. But instead of leaving it on the counter where she was supposed to, Ms. Pero fell and hit her head on one of the glass display cabinets and was killed."

"So you think Ms. Pero was in on it?"

"Probably. But unfortunately, we don't have enough proof yet. Investigations take time, Carol. However, somebody inside Westin's knew Carmen would be there that day, and whoever that is—or was—is connected to the case."

"Okay, I get how someone trailing Carmen would know which valuables she was carrying and what jewels were in the shop she was visiting. It'd be a two-for-one stop. A big win. But why me? Why did the Wigged Bandit give me a ridiculously expensive brooch, and then start calling the station?"

Eric answered, "I couldn't tell you before, Carol, but if this is our man, it wouldn't be the first time we've seen this. Several years ago there was another attack on Henry Westin's in Paris. One of the thieves, a man dressed as a woman, engaged a policeman in a conversation outside the store on the Rue de la Pais, just several doors down from the police station. The patrolman remembers she asked for directions, described her as a sweet little old lady—exactly like you did. He even shared a cigarette with her before going about his business. Minutes later, this sweet little old lady and her friends—all men dressed as women—entered the store and pulled off on the biggest heist in Westin's history. They made away with better than a million dollars in jewels and diamonds. Later, one of them even sent a letter to the police station. It was addressed to the patrolman that sweet little old lady had spoken with, thanking him for his help and enclosing a small memento, a gold cigarette lighter." Eric nodded back to the screen, at the photo of the man I thought might be the Wigged Bandit.

"And you think that might be him?"

"Could be. What we do know is that thieves like these love to brag about how close they can get without being caught. For them, it's not just about the theft. It's a game."

"So you think he's playing with me."

"Whoever he is, Carol, he's bored. And the fact that he's calling you and toying with you on the air makes us wonder if maybe he's got a bit too much time on his hands. If he's not done."

"What do you mean, not done?"

"There's going to be another robbery."

CHAPTER 22

After my meeting with the FBI, I drove back to the station in a quandary. I hadn't shared with Tyler everything I knew about the FBI and their investigation into the robberies. Tyler knew they were involved, but he didn't know Eric was working undercover, and certainly not as an escort. And I wasn't about to tell him. Nor had I mentioned everything about how the FBI suspected I'd not only met the Wigged Bandit the day of the robbery, but that she'd given me a ridiculously expensive jeweled brooch. As a thank you gift! My mind was a mass of tangled ideas and threads of thoughts all leading to a dead end.

On top of that, as I was leaving FBI Headquarters, Agent Donner suggested he call my boss, explaining that he would be sending a team of agents over to the station in the morning. He thought it would be a good idea that if the Wigged Bandit showed up, I wasn't there to greet him alone. I agreed, but not about his calling Tyler. I told him I'd take care of that. Trouble was, I wasn't quite sure where to begin.

When I got to the radio station, I grabbed a couple of colorfully wrapped Belgian chocolates from the top of my desk drawer and proceeded down the hall to Tyler's office. I wasn't about to go in empty-handed.

As I entered Tyler's office, I tossed several of the candies onto the desk in front of him. "Got a minute?"

Tyler's eyes went from his computer screen to the candy to me. "If you're here about Bunny, Carol, there's nothing more to say."

"Actually, it's not about Bunny. Or at least not directly," I said.

"Sit." Tyler snapped one of the chocolates off the top of his desk and looked at me as he popped it in his mouth. "Go on, what is it you want?"

I decided not to hold back. I told Tyler the FBI was sending over a group of plainclothes agents to the station in the morning. "They have reason to believe the Wigged Bandit may show up here tomorrow."

"What?" Tyler stared at me like I just told him the station was being invaded by aliens.

"I'm sorry I didn't come to you first with this, but I had a meeting with the FBI this morning, and they think Tomi, our mystery caller, could be the Wigged Bandit, and may try to come here tomorrow morning."

"What do you mean, come here tomorrow morning? What have you done?"

Tyler started to stand up, but I was quicker. I stood, all five feet nine of me, and leaned over the desk, my hand nearly touching his shoulder, urging him to sit back down.

"Nothing. But you're going to have to trust me on this, Tyler. I think I have a lead on Carmen's murder and the robberies, and while I know Bunny has an issue with my chasing after such things, I can't let it go. I'm going to find out who killed Carmen and how her death's related to the robberies, and when I do, KCHC's going to have the exclusive."

Tyler shook his head. I could see the disbelief at what I had just told him registering in his eyes. Anything more and I'd have to push his eyeballs back into the sockets.

"You just better hope this is something we can run." Tyler sat back down, like he was about to draw his last breath.

"I'll leave that to you," I said. "You and I both want this story. I figure Bunny's your problem. But tomorrow morning, the FBI will be here and—"

"And you, Carol, one way or the other will be on the air with Bunny Morganstern at ten a.m. tomorrow morning. You got that?"

I stepped back from the desk and gave Tyler a quick salute. "Got it."

The next morning, Tyler and I met Eric and his team in the station conference room. The agents looked like they were all dressed in the same blue suits they had on yesterday. Anyone seeing them would think they were clients coming in for an early morning business meeting. When I walked in, Eric was plugging a monitor into the station's security system. It was now possible to view anyone coming or going through the station's main gate from inside the conference room.

Eric nodded to me. Tyler and I took seats at the end of the conference table and Eric took charge of the meeting. He explained the roles each of the plainclothes agents would play. Two were to be positioned outside the station's front doors, two more in the lobby, and a fifth by the security gate facing La Cienega Boulevard. They were all equipped discreetly with a near-invisible earpiece that connected to a small lapel microphone allowing them to communicate walkie-talkie style. Satisfied Eric had the operation under control, Tyler excused himself and returned to the newsroom, reminding me I was due in the studio with Bunny at ten a.m. No exceptions.

With other agents now in place, Eric and I were alone in the conference room. I got up and took a seat next to him while he continued to monitor the security camera. Shop talk seemed like the best idea.

"Agent Donner didn't come?" I asked.

"He thought I could handle it." Eric kept his eyes on the screen.

"I guess that's good, huh?"

"It's all okay, Carol. You all right?" He glanced at me then turned his attention back to the monitor.

"Yeah, just fine."

"Good."

So much for small talk. I hated this crazy two-step we had forced ourselves into. I had questions I wanted answers to and he wasn't at liberty to comment on. On top of that, we hadn't spoken about anything personal in days. I couldn't remember when I'd ever felt so close yet so far from someone whose sentences I used to be able to finish without a thought.

We stared at the screen in silence. Then at exactly eight thirty, a woman driving a beat-up blue Toyota appeared at the station's front gate.

I leaned closer to the monitor and watched as she rolled the driver's window down. Extending her hand, she reached unsuccessfully for the visitor's bell.

"Hello?" Her voice wobbled through the speaker as she poked her head out the car's window, and I got a look at her on the security camera for the first time.

I didn't recognize her. For all I knew she might have been the same woman I'd seen in Beverly Hills or just a random fan of the station. I didn't know. She had short curly gray hair that bobbed around her face, and she was wearing big, round coke-bottle glasses. To me it looked like a disguise. I leaned closer to Eric, my shoulder touching his, and whispered, "Oh, come on, she can't be for real." He stared at the screen, cocked his head, and shrugged. He wasn't so sure.

"I'm here to drop something off for Carol Childs," the woman yelled in the direction of the buzzer.

I punched Eric lightly on the shoulder. I didn't recognize the voice, but this had to be her.

We watched as she reached again for the gate button, her short chubby fingers inches from it. The undercover FBI agent standing by the entrance walked over to her car, doused his cigarette, and smiled. We could hear the exchange through the security speaker.

"May I help?"

"I can't reach the button."

"Let me."

The agent pushed a security button and the gate swung open.

Just as the old lady was about to drive through, a young boy wearing a black hoodie on a ten-speed bike with razor-thin tires came racing through the gate. Out of nowhere, he zipped past them both. Swerving in front of the car, he stood up on the bike and pedaled fast as he could like a yellow-shirted cyclist to the finish line, making his way toward the station's big double doors. He skidded to a stop, dumped his bike on the concrete the way kids do, then ran toward the entrance. The two plainclothes agents guarding the front doors looked at each other then back at the approaching car. It was accelerating. The old lady, possibly frightened by the presence of the boy on the bike, had frozen her foot on the gas. The car, clearly out of control, was coming full speed towards the front entrance.

"Look out!" The agents dove headfirst behind concrete planters that served as barriers to the station's glass doors. At the last minute, the car swerved and careened into a concrete pillar, where it came to a stop.

"It's the kid!" Eric yelled into his lapel mic, then jumped up and raced toward the lobby. "Get him! Don't let him get away."

I followed, running down the hallway for all I was worth, but Eric was faster. I pushed through the double doors to the lobby just seconds after Eric.

He and the two plainclothes agents had already surrounded the young boy. He was maybe fourteen or fifteen years old. The hood of his sweatshirt was pushed back from his smooth round face. He looked flushed and frightened, his eyes wide, his pale skin pink with sweat. In his hands, he held a shoebox wrapped in brown paper. Eric flashed his ID and the boy froze.

Outside, the radiator of the crumpled car was spewing steam from beneath the damaged hood. The two agents who had barely escaped being hit were helping the driver out of the car. Upon entering the lobby, one of them went immediately to a phone and called an ambulance while the other offered the old woman a seat and went to fetch a glass of water.

Eric turned his attention back to the young boy.

"Do you know this woman?" He pointed to the old woman. She looked dazed, as though she were trying to absorb what had just happened. With her glasses in one hand, she ran her fingers through her short hair with the other, sighing repeatedly.

The boy shook his head.

"Why are you here?" Eric asked.

"I was told to deliver a package."

Eric stepped forward and took the box from the boy, his young hands shaking as he released it to Eric.

"Do you know what's in it?"

"No." The boy looked frightened, his eyes searching the room as though he was looking for a friendly face. "But the guy who gave it to me said it wasn't drugs. I don't do drugs. If it is drugs, I don't know anything about it, sir. I swear."

Eric put his hand on the boy's shoulder. "What's your name, son?"

"Ryan. Ryan Scott."

"Ryan, this isn't about drugs, and you're not in any trouble. But I need to know who gave you this box. Can you tell me?"

"Just some guy on the street corner, 'bout a mile back at the 7-Eleven."

"Little late for you to be headed to school, isn't it?" Eric said.

"I have first period free. I'm a senior. Got good grades and my first class isn't until nine, so my mom lets me sleep in. I stop every day on my way to school for a breakfast burrito."

I could see Eric evaluating the boy. He looked clean-cut and reminded me of my own son. I doubted he was running drugs.

"Okay, tell me about this guy. What did he look like?"

"Slim. Not tall, 'bout my height, five-six maybe."

"How old?"

"I don't know. Old. Maybe 'bout your age."

Eric looked at me. I could read his mind. *Why is it everybody thinks I'm getting old?*

I smiled back. *Kids.*

"How'd you meet him?"

"He came up to me. Said he had car trouble and needed to get something to the radio station. Asked me if I'd drop it off. Said he'd give me twenty dollars if I would."

"And why did you speed through the gate?"

"I thought I might be late for school. The station's just a little out of the way, so I was in a hurry."

Outside I could see the ambulance approaching the security gate.

Eric turned his attention back to the woman sitting in the chair. She appeared to have caught her breath and was no longer hyperventilating. He asked her name.

"Edna Bakers," she said.

"And you're here to see Ms. Childs? You said you had something to drop off?"

"A picture." Edna reached into her overly large pocketbook and took out a color photograph. Her hand was still shaking. "I was there the day of KCHC's Chocolatiers' Tour. I took this on Rodeo Drive just after you finished your report, before all hell broke out. I'd forgotten about it, and then, when I heard you on the air the other day, I remembered and thought you and your friend might like it. And since I was going to be here anyway I wanted to make a small donation for St. Mark's. There's still time, right?"

I nodded my head yes, and then looked at the picture. Sheri and I were both looking like we'd just overdosed on chocolate liqueurs, but it was something else in the background that caught my eye. A redheaded woman was carrying shopping bags, walking in the direction of Henry Westin's. I stared more closely at the photo. Was this the same redhead Churchill reported was inside Westin's the morning of the robbery? It had to be. And the shopping bags? Exactly like the ones I had helped the old lady carry back to the parking lot.

Hesitantly, I handed the photo to Eric. "You have to see this."

I saw a flicker in his eyes as he looked at the photo and then a slight fall of his shoulders. He had to be kicking himself. He'd missed the redheaded woman inside of Westin's that day and he knew it. And here it was, proof in the photo she was headed into the store. It was no wonder he'd been so distant.

"You're sure?" he asked.

"Those are the same bags I helped carry for the gray-haired old lady. She must have switched disguises right after the robbery."

The EMTs entered the lobby and Eric put his hand on Edna's shoulder and asked if he could have the photo. She said it was fine, as long as he gave it to me later. We watched as they helped her onto a gurney, and Eric promised her it would all be okay and they would take care of the car.

Eric then turned his attention back to the young boy.

"Ryan, you mind if I take this box?"

He shook his head nervously. "Not at all, sir."

Eric put on a pair of thin latex gloves from his back pocket, then placed the box on the reception counter, careful not to smear any fingerprints that might still remain.

Using a small Swiss Army knife, he slid the blade beneath the wrapping and opened the box. Inside were two smaller boxes, similarly wrapped in brown paper. On the outside of the first it said: "Attention Carol Childs."

Eric took the first box out of the carton and again opened it, exactly as he'd done with the bigger box. The paper fell away, revealing a slim blue velvet jewelry box.

"Carol, I think you're going to want to see this."

"What is it?"

I leaned over Eric's shoulder and stared down at a magnificent jeweled brooch, a silver peacock, with emeralds, diamonds, and rubies in its tail. It looked like a match to the one the Wigged Bandit had given me the day of the robbery. I reached for it.

"Carol, stop. You can't touch it. We're going to need this for evidence."

"I don't believe it." I stepped back, my hands on my hips, and stared at the box.

"I'm sorry, but you know I can't let you have it."

"I'm not talking about the brooch. This was supposed to be

cash. Cold hard cash. He said he was sending thirty thousand dollars for St. Mark's. What's in the other box?"

Slowly Eric lifted the second package from inside the box. On the outside was written, "For Carol and Sheri. Enjoy."

"What is it?" I asked.

"Chocolates."

CHAPTER 23

I watched as Eric headed out the door with the box in his hands. I would have liked the chocolates, but I wasn't sorry to see the box go. I didn't trust the Wigged Bandit. Fixated as he was with me, I feared he might have poisoned the batch, and I wasn't taking any chances. Besides, I was due back in the studio with Bunny, and unless she had downed the entire box of Edelweiss Chocolates the client had sent over yesterday, there had to be something left.

Before Kari had come down with chicken pox, she had booked Spencer Whitehall from Annabelle's Auction House for today's show. For weeks, Annabelle's had been promoting their upcoming auction, running full-page ads in the *LA Times*, plus commercials on radio and TV. Annabelle's was expecting a huge turnout, with sales estimated to be somewhere in the millions. Whitehall, a short, mousy-looking man, pushing sixty and with a graying goatee and thin wire rim specs, was talking with Bunny as I entered the studio.

Bunny seemed irritated as I grabbed a set of headphones. She snapped, "Carol, small change of schedule. I'm sure you won't mind, but I won't need you with me in the studio today." Then without missing a beat, Bunny turned back to Whitehall and told him I was their "news gal" and not on the air until the top of the hour.

I wasn't about to argue, certainly not with a guest in the studio. I smiled and backtracked into the news booth while Bunny replaced her headphones. It wasn't until I was seated back in the booth, behind the glass that divided my small space from the studio, that I noticed Bunny had changed her look. Gone was the wild frizz of curly hair and long dangly earrings. Today she looked almost corporate. Her hair was swept up into a conservative French twist, and she was wearing a much more sedate suit. Not too different from what I had on, business casual; slacks, shirt, blazer and reasonable shoes.

Matt, Kari's producer, started the counted down—*five, four, three*...Bunny looked nervous, her long manicured fingers tapping on the console. Tyler's words rang in my ear. "You have to be there, Carol." I had to back her up.

I shot her a thumbs-up and looked back down at my news stories.

As Bunny introduced Whitehall, I half listened and began to scour my notes for the top of the hour news report. In front of me I had stories about a lost dog, a press release announcing the seventieth anniversary of the Crock-Pot, and a list of celebrities celebrating their birthdays today. A blinking red light on my studio phone diverted my attention.

The news booth is soundproof and unless I opened the mic between my booth and the studio, nobody could hear what I was saying. But I still answered the phone in a whispered tone.

"This is Carol."

"Were you disappointed?" I felt like I had just been socked in the chest. The thin, raspy voice had to be Tomi, the Wigged Bandit, still pretending to be a woman. I scrambled for my notepad and scribbled the time. 10:22 a.m.

"What are you doing?" I asked.

"Why, Carol, my love, I'm doing exactly as I told you I'd do. I'm helping out. Is that wrong?"

"You sent me that brooch. Why?"

"What? You didn't like it?" He laughed, the sound of his laughter almost maniacal. "I thought after I'd given you the Phoenix you'd enjoy a pair. Lovely, aren't they? Besides, cash is harder to come by, and the brooch is worth much more than the thirty thousand I was going to send. Probably closer to fifty."

"And the chocolates?" I snapped back. "Were they poisoned? Did you plan to poison me like you did Carmen?"

"Poison?" Again he laughed into the phone like he couldn't believe I'd made such a silly remark.

"You poisoned Carmen, didn't you?" I pushed for a response.

"Miss Childs, I'm afraid murder's really not within my line of work. Like I told you before, the woman who died in the explosion was an accident. It wasn't supposed to happen."

His voice was chilling. My stomach knotted and goosebumps began to form up and down my arms.

"Neither was Carmen, but it did happen, didn't it? Just like with Ms. Pero. Seems like accidents happen when you're around, Tomi."

Now there was silence, dead air, spookier than the sound of his raspy voice. I didn't know what to say next. Finally, he spoke.

"The chocolates were from Teuscher, Carol. I thought you would have enjoyed them. But then again, perhaps it's your friend who really appreciates chocolate. Sheri, right? Yes, that's it, Sheri Billings. Perhaps she might find them more to her liking. Next time, I'll send them to her."

I hung up the phone. The fact that he knew Sheri's name sickened me. I wanted to call Eric. I wanted to hear his voice and tell him the Wigged Bandit had called again. But I knew I wouldn't be able to reach him, not with everything that had happened this morning. He would be tied up investigating the brooch and the Wigged Bandit's whereabouts.

And even if I could reach him, what good would it do? I was stuck in the studio, babysitting Bunny. Instead, I sent a text: "Wigged Bandit called @ 10:22. 'Did I like the brooch?'" Eric responded with a happy face and said he'd call later.

I felt like a prisoner, jailed in my tiny news booth listening to Bunny. The interview with Whitehall was going poorly. The call-in lines, usually lit like a Christmas tree during Kari's show, were dark. Bunny appeared to have stalled with questions and was repeating herself, referring to her notes and stumbling through the interview. I could see Whitehall's patience fading. I was tempted to interrupt, ask a question that might open the phone lines. But Bunny had banished me to the news booth. This was Bunny's show. After all, I was *just* the news gal.

Finally, after a number of false starts that ended in yes and no answers, Bunny asked Whitehall if he might like to offer a little historical background on the life of Huguette Clark and Bellosguardo, the estate Annabelle's had been selected to auction.

Bellosguardo. Huguette Clark. The names were familiar. After all the news and media ads, how had I missed putting the two together?

I remembered seeing pictures of Huguette Clark in the newspaper ads, black and white shots of her, an attractive young girl sitting on the veranda of her estate, wearing a fitted beaded hat and matching long white gown. The ads, all with banner headlines, included photos of the property on the edge of the Santa Barbara cliffs overlooking the ocean, with interior shots of the house and pictures of bronzed sculptures and jewelry. Why hadn't I recognized the name? Churchill had referenced Huguette Clark when he noticed the Phoenix brooch I was wearing the night of Carmen's murder. He thought it had belonged to her.

I adjusted my headphones and leaned closer to the window. Whitehall began recapping Miss Clark's life story in a dull, monotone voice I feared would put our listeners to sleep.

I jotted notes. Born in 1906, Miss Clark was the daughter of a U.S. Senator and wealthy industrialist. She had married once, divorced, and lived the remainder of her life quietly with few friends. She preferred to speak only French for fear of being spied upon. Then, around twenty years ago, she had checked herself into a New York hospital for a minor skin cancer surgery and never left. She died there at the age of one hundred and four, a wealthy recluse. Her Santa Barbara estate had sat empty for years. The cost to maintain it was nearly forty thousand dollars a month.

"I was privileged to tour Bellosguardo before we were assigned the auction. It was like visiting a time capsule. Things were virtually untouched, as through Miss Clark had just left and might return at any moment."

Bunny asked, "And of the things you saw from Miss Clark's estate, Mr. Whitehall, do you have a favorite?'

"Oh, absolutely." Finally, Whitehall's dull voice took on a sense of excitement. Talking about the jewels, he sounded ten years younger, his voice livelier and more animated. "There would be quite a few, but top of my list would have to be the nearly twenty-carat square-cut diamond ring left on Miss Clark's dressing table. I don't believe she ever wore it. It's estimated to be worth two million dollars. And there's a cushion-cut nine-carat pink diamond by the French jeweler Dreicer & Company. I would estimate it to be worth close to sixteen million. It's believed to have been a gift from her father to her mother. And then, of course, another favorite of mine, an emerald bracelet designed by Cartier. It's lovely, probably worth fifty to seventy-five thousand dollars."

As I listened, I realized Eric was right. There was going to be another robbery, and I knew exactly where.

CHAPTER 24

I phoned Sheri during Bunny's show. I told her under no circumstances should she accept any deliveries—specifically anything chocolate—and that I would explain later. I suggested we do dinner. I knew I wouldn't feel like going home. Charlie had dinner scheduled with his dad, and I suspected by the end of the day Sheri would be up for something, particularly after my call. She suggested Vitello's, a favorite little Italian restaurant of hers known for live entertainment and star sightings. I'd always think of it as the place where actor Robert Blake shot his wife.

The story was that after dinner, Blake had walked his wife from the restaurant down a tree-lined street to where he had parked his car next to a dumpster. Once there, he told his wife he'd left his gun inside the restaurant and returned to get it. When he came back, his wife was dead. Shot in the head. The story became LA's next big celebrity sensation, coming just seven years after the OJ trial. Like OJ, Blake was acquitted in federal court and later found guilty in civil court. The upshot being that LA was becoming known as the town where a man could kill his wife—or arrange to kill his wife—and get away with it. I hoped that wasn't going to be Carmen's story.

Sheri and I ordered a couple glasses of Chianti and an appetizer of fried calamari. I started to raise my glass for a traditional girls' night out toast when she stopped me.

"Why don't we skip the toast and you tell me what's going on?"

"I don't know where to begin."

"You could start by telling me what was behind your desperate call this morning. I've had the front door bolted shut all day long and sent Clint to his uncle's for dinner. What's up?"

I put my wineglass down and exhaled. "I can get to that, but first you need to know the FBI believes the Wigged Bandit is a man. Not a woman."

Sheri signaled the waiter for another glass of wine. This was easily going to be a two-glass story. I caught her up on everything that had happened since we last spoke.

"So, right now, I don't trust anyone or anything," I finished.

Sheri bit her lip and shook her head, her dark hair falling in her face. I could tell she was trying hard not to smile.

"What's so funny?" I asked.

"You and this bandit friend of yours."

"He's not my friend."

"Well, he's certainly an admirer. He's given you two very expensive pieces of jewelry and you can't seem to hang on to either of them. The FBI's got them both."

"That's not the point, Sheri. This creep, whoever he is, could very well be a murderer, and he's fixated on me. He's been calling the station and Eric's convinced there's going to be another robbery."

The waiter came by and filled our glasses and I waited for him to leave, then leaned forward and whispered, "And, after sitting in on Bunny's show this afternoon, I think I know where it's going to be."

Sheri tipped her glass to mine. "Where?"

CHAPTER 25

It was Sheri's idea we check out Annabelle's auction at the Beverly Wilshire. She convinced me since I had sent Eric packing with the chocolates, I owed her. And the only possible way I could make it up to her was for us to go check out the Huguette Clark estate jewels ourselves. We weren't alone. By the time we arrived, the hotel was packed with curious onlookers.

Sheri was more familiar with the Beverly Wilshire than I was. On a reporter's salary, I couldn't exactly afford to hang out there. I simply knew it as the hotel where *Pretty Woman* had been filmed.

This wasn't the first time the hotel had handled a big auction. After Princess Diana died, Sotheby's auctioned off a copy of the Heart of the Ocean, the necklace featured in the movie *Titanic*. The Coeur de la Mer was valued at two point five million, the proceeds of which went to Princess Di's memorial fund. I was certain the Santa Barbara trustees for Bellosguardo would be happy with an amount half that size. The estate taxes alone had to be costing a fortune.

We entered the Grand Ballroom, where Annabelle's had set up their public display. The room was bathed in a soft gold light. A huge Italian chandelier hung in the center of the room, adding to the sophistication and ambiance of the evening's affair. The crowd was equally as dressy.

At the last minute, I had thought to change from my business-casual attire into something a little more suited to an evening out. But despite my efforts to pull together a look, I still looked like I'd been shopping the Macy's sale rack. Sheri, on the other hand, always looked like she had just stepped out of a Gucci showroom. There was something about being born with a silver spoon in your mouth that couldn't be taught. She belonged there, while I felt like an imposter.

The room, a two-tiered split-level area with seating and tables for several thousand people, faced a large stage and was frequently used for award shows. The upper area of the theater, where ordinarily tables were set for dignitaries, had been cleared and cordoned off with red velvet ropes. It now served as a temporary showcase for the auction. From three feet behind a protected perimeter, the public was allowed to shuffle single-file past items from Miss Clark's jewelry collection. Bulletproof glass cases displaying rings, necklaces, pendants, and earrings the likes of which I'd never seen, with stones bigger than those from my son's marble collection, were set between larger pieces from her home, including brass statues and artwork. It felt like this was the Tower of London and we were viewing the Crown Jewels. Surveillance cameras were everywhere.

Sheri tapped me on the shoulder as we passed one of the display cases. "Next time your mystery man calls, tell him you want that." She pointed to a large diamond ring mounted on a pedestal behind the glass. I stepped closer to the glass, and without disturbing the velvet rope, squinted at the large stone. "I'm serious," she said.

Beneath it, a card read: "20 carat colorless diamond ring. Found in its original Cartier box. Estimated value: $2.5 million." It was the largest diamond I'd ever seen, a brilliant square-cut stone reflecting a rainbow of colors against the glass.

"If I didn't know better," I said, "I'd say that ring looks exactly like the one Carmen sent Eric to get from her hotel room the night she died."

Sheri leaned over my shoulder and stared at the ring. "Do you think it is?"

I laughed. "No. Absolutely not. But if I were going to skim off the top of my husband's deliveries, believe me, that's the ring I'd take."

With my eyes still on the ring, I stepped back and bumped into someone behind me. I was about to turn around and apologize when I felt a sure set of hands on my shoulders, steadying me. A voice I knew too well whispered in my ear.

"We can't keep meeting like this." There was no mistaking the voice. My body responded viscerally. My pulse quickened and I felt a warm flutter in my stomach. Eric.

I turned around and looked into his eyes. Any other time, I would have kissed him hello and folded myself into his arms. But instead, realizing he was working, I said, "I'm not here because of you, honest. Sheri and I wanted to see the exhibit."

Eric winked, a sign barely visible to anyone passing by, then teased, "You sure you weren't shopping?" His body posture was still like that of a soldier at attention, his eyes scanning the crowd. "Lots of nice things here."

I looked back over my shoulder. I wondered how many other agents were in the room and how many scanning devices were running facial recognition programs at that very moment.

"And you," I teased back, "are *you* shopping for someone special?" I meant the Wigged Bandit. With the number of agents I suspected were in the room, they must have thought the Bandit was here shopping too.

"Maybe," Eric said. Then placing his hand back on my shoulder, he squeezed it. Giving me a subtle grin that could have meant anything, he turned and walked away. Maybe?

Sheri suggested we get dessert at The Blvd Lounge across the courtyard at the hotel's five-star dining facility. As we made our way through the lobby toward the exit, Sheri nudged me. Ahead of us was the auto court, a cobblestoned parking entrance that divided the hotel and the Grand Ballroom from the restaurant. It was filled with arriving cars and red-vested valets who bobbed between vehicles and drivers, exchanging keys for receipts while helping passengers to the curb.

"Do you see that?" She pointed in the direction of one of the valets. He was holding open the passenger door of a large black SUV Hummer. A small woman, whose petite frame was hidden by the car's oversized door, climbed out.

All I could see from beneath the bulk of the gas-guzzling truck were her shoes and legs. But the driver, standing on the curb with his black hair slicked back and wearing a cape, I recognized. It was Diaz, handsome as ever. And getting out of the truck, with a great deal of difficulty as she shimmied her short skirt over her plump legs, was Mimi. I grabbed Sheri's hand to avoid saying anything. Was this a lovers' escape? Or were they here, like so many others, to view the glitz and glamor of Huguette Clark's personal collection?

I was about to cross the parking arcade to find out when Sheri pulled me back. They weren't alone. Standing a few feet away from Diaz, just outside the entrance to the hotel's restaurant, was Donatella, and with her was Paley. Was this her date, or perhaps her beard, a cover to throw off any suspicion of impropriety?

I needed to talk to them. I couldn't believe my luck. Here they were, the four people I thought knew something about Carmen's murder and very likely the robberies, standing just a hundred feet away from me.

I was about to step into the street and ask for a few minutes of their time when Bunny pulled up in front of the restaurant, threw her keys to the valet, and came running up to Mimi like a long-lost friend.

I couldn't believe it. I stood there and watched as the five of them disappeared into the hotel. "What's that all about?"

Sheri looked at me. "I don't know, Carol, but I've suddenly lost my appetite. That woman's up to something, and I've got a hunch you should watch your back."

"Maybe," I said. "But right now, I've got something more I need to do." I stepped across the street, Sheri just a few feet behind me.

"Carol, what are you doing?"

"I'm going to find out what's going on. That's what I'm doing." Sheri stood with me at the entrance to the restaurant. A small crowd between us, Diaz and his entourage blocked any view of either Sheri or me as they waited to check their coats.

Sheri put her hand on my shoulder. "What are you thinking?"

"I need to know why Bunny's here, but even more than that I want to talk to Donatella, and there's no way she's going to talk to me in front of Diaz or any of his friends."

"Maybe I can help. None of these people know me. Watch this."

Sheri stepped confidently in front of me, cut through the crowd and approached Donatella. I watched as she talked animatedly between Diaz and Bunny, touching Donatella's face as though it were a piece of artwork. Then covering her own heart with hand, she sighed and pointed in the direction of the ladies' room. It was an Oscar-winning performance. I bit back a smile as she ducked back between diners waiting to be seated and returned to my side. On her face was a look of confidence, like she'd just accomplished mission impossible.

"What'd you do?" I asked.

"I simply told her I was a talent agent and that she looked exactly like someone we were looking for. That she'd be perfect, but I was about to leave town and asked if she'd meet with my business partner for a few minutes in the ladies' room."

"And she bought it?"

"I don't know if she did, but Diaz was all excited for her and both he and Bunny told her to go. I'm sure she's waiting for you now. But between you and me, the girl's no actress, Carol. There's nobody home behind those dark eyes of hers."

Sheri's ability to improvise amazed me. Growing up the daughter of a successful movie mogul, I didn't think there was a scenario she hadn't seen or used when it came to making up excuses to get to people.

I found Donatella in the ladies' room, sitting on an old-fashioned fainting couch beneath a huge gold-ensconced mirror. She was on her cell phone and glanced up at me when I entered. For a moment, I thought she might recognize me, but I reminded myself there was no reason she would. We'd never been introduced and both the day of the polo match in Santa Barbara and Carmen's memorial she'd been busy with the horses and hadn't mingled with the crowd.

"My business partner thinks you have the face we're looking for to launch our campaign for BellaCina, a new cosmetic line." If Sheri could make things up, so could I. I mentally crossed my fingers there was no such line and that if there were Donatella didn't know it. "We plan to introduce it in Europe this spring."

"I've never heard of such a line." She stood up and glanced in the mirror, adjusting her hair as she spoke. Her accent was heavy. I couldn't place it, but thought it might be from somewhere in Eastern Europe.

"You look like you could be from Europe. I suppose that's why she thought you looked like you'd be perfect for our model. May I ask where you're from?"

"Does it matter?" She turned and looked at me, clutching her cell phone in both hands against her stomach, as though it were a security blanket.

"Not really. I just assumed you were European from your accent. Have you modeled before?"

"Some."

I was getting nowhere. I told her I had seen her coming into the restaurant and asked if she with Diaz. "He's a very attractive man," I said. "Are you a friend?"

"I work for him. I'm a trainer."

"I thought perhaps you might be a girlfriend. You look a lot like his ex-wife."

Donatella looked even more unsettled at that remark and glanced back over her shoulder into the mirror, pushing a loose strand of her dark hair behind her ear.

"No," she said.

"Well, it must be interesting work. Polo, the sport of kings and right-handed people."

"Excuse me?"

"Right-handed people. To play polo you have to be right-handed or at least able to play with your right? I take it you must be ambidextrous."

"I don't know what you mean." She hugged herself tightly and started subtly rocking back and forth on her feet.

"It's just I noticed you're wearing your watch on your right wrist. Most lefties do that. I know I do." I smiled and raised my right arm slightly to show off my wrist. "Must make it a little tough to train players as a lefty."

"I thought you wanted to talk to me about modeling?" She squeezed herself tighter, the knuckles on her hands growing white as she pinched her forearms.

"I did. I'm just making conversation. You looked nervous; don't be. I just like to know something about our models before we introduce them to a possible client."

Donatella glanced down at her cell phone, her lips pressed tightly together, the look on her face like she was willing it to ring.

"I'm sorry," I said. "I know you weren't expecting this and I'm probably taking up too much of your time. Perhaps if you give me your number we might talk later."

I noticed a look of relief wash over her face as she glanced down at her bag and reached into it. With her hand shaking, she scribbled a number on a small piece of paper and handed it to me. Then, as though someone had sounded a fire alarm, she rushed for the bathroom door. Before she got there, I asked one more question.

"Oh, I almost forgot. Donatella, that's a beautiful name. But I'm afraid I didn't get your last name. What is it?"

"Pero," she said. The door closed and I knew as she disappeared behind it Donatella was neither a horse trainer nor an actress. With a name like Pero, I knew it couldn't be a coincidence. It had to mean something that both Donatella and Churchill's assistant had the same last name. Cousins maybe? It was just a hunch, certainly not concrete evidence, but I felt like I had just gotten a thin thread, painstakingly woven into an intricate pattern of deceit, and if I started to pull at it, it might unravel a lot of the mystery surrounding Diaz and his team.

CHAPTER 26

The next morning, I tried to call Donatella from my cell phone as I drove into work. I was certain the girl wasn't interested in pursuing a modeling career, but I thought I might try my luck to see if I could get her to reveal anything else about her past. The number went immediately to a prerecorded announcement. "The number you have dialed is no longer in service..." I glanced at the number Donatella had given me and redialed. I hadn't misdialed the number, it was bogus. No surprise there.

What did surprise me was the condition of my desk when I walked into my small office. It looked as though it had been rifled through. My first thought was that Tyler had come looking for more chocolates. The top drawer was ajar and my candy stash definitely violated. But it was the pencils and papers that appeared to have been rearranged and the phone's receiver laying upside down in its cradle that caught my attention. The message light on the phone was blinking and somebody had obviously accessed my computer files. Several Word docs I'd closed and saved were open. It could have been anyone from the newsroom. Tyler insisted the staff all use the station's call letters as our passcode, just in case there was an emergency and he needed to retrieve any messages. Expectation of privacy was nonexistent. I picked the phone up and listened to my voicemail. A call had come in just after midnight.

"Sorry to have missed you last night at the hotel, Carol. Did you see anything you liked?" There was a muffled chuckle, as though the receiver was shoved too close to the caller's lips. I could almost feel his ragged breath coming through the phone, assaulting my ear. "I thought Miss Clark's ring was exceptionally lovely. Didn't you? How nice that might look on your long fingers. Have you ever thought of wearing one again? On your left hand? Oh, I hope I'm not getting too personal, but you looked so cozy with your handsome agent friend, like you wanted to snuggle up next to him." He laughed again. "Did you think I wouldn't notice? Or that I wouldn't know who he was? I know everything, Carol. Maybe one day we'll talk, but for now, I called to say goodbye. Business has been good and it's time to go. Perhaps I'll consider a return visit, same time next year. Until then, my pretty. Ciao."

I saved the call to voicemail. I needed to let Eric know that not only was I being watched, but so was he, and he'd been made. As for the implication concerning the ring—an engagement ring—was he kidding? I certainly wasn't considering marriage. What a silly thought. I dismissed it and headed down the hall to the studio. I planned to call Eric during the station break, but right now it was almost nine forty-five. Tyler insisted all on-air talent be on deck at least fifteen minutes before show time.

I entered my small news booth and noticed the studio was empty. Matt sat in the control room on the opposite side of the studio behind another glass window. He was reading the newspaper. Bunny was running late. We glanced at each other across the empty studio. Matt shrugged and I pulled up a list of chick-lite news stories to read and waited. Twelve minutes later, three minutes to show time, Bunny walked in.

She was dressed in camouflage fatigues, a t-shirt, and carrying a black backpack. It was a complete transformation from the woman I'd seen last night standing in front of the Beverly Wilshire Hotel in a gold lamé cocktail dress. I watched as Bunny dropped the backpack on the floor and took her seat at the console.

Glancing over at me as though I was an afterthought, she opened the mic between our two studios. "Carol, I'm not going to need you to assist today. I'll be doing the show solo. It's come to my attention that we're really not doing the best job we can with our coverage of Carmen's death and the recent robberies. And going forward I'd prefer to work alone. I've got some things I'd like to do. I'm sure you understand."

Like to do? I could feel the hair rise on the back of my neck. At that moment I could think of a few things I'd like to do, including strangling her with the cord from her headset. What did she mean we weren't doing our job covering the robberies or Carmen's death? Considering the constraints of Bunny's chick-lite news format, I thought we were doing the best we could.

Kari had included both Diaz and Mimi on the air in a salute to Carmen's life, and I'd updated what the police knew of her death in my new reports, albeit carefully, knowing Bunny would be listening.

"Excuse me?" I said. "I thought you didn't want—"

"Carol." Bunny stared at me, her eyes steely, daring me to challenge her. "You don't really think *you* can possibly cover this story, do you?" She laughed dismissively. "Oh, I know you're trying, slipping updates into your news report when you think I won't notice. Sweetheart, you're dating an FBI agent. Just how effective do you think you can be?"

I felt like Bunny had just dumped a bucket of ice water over my head.

"Tyler told you that?"

"He didn't have to."

I stared at her through the glass. Bunny Morganstern, the owner's wife, dressed in her combat-ready attire and daring me to challenge her. It didn't get any more imposing than that. Without a doubt, I knew she was the person who had rummaged through my desk, gone through my files, and listened to my voicemail.

"So it's you, you're the one who broke into my computer—"

"Stop right there. Why shouldn't I? Certainly you haven't forgotten it's my husband who owns the station. In essence, Carol, you work for me. And you're right. I did go through your files, and now I know exactly what you think about me and my idea for chick-lite radio."

I felt as though I'd just been strip-searched and busted. Of course she knew what I thought. On more than one occasion I had included a disparaging remark concerning KCHC's news coverage in my personal emails. We sucked when it came to hard news, candy-coating anything remotely serious. I blamed Bunny, frequently ending my emails with a sour-faced icon akin to someone sticking their tongue out. I should have been more careful.

"Don't think I don't see right through you, Miss Childs. Acting all sweet and helpful. What you don't understand is that I have the advantage of age. I've been where you are. I know how you think. And unlike you, I know what lies ahead. I know you think I'm old and that I sold out, married the boss, that I have it all and should just sit back and be grateful. But believe me, I'm a long way from being done."

I felt like I'd stepped on a landmine. There was no way I could salvage this conversation. What could I say?

"And the good news is, I'm not too old, and I still have a foot in the game. You see, Carol, I've been thinking—maybe you're right. Soft news, particularly in this instance with Carmen and the robbery, doesn't make sense. But you, my dear, you're stuck. You've got this FBI boyfriend, and you're treading lightly. Instead of pursuing leads you ought to be chasing after and nailing the FBI for what they're not telling us, you're playing it safe. You're too busy trying to balance your professional life with your personal. Whereas I don't have that problem." Bunny started to put her headphones on and paused. "Now that I've said my piece, if you like, you can sit back and listen, or you can get up and leave and come back when it's time for you to read the news. I really don't care. I plan to cover this story myself, and you, dear Carol, can't do anything about it."

I couldn't remember when I'd ever been told off so viciously, but I wasn't about to get up and leave. Instead, I took out my phone and sent Eric a text. "Tomi left a voicemail last night. We need to talk."

Eric responded almost instantly: "Annabelle's Auction has been hit. Check your email."

I pulled up my email on my phone and smiled. Moments ago, the auction house had issued a brief statement, "Jewels from the Huguette Clark Estate Sale Missing." Investigators believed jewel thieves had targeted the estate. There was a brief summary of what was believed to have been stolen, but because of the late-breaking news, there was no way Bunny knew. I sat back and listened as an ascending scale of notes with a chorus of voices singing "The Kari Rhodes Show" announced the start of the hour.

"Good morning, this is Bunny Morganstern filling in for Kari Rhodes, and you're listening to Hollywood news, views, and inside clues. But before we get started, I'd like to welcome back a guest who's with us today from his ranch in Simi Valley. You know him best as that handsome polo player from Spain, Umberto Diaz de la Roca. Diaz?"

"Thank you, Bunny, it's an honor to be here. As you know, being a celebrity isn't always the bright and shiny world we try to project. And I appreciate the opportunity you're giving me to update your listeners on some of what my family and I have been going through. This has been a tough time."

I rested my elbows on the console in front of me and shook my head. I thought we'd heard enough of Diaz talking about Carmen the day of the memorial. Was this going to be more of same, Bunny-style? Bunny shot me a look like she'd read my mind. A thin smile crossed her face, like that of a grinning poker player with a winning hand.

"I can only imagine," she said.

"And as I prepare to leave, I'm most appreciative of the opportunity to talk frankly about the events which have so marked this visit."

Leave? It hadn't occurred to me that Diaz might try to leave the country. In my mind he was a probable suspect, if not for the robberies, then certainly for Carmen's murder. The FBI had to be looking at him; the husband is always a suspect. How could they allow him to leave? Diaz may have had an alibi for the night of Carmen's murder, but that relationship was anything but hallmark.

As for the robberies, I didn't see Diaz stealing from himself, even if there were some type of insurance policy to cover his loses. It'd be a red flag. Insurance adjusters would be all over him. Diaz was too smart for that. And now he was leaving. Eric hadn't mentioned anything about Diaz leaving. Why?

I tuned back into what they were saying. Bunny explained that Diaz would be returning to his home in Spain on Sunday and that she'd had the good fortune of running into him last night at Annabelle's pre-auction display, where she'd joined him and several friends for a small intimate farewell dinner. "But let's cut to the chase, shall we? You're leaving and Carmen is...well...I hate to say it, but unfortunately, she's dead. To some out there, I'm sure this looks suspicious."

"I know it may, and I hope people understand this isn't easy. I don't live here full-time. Carmen and I each maintained our own lifestyles. We were very much in love, but my schedule with the horses, charity events, and such is quite demanding. My return trip was arranged long before we arrived here."

"I think anyone who knows you knows your horses are your world."

"No, Bunny, Carmen was my world, and she always will be."

"Of course she was. But if I might, I'd like you to share a story with us about a previous visit to the U.S. One you told me last night, that I believe may help to explain why you feel Carmen would want you to go on."

There was a long uncomfortable silence. I wondered if perhaps Bunny was pushing Diaz beyond where he was prepared to go. I thought she was about to speak to fill the void when Diaz started talking.

"You're quite right, Bunny. It was another visit, also very sad. It happened three years ago. Carmen and I were having troubles. It's no secret we were separated. I was spending more and more time in Europe on business and then returned to the U.S. for a competition in Florida. Carmen was here in LA when I called. There was an accident with the horses. We had flown directly from Spain.

It was a long flight and the horses were fatigued. You may remember hearing about it in the news."

I quickly Googled "Diaz de la Roca polo accident Florida" and a page came up that caused me to catch my breath. I couldn't believe the photos. Diaz described the scene.

"In Europe we have a supplement we give the horses to help with exhaustion, but this same drug hadn't been approved for use in the U.S. I had a local pharmacist mix something up, and the results, I'm afraid, were devastating. Something went wrong with the preparation. I lost my entire team. All twenty-one of my horses died, right in front of me. Collapsed just before taking the field. It was, aside from Carmen's death, the worst day of my life. I thought I'd lost everything, but Carmen came back to me and together we rebuilt the team. The team was everything to her. She'd want me to go on."

I stared at the pictures of horses collapsed on the field. It was unbelievable. I had never heard about the accident, but then why would I? It had happened on the east coast. I didn't follow polo. It was a tragic accident for sure. Like so many stories, it had its fifteen minutes of fame and then, like so many other tragedies, quickly faded with yesterday's news. But as I looked at the pictures and listened to Diaz, I knew something about this wasn't right. I could hear it in his voice. This had to be more than an accident. I wondered if somehow Carmen's murder, the robberies, and the death of these horses were all tied together.

I listened even closer as Bunny continued.

"And of course, the police have told you there's no reason for you not to leave?"

"None whatsoever. And I'd like to thank them. I believe they're doing everything possible to find Carmen's killer."

I listened as they chatted casually back and forth. Scribbling notes on a pad in front of me, I could think of a hundred questions I'd like to ask, but couldn't. This was Bunny's show, and from the giddiness in her voice—like that of flirtatious schoolgirl—I knew she was no match for this Spaniard and his smooth Castilian accent. He was as charming on the air as I knew he could be in person. And no matter what she thought, Bunny was ill-equipped to put him on the spot.

As we approached the top of the hour, Bunny nodded to me. She wrapped the show, promising her listeners she planned to pursue the Beverly Hills robberies and Carmen's murder. "Stay tuned for exclusive updates from KCHC. Until then, this is KCHC investigative reporter Bunny Morganstern."

I bristled at Bunny's use of the term "investigative reporter" and tossed the stack of chick-lite news stories over my head. It felt exhilarating to be rid of them. I pulled up the email Eric had sent alerting me to Annabelle's robbery. I adjusted my headset and glanced in her direction. Two could play at this game of hers.

"This just in...a spokesperson for Annabelle's Auction House announced early this morning they have been robbed. While preparing for the live auction this weekend of the Huguette Clark estate, auctioneers noticed several pieces appeared to have been replaced with copies of Miss Clark's personal jewelry. Reported to be missing are a pair of diamond and emerald earrings, estimated to be worth about eighty-five thousand dollars, an art-deco diamond bracelet by Cartier, circa 1925, valued at one hundred and twenty-five thousand dollars, and a rectangular square-cut diamond ring estimated to be worth nearly two point five million dollars."

CHAPTER 27

My cell phone buzzed as I was about to leave the news booth. I glanced quickly at the caller ID, noticed it was Nina, and answered immediately. From the tone of her voice, I could tell she wasn't happy.

"He's lying!" she screamed.

"Nina, slow down. What's wrong?"

"I'm sick of this family, that's what's wrong."

"What's going on?"

"That radio show a few minutes ago. I was listening, and the story about Carmen and the horses? That's not why Carmen stayed with Diaz. She didn't come running back to him because of what happened in Florida. He makes it sound like there was some big tearful reunion. That the horses died and that's why they didn't get divorced."

This wasn't a conversation I was prepared to have on the phone. Whatever information Nina had about Diaz and the horses and what happened in Florida had more than piqued my curiosity. And right now, Nina sounded ripe for the picking of a few family secrets she might not have been so willing to share before. That and the fact that I had just learned Diaz was preparing to leave the country made it all the more pressing I talk with her right away, in person.

"Nina, where are you?"

"I'm at the ranch."

"Does Diaz know you're there?"

"Like that matters," she snapped sarcastically. "I'm at the

barn. Diaz, if you want to know, is probably up at the main house."

I asked Nina if she could stay at the ranch. I told her I would be there within the hour, but first I needed to see Tyler. I had a few choice words I wanted to share with him about Bunny's new commando role.

I hurried down the hall and found Tyler seated behind his desk with his nose to the computer screen. I sat down in a huff and waited, feeling like a volcano about to explode. When he didn't notice me, I unleashed like Mt. Vesuvius, spewing news of Bunny's decision.

"Were you listening to the show just now? Did you know Bunny decided to investigate Carmen's death? And the robberies? That she suddenly thinks it's newsworthy?"

"I did." Tyler's answer was almost too quick and simple. He refused to look at me. But his hands came off his keyboard and he held them together in a fist beneath his chin. His jaw clenched.

"You knew?"

"I told you yesterday, Mr. Morganstern called and said he liked hearing Bunny on the air. He thought it made her happy." Tyler looked up in my direction for the first time. "Then this morning, he called back and suggested Bunny might like to return to broadcasting. Said she wanted to use the Beverly Hills robberies and Carmen's death as a test case for the station. Apparently, she's rethinking the whole chick-lite news format. Good, huh?"

"Good? Tyler, this is my story, and—"

"And what, Carol?" Tyler put both hands on the edge of his desk and leaned back in his chair. "You planning on actually going around that FBI boyfriend of yours? And maybe uncovering something every other reporter in town doesn't have fifteen minutes after we do?" He had me there. My privileged information was tantamount to little more than a press release with a promise of more down the road. Until then, Eric wasn't about to compromise an open investigation, and I wasn't about to ask him to for the sake of my reports. "You want this story, Carol, you are going to have to go get it. If you don't, Bunny will."

* * *

I met Nina at the ranch. She'd left word at the front gate I'd be coming, and I was directed to the barn, where she was grooming a horse in the crossties. She held the horse's halter in her hands and whispered in his ears, steadying him as I came closer. "Be careful where you stand. Diego's a bit skittish. He's been known to kick."

I took her at her word. The horse jerked his head in the halter, laying his ears back as I approached. I could see the white around the horse's eyes. This was one nervous animal. Cautiously, I leaned up against one of the barn's supportive posts, several feet from the horse's head, and asked if we could talk.

Nina looked around to make certain we were alone.

"I didn't like what Diaz was saying this morning. And the fact that he's leaving before there's even been an arrest for Carmen's murder worries me."

"Are you having second thoughts about Diaz? Do you think maybe he had something to do with your sister's murder?"

"Maybe. Truthfully, I've gone back and forth on it, and I don't like what I'm thinking. I mean, it's always the spouse, right?"

"Nina, on the phone you said Carmen didn't come running back to Diaz because of the horses. That the accident wasn't the reason she stayed. Why did she?"

"Because she couldn't leave." Nina stopped brushing the horse and looked at me. "Carmen came to Florida to serve Diaz with divorce papers. The press has photos of her getting off the plane in dark glasses and meeting Diaz. Everybody thought it was because she was so upset about Diaz and his horses. Truth was, she hadn't even heard about the accident."

"But if Diaz was at the airport, he had to know she was coming."

"Penny told him. He called and wanted to talk to Carmen, and when he couldn't get her, he tracked down her agent. By then she was already on a plane, just not for the reason everybody suspected. When Diaz met her at the airport, he had flowers and they were swarmed by the press. His fans thought she was coming to be with him. In reality, she had the divorce papers with her."

"But there's no record of them ever being divorced."

"Diaz's money is in a trust. He would have signed, but if she left him, Carmen got nothing. And Carmen wasn't about to leave empty-handed."

I picked up a grooming brush from the bucket in front of the crossties, pulling horse hairs from the combs as I thought about Carmen and Diaz and their relationship.

"He had to know she was stealing from him. You knew. You told me."

"Yes, and the FBI found out and came and emptied out her security box. Took a bag full of things. Big as a feedbag." Nina pointed with the horse's brush to one of the feedbags outside one of the stalls.

"Maybe Diaz got tired of it all. Maybe she crossed a line," I said.

"That's just it." Nina started to groom the horse again. "I don't think for Carmen there was a line. Diaz may have known what she was doing, but I think he liked keeping Carmen right where she was. Mrs. Umberto Diaz de la Roca. It kept all his lady-friends at bay."

"Like Mimi and Donatella?"

"At least." Nina began to pick the loose hairs from the rubber brush in her hand and let them fall to the floor. "But if either of them did it—killed Carmen—and I'm not saying they did, but *if* they did, I'm not convinced they had anything to do with robberies. That's what bothers me. I can see either one of them killing Carmen. They both hated her. But why steal from the man who supports them? Neither of them was hurting for money."

"LA's an expensive town, Nina. Maybe Mimi wanted more than Diaz was willing to give. Could be there was a limit."

"Hardly." Nina started brushing the horse again, this time with stronger, more circular motions. "What Mimi wanted, Mimi got. It's easy for Diaz. Half the time it isn't even his money. When Mimi needed extra cash, Diaz would arrange for her to show up at some charity function and get a few photos taken. That's how it works, you know. Nobody *donates* their time. There's a cost for attaching a celebrity name to any charity in this town. It happens all the time, and Diaz just made sure Mimi got her fair share."

"And Donatella? He takes care of her too?"

"She sleeps with him. What do you think?"

I had my suspicions about the girl, the last name Pero for one. But sharing a last name alone was hardly enough to convict one of both murder and robbery. I needed more, and from what little I had been able to learn about Donatella, it was obvious the girl was dependent upon Diaz for everything she had. If she were a struggling actress, I'd seen no evidence of it. After meeting with her in the restroom of the Beverly Wilshire, I'd researched IMDb and found no listing of her ever working. Far as I could tell, the only acting she'd been doing was that of Diaz's girlfriend. She may have gone out on a few auditions locally, just to keep her cover, but nothing had come of it. And if what Nina said about Diaz was true and he had picked her up in Europe to work as a horse trainer, other than seeing her with a groom's brush in her hand, my guess was the girl knew little more about horses than how to muck a stall. From all appearances, I thought Nina was right; Donatella was a wannabe actress who had come from nothing, landed in the arms of one of the world's most flamboyant playboys, and wanted nothing more than a leg up in life, and Diaz was happy to offer her the boost she needed.

I looked around the barn. It was messy, unlike the day of Carmen's memorial when there wasn't so much as a stray piece of hay on the floor. Up and down the aisle some of the stall doors were open. Half the horses appeared to be out of the barn. Their gear, blankets, bridles, saddles, and pads had been placed on the top of monogrammed tack boxes outside each of their stalls in preparation for their trip back to Spain.

What if the answer was right under my nose? Right here in the barn, so close to Diaz that even he didn't suspect.

"What about someone on Diaz's team? You think any of them might be involved?"

Nina shook her head. "If you'd asked me three years ago, I'd have to say definitely no. Diaz's team, they were like brothers to him. But after the horses died, none of his teammates wanted anything to do with him. They thought he was jinxed, and they deserted him. He had to start over."

"You mean build a new team?"

"Yeah. Horses. Riders. Trainers. Everything. They're all new. All except for Six Pence. He's Diaz's horse. He was in the barn the other day when you were here. A couple of Diaz's teammates were working on his hoof. When the accident happened in Florida, Six Pence was still here. Diaz had left him on account of an injury. The horse is accident-prone. It's the only reason he's still alive. He's the lone survivor and because of it, Diaz will never part with him."

I wondered about those things Diaz wouldn't part with, and I didn't want to share with her my thoughts about Diaz's new team. I wasn't even sure myself if they were involved, but the idea starting to form in the back of my mind concerned me. Were they all in on it? Were they a team of traveling thieves?

Instead, I asked, "Was Donatella with Diaz when the accident happened?"

"That's the first I remember hearing about her. Carmen flew down to Florida, and Donatella was with him when she arrived. Carmen was furious, but what could she do? For all practical purposes, they were separated, and you don't leave a man like Diaz alone. You'd think the fact Diaz had Donatella with him would be enough to make Carmen want to walk away, but it wasn't. Not without his money. Instead, she agreed to look the other way, and they continued to live separate lives. Donatella was with him from then on."

Something about what Nina said about the timing of Donatella's appearance and that of Diaz's new team bothered me. I had no proof, but what if Donatella didn't care about being the next Mrs. Umberto Diaz de la Roca as much as she let on? What if she cared more about her teammates? Could she be but one of the players in a team of thieves? Something like Lewis had described when talking about the Pink Panthers in Paris? A well-organized group of international jewel thieves? "Nina, do you think Donatella knew when Carmen would be making deliveries for Diaz?"

"I don't know, maybe. Why?"

"Because if what you just told me is true, I don't think Diaz killed your sister. And I don't think he did anything to cause her to be killed either. If he did that, Donatella would be in line to be the next Mrs. Umberto Diaz de la Roca. And I don't think that fits his lifestyle. I think he's a playboy and a gambler, but murderer and thief? I'm not so sure. I suspect Diaz, just like you said, likes things exactly as they are, and I doubt he wants to do anything to upset it."

"Then who killed my sister?"

"I'm not sure," I said. "It could be Donatella, or someone else close to Diaz. Maybe even several someones who knew when Carmen would be making deliveries and followed her around so they could not only steal the jewels she was delivering for Diaz but also knock off the stores she was visiting."

"And double their take?" she asked.

"Exactly, Nina. And if Carmen found out about it—"

"It might be what got her killed."

CHAPTER 28

It was dark by the time I left Nina at the barn. The sun sets early in December, and the skies were inky black and the traffic was a slow crawl back to the valley. It wasn't until I approached the crest of the Santa Susana Pass that I noticed the headlights in my rearview mirror. The car behind me was on my tail like a dog in heat.

I sped up, and he sped up. I slowed down, and he slowed down. Then the lights blinked. Whoever was behind me wanted my attention and wasn't going to give up until I did something to stop it. I pulled off the freeway at the first exit on the valley side and found a gas station. I figured a well-lit area beneath a street lamp with lots of people was as good a place as any to confront my tailgater. I locked the doors, sat back behind the wheel, took my phone from my purse, and with my thumb ready to hit the emergency speed dial, waited.

I watched in my rearview mirror as a big truck pulled in behind me, its front wheels hitting the curb and jostling the cab as it came to a stop. Between the dust from the mountain pass and the cab's blackened windows, I couldn't make out who or how many people might be in the cab. Then the driver's side door swung open. A boot hit the ground, followed out by a cowboy hat and a pair of broad shoulders. I held my breath as the stranger approached and, with the back of his hand, knocked on my window.

"Carol, roll the window down, will ya?"

If the stranger hadn't said my name, I might have hit the gas and sped off or, at least, leaned on the horn to attract attention. Instead, I rolled the window down partially and peered out a slim crack at the top of my door. From beneath the broad brim of the cowboy hat was a face I knew. It was Paley, Westin's security guard.

"Sorry if I scared you Ms. Childs, but I need to talk to you. It's important. About the case you're working on."

"Excuse me, but how did you even know who I am? Are you following me?" I took my thumb off the emergency dial. I was more angry than frightened. I had left numerous messages for Paley; after the robbery, several times after Churchill and I spoke, and again the day of the polo matches in Santa Barbara, all of which he had ignored. The fact that now he wanted to talk to me and had chased me down in the dark of night made me think something urgent was bothering him.

"I saw you leave the barn, Ms. Childs. And I know you're the reporter who covered the robbery at Westin's. Look, we can't talk here. Can I buy you a drink?"

If I wasn't so desperate to get answers, I might have turned him down. But a reporter can't always pick the place and time for an interview, and I needed to know more about Paley if I had any hopes of understanding what was going on with this case.

I mentioned I knew there was a bar, the Cowboy Palace Saloon, a few blocks south off Devonshire. From time to time, Sheri and I would hang there and enjoy two-stepping to the music. And right now it seemed like a much better place to talk than in the parking lot of a gas station.

"Perfect. I'll follow you," he said.

I led the way, my eyes going back and forth from the road ahead to the lights in the rearview mirror the entire time, wondering what this was all about. As I pulled into the parking lot at the Cowboy Palace, I realized I really didn't know much about Paley. I had no idea if he was involved in the robberies or if he might even be connected to Carmen's murder.

We settled ourselves in one of the red booths and I ordered myself a glass of white wine, something to help settle my nerves. While I might have looked cool and calm on the outside, I was still shaking from our freeway pursuit. Paley ordered a beer.

"Look, Ms. Childs, I owe you an apology. I know you've wanted to talk to me. You called after the bombing, and I never called you back. I didn't think I should be talking to reporters."

I waited as the waiter set down our drinks. "And now you want to talk? Tonight?"

"Let me finish. In my defense, the police and FBI were all over the robbery and the bombing. They didn't want me talking to the press. They told me not to talk to anyone, and Mr. Churchill, he wanted to keep things on the quiet side. So I did what I needed to do. You know, to keep my job. But now, I think I need your help."

I wondered why the man hadn't just picked up the phone and called me. Chasing after me in the dark of night seemed like a desperate attempt to get my attention.

"What is it you'd like me to do?"

"The investigators think it was an inside job. Whoever this Wigged Bandit is, she knew someone on the inside." She? Paley's reference made me think the FBI hadn't shared much with him concerning the Wigged Bandit's identity and probably had plenty of reason not to. "And I think they're looking at me."

"Why?" I wrapped my hands around my drink and leaned back against the red Naugahyde seat. I wasn't about to let my guard down.

"It's Diaz. He's always been very good to us at the store. Sometimes when Carmen would come in he'd come with her, and we'd get to chatting. I love horses. I have a couple of my own. Anyway, after the robbery he sent over tickets for the polo matches. We talked more at the game, and before I knew it, he'd offered me one of his horses, a retired polo pony named Six Pence."

"I was under the impression Diaz would never part with that horse."

"That's just it. He always made a big deal about how much he loved that horse. He's got photos of the horse in all his programs and has been quoted saying how he'd never sell him."

"And then he gives him to you, and the FBI starts to wonder why?"

"Exactly. Diaz sent him over yesterday. Up until then I thought he was joking."

I had to admit, knowing what I did about Diaz and how Nina said he'd never part with Six Pence, this raised my suspicions as well.

"If it's not you, just who do you think the inside contact is?" I knew I sounded snippy, but the fact that Paley hadn't returned any of my calls and had chased after me on the freeway put me on the offensive. He could sweat a bit. I needed answers.

"I've been trying to figure that out. It's not me, I promise you. And I don't think Churchill's involved. The only one it could have been was Ms. Pero."

I wasn't about to reveal that the FBI thought so too. But I was interested in knowing what suspicions Paley had concerning the woman. "Why do you say that?"

"Because Ms. Pero and Mr. Churchill went out to dinner together the night before the robbery. That in itself wasn't unusual. They did from time to time, but the next morning Churchill calls in, and I hear Ms. Pero talking to him on the phone. Suddenly he's sick. She tells me he must have eaten something bad last night and he won't be in until much later in the day. Then she starts talking about Carmen Montague, that she's expected in the store early and Churchill wants to make sure she's not disturbed."

I hadn't heard this part of the story before, and I wanted to understand exactly what had gone on inside Westin's prior to the explosion. Something either Churchill or the FBI hadn't already shared with me. "Then what happened?"

"Ms. Pero asked if I'd keep the showroom quiet until Ms. Montague left. You know how stars are. They like to shop by themselves, with no one else in the store to bother them. To tell you the truth, I didn't think much about it until the FBI started asking all kinds of questions."

I knew Paley was right about celebs and their shopping habits. Before he died, Bob Hope used to grocery shop at Gelson's after the store closed. The managers kept it open just for him so he wouldn't be disturbed. A lot of merchants do the same for some of their bigger names.

"But you definitely remember Ms. Pero telling you Churchill said Carmen would be in the store that morning?"

"Yes, but I don't think Mr. Churchill told her that. I think she was lying about it."

"What makes you so sure?"

"The day before the robbery I heard Ms. Pero on the phone with Carmen. I could tell by the conversation Carmen wanted to speak to Mr. Churchill, but Ms. Pero kept saying he was busy. I thought that odd because I knew he was in the office napping. He did that sometimes. The old guy got tired standing on his feet all day. Anyway, later that morning, I heard Ms. Pero on the phone again. Only this time, she was calling Carmen back confirming her appointment with Mr. Churchill the following morning. I didn't think anything of it, but now I wonder if maybe she never told Churchill about Carmen's call or her plan to visit the store."

"You think Ms. Pero set the appointment up and never told Churchill about it? And that she took Churchill out to dinner the night before and got him sick deliberately?"

Paley nodded. "Something like that. All I know for certain is that Ms. Pero was very upset when Mr. Churchill came in that morning. I don't think she expected him to rally so quickly."

"And what about the Wigged Bandit? Did you see...her?"

"I know there was a redheaded lady waiting in the showroom that morning. Ms. Pero had gone to the vault for something. When she came out, Mr. Churchill was there. She seemed very surprised to see him."

"Did she say anything?"

"I don't remember. Carmen arrived a few minutes later with some man, and she and Churchill started talking. Churchill was showing her something, or she was showing something to him. I'm not sure. Either way, Carmen was in a rush. Next thing I know, Carmen's gone and there's this explosion. The police say it was a flash bomb. Whatever it was, the air filled with smoke, and I threw open the front doors so we could breathe. Everything after that you pretty much know."

"I assume you've shared this with the cops and the FBI?"

"I have. I met with them this morning, but like I said, I don't think they believed me."

Paley's story backed up what I knew the FBI had on Ms. Pero, and I could understand why the old security guard was nervous. Diaz's gift horse certainly aroused suspicion, and the FBI had no reason to believe Ms. Pero acted alone.

"Anything else you want to tell me? 'Cause if you've already shared this with the investigators, there's not much I can do."

Paley took a long swing of his beer. "It has to do with the delivery of the horse, or the driver anyway. Could have been a groom or a trainer, I don't know. But he was overly curious about me. He seemed to know I worked security at Westin's and that I was there the day of the robbery. You'd think he'd be asking all about my barn and the setup, but instead he kept asking questions about the explosion and Ms. Pero."

"Like what?" Now Paley had my attention.

"He wanted to know if I thought Ms. Pero had suffered."

"Odd question for a delivery driver. Did you get his name?" I took a sip of my wine.

"Tomas."

I nearly choked. Could Tomas be Tomi? My mystery caller, the Wigged Bandit? Was he the connection I was looking for? That would tie Diaz's team to the robbery? "Tomas? You sure he said his name was Tomas, not Tomi or anything like that?"

"I don't know anything more than that, other than he seemed to know a lot about horses and was helpful getting Six Pence set up in the barn. Truth was, I didn't want to keep talking about the robbery. It bothered me."

"And you shared that with the police?"

"Absolutely. But I'm not sure how much good it did. I mean, Ms. Pero's dead, I worked security at the store, and now I've got Diaz's horse. I'm pretty sure they think I'm lying."

The waiter brought us a second round of drinks. I switched the topic back to why Paley had followed me down the freeway. I wanted to know how he had found me.

"It was an accident. I was going to call you, but then this Tomas guy, he forgot to bring some of Six Pence's gear by when he trailered the horse over. So I came back to the barn to pick up his bridle and a few extra things. And that's when I saw you talking to Nina. I decided to wait around until you left. I didn't mean to scare you on the freeway. I'm sorry. But I figured if the FBI's going to finger me for this, I could use a reporter on my side."

"I'm a long way from being on anyone's side, Mr. Paley."

"I get that. But Diaz and his people, they're getting ready to go back to Europe. And the fact the Feds are going to let them go tells me they don't think Diaz has anything to do with any of this, and I've got nowhere to turn."

I had to agree. I couldn't believe Diaz was leaving the country. On the other hand, I still had questions about Paley and Donatella. I didn't know what their relationship was, and I had seen them together on more than one occasion—the polo match, inside the barn at Carmen's memorial, and last night at the Beverly Wilshire.

"Tell me, what do you know about Donatella? I saw you with her in the barn the day of Carmen's memorial. How well do you know her?"

Paley looked at me like I'd accused him of skirt chasing.

"Not at all." He held his hands up in surrender. "She's Diaz's trainer. Other than that, I barely know the woman."

I put my glass down then raised a brow. If I was going to be lied to I needed something better than that.

"Look, if you must know, I was at a dinner with her at the Beverly Wilshire last night. But only because Diaz insisted I come. He said it was to celebrate the transfer of the horse, although I suspect I was there more as a cover for their relationship. I don't want to get involved. What the man does, who he does it with, it's not my business. I felt I owed him, but other than last night, the only other time I saw her was in the barn the day of Carmen's memorial. We were all watching the farrier work on Six Pence. I spoke with her a little about the horse, but that's all. Other than that she was talking mostly with the other trainers. They all appeared to be pretty close and were speaking some language I didn't understand. Czechoslovakian or something like that."

CHAPTER 29

When I got home, Charlie met me at the front door with the house phone in his hand. He was dressed in his football jersey, despite the fact he'd been benched from practice because of his broken arm, and he looked like he was ready to tackle someone.

"You okay?"

"There's a message on the house phone, Mom. You need to listen to it." He handed me the phone and I put it on speaker. I couldn't imagine why he was so concerned.

"Ms. Childs..." My heart froze the minute I heard the soft, raspy drawl. I knew immediately it was Tomi. I feigned a cough and took the phone off speaker.

"Charlie, could you get me a glass of ice water from the kitchen? I've been talking all day, my throat's dry."

While Charlie fetched me a glass of water, I played the rest of the message.

"You need to watch out for your friend. All the digging she's doing; she's becoming a nuisance. You might want to call her off. Accidents happen, you know."

Accidents happen? I had said those very words to Tomi when I last spoke to him.

Charlie returned with a glass of ice water and a look of concern on his face. "What's that about, Mom? It sounded serious. You okay?"

I saved the message and turned my attention back to him.

"It's nothing to worry about, I promise."

I didn't want to worry him. Since my first experience investigating a crazed psychopath I knew I needed to keep my work life and my personal life separate. But in the back of my mind, I also knew I was in trouble. Tomi had my home phone number, and it was my own fault. Like a lot of single women, I was listed in the phone book with my first initials only, family name, and no address. I should have known better; it was like a red flag to anyone trying to track down a single woman. It would have been better to be unlisted. It made it too easy.

"Hey, I've got a coupon for Ben & Jerry's. If you're completely done with your homework, what do you say we call Sheri and Clint and treat ourselves to a little Cherry Garcia?"

I knew Charlie couldn't resist his favorite ice cream. The thought of something sweet was almost Pavlovian and guaranteed to redirect his teenage attention. I picked up the phone and left a message for Eric on his cell phone. I told him about the suspicious voicemail and then called Sheri. We needed to talk. If the "friend" in the voicemail was Sheri, I needed to find out why she was becoming such a nuisance.

Sheri sat across from me at one of the small Ben & Jerry's tables with a triple scoop of Tonight Dough, a blend of caramel and chocolate ice cream with chunks of chocolate and peanut butter cookie dough mixed in with chocolate chips. I splurged on my usual, a double scoop of Cherry Garcia, and then told her about the voicemail I had received on my home phone from Tomi.

"He couldn't have meant you, could he?"

"Me? Are you kidding, Carol? I'm still waiting for my box of chocolates."

I loved that Sheri dispelled fear with humor, but this was serious. I reminded her that the caller could very well be the person who had murdered Carmen. "And any box of chocolates from this crazy Wigged Bandit, Tomi, Tomas, or otherwise, you don't want."

Sheri closed her eyes and turned the small plastic spoon over in her mouth. The look on her face was somewhere between sweet ecstasy and deep meditative thought.

"Sheri?"

"Maybe it's Bunny. Did you ever think of that? She's pushed herself into the story. She's probably pissed off your Wigged Bandit friend, and now he's after her."

I couldn't eat anymore. I pushed my ice cream away. My stomach clenched at the thought of the Wigged Bandit in pursuit of Bunny. Sheri looked at me then back at my half-eaten bowl of ice cream. "You're not going to eat that?" I shook my head.

"If it is Bunny, how am I going to tell her? It's not like she's going to believe me. She'll think I'm trying to steal the story back from her."

"But just the same, Carol, you have to try."

I agreed, and after Charlie was in bed, I called Bunny's cell. She didn't pick up. Not that I expected she would, but I left a message all the same. "Bunny, it's Carol. Look, we need to talk. I can't get into everything right now, but I think you're in trouble. It concerns the robberies and maybe Carmen's murder. Call me. It's important."

She never returned my call.

The next morning, I came into work early. I wanted to talk to Tyler about the voicemail I had received at home, and I hoped I might find Bunny wandering the halls. Instead, it was unusually quiet, void of the usual buzz of activity with interns running in and out of the studio and sales reps mixing it up with on-air talent. This morning, it was as though everybody had left the building.

I walked past the studio where KCHC's new morning team, Mitzi and Charlie, were in the midst of their broadcast. I waved and got no reply and continued down the hall towards Tyler's office.

Tyler stood up when I walked in, as though he'd been expecting me. His slim, pencil-thin frame leaned against the desk, his freckled face unusually pale.

"Good. You're here."

"What's up?" I asked.

"Bunny's missing."

"Missing?" I felt my stomach tighten. "What do you mean, missing?"

"Morganstern just called. Said Bunny left early this morning before he got up. They were supposed to meet for breakfast—something about Bunny wanting to discuss some programming changes here at the station. He thought maybe she was upset about something and had just gone out for a walk, but she never came back. And she's not here."

"Maybe she's stuck in traffic or just running late. She does that, you know."

I wanted an explanation, anything that wouldn't feed that growing feeling of dread I felt forming in the pit of my stomach.

Tyler shook his head. "Morganstern's got a bad feeling about it."

I sat down in the chair in front of Tyler's desk.

"So do I."

I told Tyler about the voicemail from last night. How I thought for certain the caller had been Tomi, and how he had said my friend was becoming a nuisance.

"At first I thought it might be Sheri, but Sheri hadn't done anything and suggested it could be Bunny. I'm tempted to agree with her. He was making a threat, Tyler. I think he thought I could call her off."

"You're certain it was the same voice, the same mystery person—this Tomi—who's called here before?"

"He said accidents happen. That's the same phrase I used with him the last time he called me. Only this time he used my name, Tyler, and he has my home number."

Tyler sat down. "We need to call the police."

I was about to explain that I'd left a message for Eric when Tyler's inside line rang. A number only those who worked at the station, including Morganstern, had.

Tyler looked over at me. "It's Morganstern. Stay put."

Tyler stood up again and took the call. From the look on his face, and the half of the conversation I could hear, the news wasn't good.

"The police?...They're sure?...I see. Diaz's ranch?...Got it. I'll get Carol out there right away, sir....and Mr. Morganstern, I'm sorry for your loss."

"Loss?" I gripped the railing on the chair and leaned forward. "Is she—"

He hung up and looked at me. "Bunny Morganstern is dead."

The words burned my ears. I couldn't believe it. We weren't friends. In fact, the feelings between us were growing more adversarial by the day. But dead? I didn't want Bunny to be dead. I felt as though the air had been sucked out of the room.

Tyler sat back down behind his computer and began typing on autopilot. I knew he'd be pulling together a news story. Bad news happens, and newspeople focus on the work. In Tyler's case, his feelings were coming from the tips of his fingers and out onto the keyboard. He kept typing as he spoke.

"Morganstern says she was investigating Carmen's death. Something about it led her to Diaz's ranch. She was found dead in the barn this morning by one of Diaz' trainers."

I closed my eyes. Of course she was investigating. Bunny had gone through my files and seen my notes. She knew the contributing cause of Carmen's death had been copper sulfate, a chemical commonly used by vets for the treatment of thrush with horses. She had gone to the ranch to find the killer. Only the killer had found her first.

CHAPTER 30

I would have known something was wrong at Diaz's ranch even without the early morning inside tip from Morganstern. Traffic headed west along the 118 had slowed to a near stop and police cars were parked everywhere, catawampus next to the hillside, their lights flashing. Halfway up the hill, off road, a silver-colored Land Rover with the driver's door wide open had been deserted. Bunny's car? It looked as though someone had put the vehicle into four-wheel drive and then plowed up the hillside in an attempt to avoid the main gate. Muddy footprints led from the vehicle to the white corral fencing surrounding the estate. On the side of the hill, slide marks indicated the climber had tried several times to sneak onto the property, avoiding the main entrance, before successfully crawling beneath the barrier.

I passed two patrol cars parked outside the main entrance and proceeded towards the gate. Carmen's former PR person, Penny Salvatti, was standing in the center of the road wearing a hooded windbreaker. Her red hair was frizzy from the moisture in the air, the gate wide open behind her. I flashed my station ID and said I was here to talk with Diaz. She nodded and pointed solemnly in the direction of another small brigade of early responders. An unmarked black SUV—possibly the FBI's—and an LAPD patrol cruiser were parked outside the barn.

I knew with the presence of the black SUV, Eric would be inside. Anything unusual that went down on the ranch at this point was bound to be on the FBI's radar. I spotted Eric as I entered the barn. He was squatting down in front of Donatella, his back to me. She was seated on a bale of hay crying uncontrollably, her head in her hands. Across from her, next to the area where Nina had been grooming the horse, was a body. It was covered with one of the barn's green horse blankets and appeared to be lying face up. From beneath the blanket, I could see the tips of Bunny's brightly painted red fingernails and the bottom of her work boots. The same ones she had worn into the studio the day before. The only difference was today they were covered with mud.

It didn't take an investigator to know someone had moved the body. A trail of blood was smeared across the floor from the empty crossties to where the body now lay. Bloody hoof prints and footprints from a small pair of boots were everywhere. A torn bag of blue crystals I assumed to be copper sulfate had spilled open and mixed with the blood. It bled like little rivers into a bloody purple mass where it pooled beneath the crossties. Someone had removed the horse, taken it back to its stall, and dragged the body to its current position, then covered it with the blanket.

I replayed Tomi's voicemail in my head as I stared at the scene and imagined how it had all gone down. Bunny had probably received a call from Tomi, exactly like I had. Only to her, it would have been an anonymous caller, luring her to the barn with the promise of helping to solve Carmen's murder.

Bunny probably arrived early, before dawn, and found Donatella, or perhaps Tomas, grooming a horse in crossties with a small bag of copper sulfate at his feet. It would have been perfect. Bunny knew about the copper sulfate. She had stolen my notes and would have read how the coroner had found evidence of the chemical in Carmen's system, and that the crystals were used for veterinary purposes. And there they were, like bait, beneath the horse's hooves. Maybe Donatella or Tomas even pointed them out to her and asked if she could hand them the bag. If it were Tomas, I could almost hear him say it with his thin, raspy voice. "Would you mind, love?"

But Bunny knew nothing about horses. A city girl from

Chicago, she probably thought with the horse in crossties and Tomas holding his halter, it was fine. Except, if the horse had been Diego, the horse I had seen Nina with the day before, Bunny wouldn't have stood a chance. The animal would have spooked and kicked her the minute she bent down behind him, his powerful rear legs smashing into her skull. Death would have been instantaneous. It would have looked like an accident. Exactly like Tomi had said on my voicemail. "Accidents happen."

Only I knew this wasn't an accident.

I took out my notepad and wandered down the aisle.

The stall doors that yesterday had all been open were now shut, their barred, yoked windows bolted tight. The only view I could get of the horses was through metal bars. I found Diego's stall, his brass nameplate above the door, and peered into his cell. The horse's back was to me, his head hung low as he nibbled at a flake of hay in the far corner. My eyes went to his back legs. I scanned his haunches, his hocks, his hooves. At the base of his heel, I spotted evidence of trauma. There was blood on it, and more spots of blood on the bedding beneath him. I made a note and proceeded down the aisle. I needed to find Diaz.

I found him inside the tack room at the end of the aisle. He was standing in the center of the room, dressed in his riding boots and jodhpurs. The walls of the room were lined with bridles and riding gear. Grooms and teammates sat on tack boxes like they had just been called for a meeting. They all looked dazed, as though they had just been slapped across the face and were still trying to absorb the blow. I wondered if one of them was Tomas. Diaz stopped talking and looked at me as I leaned against the door.

"May I help you?" Diaz looked at me. His eyes and brows narrowed to a frown. I could see he was trying to place me.

"I'm Carol Childs," I said. I extended my hand and reminded him I was with the radio station. "Bunny Morganstern and I worked together."

He bowed his head and pinched his eyes shut like he might be holding back tears.

"Yes. You were here for the memorial. Tyler Hunt said you'd be coming." He pointed toward the door, and we walked back out to the aisle.

"Can you tell me what happened?"

He looked back down the aisle at Bunny's covered body and shook his head.

"Donatella came and got me. She was in the barn this morning working with Diego. She was hysterical. She kept saying there had been an accident. When I got here, I found Bunny slumped in a ball beneath the crossties. Her head was bashed in."

"Did Donatella tell you what happened?"

"She said she left Diego in the crossties. She'd forgotten a hoof pick and went back to the tack room to get one. Next thing she knows something's wrong with Diego. She hears someone scream and the horse is whinnying and kicking like crazy. She comes running and finds Bunny on the ground, beneath his hooves."

"And she moved the horse?"

Diaz nodded. "Of course. She put Diego back in his stall and then came running to get me. She was terrified. Still is, look at her."

I glanced back to where Donatella sat with Eric. She had a tissue in her hands and was gesturing frantically. She looked more emotional now than when I'd first seen her.

But it wasn't Donatella I was concerned about. Diaz was lying. Either that or Donatella was a better actress than anyone credited her to be. No trainer worth his boots would ever leave a horse in crossties alone. Certainly not a horse like Diego. Diaz had to know that. It was inviting disaster. Anyone who worked around horses knew better.

"And who moved the body?"

"I did," Diaz said. "And then I called the police."

"Do you have any idea why Bunny was here?"

"None. I'd invited her to come out to the ranch for riding lessons. It was an open invitation. I always ask friends. But she hadn't told me anything about coming. She may have called and set something up, but I didn't have it on my calendar."

"So you had no idea she'd be here?"

"Not at all." Diaz shook his head and glanced back at Donatella. He was clearly worried about the girl.

"And Donatella, she was alone in the barn? Your other riders, they weren't around?"

"Mornings are busy for us. They all would have been in and out of the barn, exercising the horses."

I looked back down the aisle. I didn't notice any empty stalls. Diaz must have called all the riders in when he discovered the body.

"And what about Tomas?"

"Tomas?" Diaz seemed surprised I knew any of his people by name.

"Yes. Tomas and Donatella are both trainers, right?" I paused to see if Diaz reacted, hoping I'd see some tell or facial tic that might indicate he knew Tomas was involved in the murder. There was nothing. "Was he around this morning?"

Diaz glanced back into the tack room and shook his head. "I haven't seen him. He may have taken a horse from one of the other barns out into the hills for an early morning trail ride. He does that from time to time."

I was about to ask Diaz more about Tomas when I heard a scream coming from the other end of the barn. I turned to see Morganstern burst through the barn doors like a madman. Two cops were on him instantly. I knew it was procedure for the police to hold relatives back when a body was discovered. But Morganstern had somehow escaped their hold. He cried out Bunny's name, clawing at the air as though he were trying to pull his way closer to her body. Overpowered by emotion and the strength of the cops, he fell to his knees, sobbing.

"You're going to have to excuse me. I need to go to him." Diaz pushed past me and jogged in the direction of where Morganstern had collapsed.

Halfway down the aisle, where Eric and Donatella were talking, he stopped and said something to Eric. There was a quick exchange, then Diaz lifted a tearful Donatella to her feet and the two walked over to Morganstern. Diaz stopped momentarily, leaned down and touched Morganstern's shoulder, and whispered something into the grieving man's ear. Then putting his arm back around Donatella and pulling her to him closely, they disappeared through the barn doors.

Eric looked back at me. Our eyes locked like we were the only two people in the barn. He stood up and I watched as he approached.

"Carol, you got a minute? There's something we need to talk about."

I decided to beat him to the punch. The events of the morning were overwhelming. I was frustrated, angry and confused. I lashed out.

"Didn't you get my voicemail last night? About the message on my home phone? That I needed to watch out for *my friend*?"

"I got it this morning, Carol. You left it on my cell phone. I thought it was personal. It wasn't marked urgent. I had no idea it had anything to do with the case. I've been up all night with the investigation and I'm beat. I didn't play it back until an hour ago. By the time our guys checked it out, Bunny was already dead." Eric sounded like he was measuring his words, being careful to control any sense of emotion. His voice was monotone.

"Dammit." I couldn't look Eric in the eye. I turned my back to him. I was angry at myself. Why hadn't I marked the call urgent? All I had to do was hit the pound sign and he would have known. Had I just assumed Eric would see the call was from me and answer it? I looked back at the body. I wanted to erase the scene, but I couldn't unsee Bunny's dead body lying in the center of the aisle. If only I had tried to call her again, gotten hold of her instead of just leaving a message, maybe none of this would have happened. With my fists to my mouth, tight like I wanted to punch something, I said, "I feel responsible."

I could feel Eric standing behind me, the heat of his body just inches from my own. Another time he might have put his arms around me, but, for now, we were maintaining our professional roles. Instead, he put his hand lightly on my shoulder, like he might a colleague.

"Carol, this isn't your fault. Investigations aren't easy. Bad things happen. Things don't always wrap up in nice neat little packages with the bad guys going to jail."

I stared into Eric's eyes. He looked tired, his eyes bloodshot. For the first time, I had an idea of what he must feel like to chase after criminals, knowing, in the end, they just might get away with everything. It had to be tough.

"The good guys don't always win, Carol."

I shook my head. "Does Diaz know who you are?" I was angry. I needed to know.

"He thinks we're all part of the investigation. That's all I can tell you."

"And Donatella? You just questioned her and let her go?" I pointed back in the direction of where Eric had been sitting with Donatella. "You can't possibly believe this was an accident. That she's not somehow connected to everything you're investigating. She's got the same last name as the woman killed in the jewelry store. Pero. That can't be a coincidence."

"It's a name, Carol. And it doesn't matter what I believe, not right now. We need proof and that isn't always easy. It's not like it is on TV. Things don't come out in an investigation when you want them to. It takes time to find evidence and to make it stick. And off the record—between you and me—sometimes it takes a little help. But I can tell you we're getting close. We've got another videotape with the Wigged Bandit on it."

"You mean Tomas?"

I caught a flicker of surprise in Eric's eyes. "So you know his name?"

"That Tomas is probably Tomi, a.k.a. the Wigged Bandit, and works for Diaz? Yeah, I do. And if I'm right, he's not alone. He may have a few of his buddies traveling with him."

Eric smiled. "You're a good investigative reporter, Carol. Better than anyone gives you credit for."

Right now I felt like I needed to be a better reporter than a girlfriend, and the two, just like Bunny had said, made for a difficult mix.

"So what? Why are you telling me this? I can't do anything with it."

"I wouldn't rule that out. Not yet. There's something more you need to know. This other videotape is from the Beverly Wilshire. It was taken when Annabelle's was setting up the auction for the Huguette Clark collection. The missing jewels you reported on from the collection, they were stolen from the auction *before* the public showing. Before the show was open to the public and the jewels were all officially mounted in the display cases."

"But Annabelle's reported it after the auction opened."

"That's when we discovered it. Someone switched out some of the jewels prior to the auction."

Eric explained how the cameras inside the Beverly Wilshire Hotel had caught Tomas on tape, working as an assistant to the auctioneer, just as Annabelle's was setting up the auction. Annabelle's had believed Tomas was an employee of the Clark Estate while the Estate claimed never to have seen him before.

"But it gets better, Carol. As a matter of practice, Annabelle's invites potential big buyers for a private viewing. It's a big deal, happens a couple days before the public viewing, and guess who was one of those buyers invited to the event?"

"Diaz," I said.

"And who do you suppose he brought with him?"

"Donatella?"

"Exactly. And according to Diaz, he also brought along a ring, similar to Ms. Clark's two-million-dollar diamond ring, that he had purchased from an estate sale in Europe. It appeared he wanted to compare the two. It's an old sleight of hand trick. Diaz looks away, something or someone diverted his attention. On the tape, it looks like Donatella has pulled him away. At that point, the assistant, Tomas, switches the rings, and Diaz goes home with a two-million-dollar ring in his pocket, thinking it's the ring he brought to compare. The ring in the display case is valued at a fraction of the one the late Ms. Clark owned. It's a two-hundred-thousand-dollar fake."

"A big difference," I said.

"But not something the untrained eye looking through a glass display case is going to notice."

"And Diaz knows?"

"He does now."

"Which means he knows he's been set up."

"Possibly. And that's one of the reasons the FBI needed you not to say anything about what we've been doing. Like I said, we're getting close, Carol. We're just not there yet."

"And what about the ring? Where's it now?"

Eric suggested I sit down. I found a tack box outside one of the stalls and sat on top of it.

"It's the ring Carmen was wearing the night of the awards show. The ring she left in the hotel room—in her bag—before joining Mimi at the after party. And, more importantly, the ring she asked me to fetch for Churchill the night she was murdered."

"It was Huguette Clark's ring?" I slapped my hand to my chest. My heart was beating like a racehorse.

"She believed it was just another ring Diaz wanted to sell. And as you thought, she was trying to skim off the top from those jewels she delivered from Diaz."

"She didn't know it was a two-and-a-half-million-dollar ring?"

"Diaz is sure she had no idea."

"And you still have it?"

Eric laughed. "Not on me. But trust me, we have it."

I stood up and stared into the stall behind me. Inside, a bay-colored polo pony with a dark cropped mane and tail cribbed at the door, biting the rough wood beneath the bars. I reached for a handful of hay from the feedbag and extended my flat hand beneath the bars. Then, turning around, I looked at Eric and brushed my hands clean.

"And yet come Sunday, the FBI's just going to let Diaz and his team get on a plane and fly back to Europe. When it's becoming more and more apparent Diaz is either involved or being played and hasn't got a clue what's going on around him."

"You know that's not something I can talk about."

I stared into his eyes, leveled and focused on my own. He didn't have to tell me. I was getting good at reading his masked expressions. This was a setup.

"Because Diaz isn't just going to fly out of the country, is he? That's why you want to talk to me. The FBI's giving them all—Tomas and Donatella and anyone else involved—just enough rope to hang themselves."

"No comment."

"So we are on the same team."

"I hope so. But you and I? We never had this conversation."

I looked into Eric's eyes. I missed our conversations, those late night phone calls when he would call for no other reason than to say goodnight or just to hear my voice.

"We haven't had a lot of *conversations* lately, Eric. In fact, we haven't had much of anything."

Eric looked away quickly then back again, as though to check no one might overhear us. "I'm sorry about the way things are between us right now, Carol. I didn't plan it this way."

"No. I know you didn't." I stood up a little straighter and backed away an inch, enough to give me a little space. "We each have our roles to play, don't we?"

"Which is one of the reasons I needed to talk to you. We need you to broadcast something."

I took my notepad from my bag. My pen was poised and ready.

"So what is it the FBI would like me to report?"

"Ms. Morganstern's death was an accident and Diaz and his team will be returning to Spain on Sunday as previously scheduled. And you can include a quote that a source close to the investigation has told you they have no reason to suspect either Diaz or his team has any connection to Ms. Montague's death or to the recent jewelry store heists in Beverly Hills. They are cleared to go."

I finished writing. "Anything else?"

Eric glanced back over his shoulder and in a voice barely above a whisper, said, "About that conversation, the one we haven't had lately? Just so you know, I miss it too, Carol. I promise we'll have plenty of time to talk after this case is over. I'm planning on it."

I called the station from my Jeep. I didn't want to file news of Bunny's death from the barn. I had the uncomfortable feeling someone too close to the crime might not only be listening but also watching.

"Police were called to the ranch of Umberto Diaz de la Roca in Simi Valley this morning after a body was discovered in the barn. The body, believed to be that of Bunny Morganstern, wife of KCHC station owner, Howard Morganstern, appears to have died after being injured in a horse-related incident. When asked to comment, Mr. Diaz claimed he had no idea Ms. Morganstern was visiting the ranch and says he is devastated by the loss.

"In other news, Mr. Diaz has confirmed he is expected to return with his polo team to Spain on Sunday. Sources close to the investigation into the death of his wife, Carmen Montague, confirmed there is no evidence either Diaz or any member of his team is responsible for Ms. Montague's death. And that rumors suggesting Ms. Montague may have been a target or possibly connected to a string of jewelry store robberies in the Beverly Hills area completely false. This is Carol Childs reporting live from Simi Valley."

CHAPTER 31

I knew the FBI and the police had a lot to do before there could be an arrest. Far as I could tell, the FBI had nothing on Donatella, and Tomas was nowhere to be found. Suspicion was one thing, but only hard evidence would secure an arrest warrant. Cases that moved too quickly risked getting kicked out of court for lack of proper procedure.

As for me, I still had a lot of dots to connect before the big picture made any sense. Right now, it was just a bunch of moving pieces: Ms. Pero and Donatella had the same last name. No way was Donatella a horse trainer, and far as I knew, Ms. Pero had to have been Tomas' inside contact, but I didn't have any real proof they even knew one another. And Paley, if he was to be believed, may have simply been in the wrong place at the wrong time. As for Diaz and his relationship with Donatella, I had my suspicions, but who was using who? Was Diaz just using the girl to satisfy his male ego or perhaps to knock off Carmen, maybe even promising Donatella marriage in return? Or was she using him, helping position a team of international jewel thieves?

The only thing I did know was that the clock was ticking. And if Diaz and his polo team got on their plane Sunday and left LA, we might never know who had killed Carmen, who was behind the robberies, or where the jewels were. It would just be another unsolved case. Exactly like those in Europe. And if I was right, Donatella, Tomas, or the Wigged Bandit, and his team of thieves would win. All I knew for certain was that I had promised Nina to find her sister's killer. And now with Bunny's death weighing heavily on my mind, I owed that much to her as well.

After leaving the ranch, I went back to Henry Westin's. I wanted to return to the scene of the crime and talk with Churchill. I had questions about a couple of the women in his life, specifically Ms. Pero and Carmen Montague.

Churchill was behind the counter when I entered. He was dressed in a double-breasted blue blazer, a red bowtie, and gray slacks. He looked spiffy, every bit the British gentleman he was, right down to the pocket square in his left front pocket. I explained I wanted to talk to him more about the day of the explosion.

"Mr. Paley told me you weren't expected in the store that day. He said you had called in sick with an upset stomach. And that you informed Ms. Pero Carmen Montague would be coming in."

"That's partially correct. Ms. Pero and I had dinner together the night before the robbery. We do, or rather we did, from time to time. I'm afraid I still can't come into the store and not think about her. I miss her dearly. But that night, I got food poisoning. I must have eaten something at dinner that didn't agree with me. I had ordered the Chicken Amandine and woke up with a nasty case of the runs about two a.m. But by ten o'clock the next morning, I was feeling much better and decided I'd best go in. I remember Ms. Pero seemed quite surprised to see me."

"Did you share that with the investigators?"

"Oh, yes. And they seemed quite concerned. I believe they think she was involved. I have trouble with that, but you never know. People can surprise you."

I believed Churchill was surprised. In his orderly world of ascots and matched pocket squares, I didn't imagine he was much for personal conversation. It would make him too uncomfortable. But still, he had to know something about the woman.

I asked, "Can you tell me anything about her?"

"Not much." Churchill ran his fingers through his thinning hair as though it might help him to remember. Then as though he'd stumbled upon a thought that might help, he said, "I can tell you we spoke French together, and a smattering of other languages. She said she had grown up somewhere in the south of France. She teased she was a gypsy. Said she'd traveled a lot, never really settled anywhere. I think the longest she'd ever been anywhere was here in California, and she'd only been here a couple of years. I'm afraid our conversations really weren't personal. We talked mostly about art and jewelry." Churchill paused and placed his hand on his heart. "We weren't...involved, if that's what you're thinking."

"No." I laughed to myself. I was certain Churchill hadn't been involved with anyone in years, much less a woman. "I just was hoping to get a better idea of who she was."

"Well, I can tell you she had quite a good eye for detail. In fact, I think I may have something of hers. I probably should have given it to the detectives when they were here, but I'm afraid it slipped my mind. Let me check."

Churchill walked back into a small office at the end of the showroom and returned moments later with a jeweler's loupe.

"It's really of no value. She often wore it on a chain around her neck. I found it on her desk after the explosion. Poor dear, she must have taken it off and left it there. I remember she said it had been a gift from a friend from the old country. I got the feeling it was maybe from an ex-lover or husband."

"May I see?" I held my hand out, hoping to get a closer look.

"Here, you can have it." He piled the loupe and chain loosely in the palm of my hand. "Like I said, it's not worth much. The chain maybe, but it was mostly sentimental value."

I took the loupe from the palm my hand and studied it. On the rim was a small inscription. *To Celine, from Tomas with love.*

I cupped my hand around the loupe. Finally, I had proof. The Wigged Bandit, the redheaded woman, Tomi, and Tomas, I knew they were all the same person. I had identified photos and knew the voice. And now, with the loupe in my hand, I had evidence that tied Tomas to Ms. Pero. My excitement was almost palpable.

"Was Ms. Pero's first name Celine?"

"I suppose. I never called her by her first name. Like I said, our relationship was professional. To me, she was always Ms. Pero."

"Do you remember where Ms. Pero was before the explosion occurred?"

"She'd been in and out of the vault. There were some items on the counter she was showing a customer. I got the feeling she was about to finish up, and when Carmen came in, I asked her to fetch me Miss Taylor's necklace from the vault. I thought Carmen would like to see what her sister was wearing to the awards show."

"Are you certain you asked her? And that Ms. Pero didn't suggest it?"

"Oh dear." Churchill paused, his eyes squinted as he furrowed his brow and tried to recall. "I'm afraid, Ms. Childs, I'm really not sure."

I desperately needed him to remember. I wanted him to help me recreate the scene. I needed to have a clear idea where everyone was leading up to the explosion.

"Mr. Churchill, I know things happened very quickly, and that it was all very upsetting, but can you walk me through everything, exactly as you remember it? Starting from when Carmen came in that morning?"

"I remember Carmen was in a rush. I asked if she'd like to see the necklace her sister planned to wear and suggested Ms. Pero get it, but Carmen said she didn't have time. She handed me the eyeglass case with the jewels inside like she always does, then asked if I'd fix the clasp on a necklace she had and double-check the mounts on a pair of earrings. She slid them across the counter and next thing I know, she and her escort were out the door."

"And then what happened? I mean, before the bomb went off. There had to be a couple of seconds before the explosion, because I remember seeing Carmen get into a limousine parked outside and leave before anything happened."

"Yes, I guess there was." He paused. His eyes glanced down at the counter between us and then back to me. "I'm afraid it's a bit embarrassing. After Carmen left, my stomach started acting up again. It wasn't something I could postpone. I left the black case with Carmen's jewels beneath the counter and told Ms. Pero I had an emergency. I remember shutting the door between the showroom and office suite in the back. I suppose I was embarrassed and didn't want her to see me going to the loo. The result, I'm sorry to say, was devastating. Ms. Pero was locked in the showroom. If she'd just stepped into the back office, behind the security door, she would have been fine."

I looked behind the counter at a doorway leading to the back of the store. The door was heavy metal and stood as the first line of defense between the front of the shop and the vault. It would have been more than enough to withstand the explosion, and if Ms. Pero had been behind it, she might be alive today. Churchill's unexpected return to the store that morning and his sudden dash to the washroom had cost her life.

"And what about the redheaded woman? The one the police have on videotape? Where was she when the bomb went off?" I couldn't imagine the Wigged Bandit would have been in the store at the time of the explosion. The sound shock alone might have caused her a concussion.

"That's just it. She wasn't in the showroom when the bomb went off. She followed Carmen out the door when she left. I didn't think much of it. Just thought she might have been a fan. You know, chasing after a celebrity for a signature. You see it all the time. But the police tell me they think she's the one who planted the bomb. That she dashed out and then came back in and stole the jewels Ms. Pero had left on the counter along with Carmen's black eyeglass case."

"Except she didn't get Liz Taylor's La Peregrina necklace. It wasn't on the counter."

"I've wondered about that. When I realized Carmen didn't have time to see it I asked Ms. Pero to put it back in the vault. But the coroner found it on her person. The police think Ms. Pero panicked when she realized I'd shut the door to the back and forgot to leave it on the counter with the other jewels and Carmen's black case. Whatever happened, it appears the explosion either caused her to fall into one of the glass display cases and cut her neck or she was hit by flying glass. I don't suppose I'll ever know."

"And the security guard, Mr. Paley, where was he when the bomb went off?"

"He'd gone outside for a smoke right after we opened. Usually does in the morning. Always about the same time. I didn't see him again until after the explosion."

I walked the showroom and studied the outside double-door entrance. It would have been easy enough for the Wigged Bandit to slap a small explosive device on Westin's front door and maybe even another smoke bomb beneath one of the counters inside. All the Bandit had to do was wait until Carmen made her delivery and when she left, follow her out the door. Exactly like Churchill had described.

After that—depending on the type of explosive device used—she probably hit a remote button on her cell phone and triggered the explosion. The sound, not to mention the commotion of such a thing, provided just enough of a cover for her to dash in, steal whatever jewels Ms. Pero had left out for her, plus the black eyeglass case, and leave. The smoke would have been so thick she probably didn't even notice Ms. Pero's body on the floor behind the glass counter.

I shook my head. She had to have been hanging around somewhere safely down the street, watching me cover the scene while she changed her identity. And when I finished my report, there she was, this little old lady with shopping bags, walking back toward the parking garage, in need of my help. I stared at the big double doors, the entrance to Westin's. Strong and secure. She must have been surprised by my offer and delighted at the same moment. I was exactly what she needed, the perfect cover, and she used me. While I didn't have a clue about who she really was or what she had in her bags, she knew exactly what she was doing. She had everything she needed in those bags: the stolen jewels, a change of clothes, and probably another wig.

I was about to leave when an antique grandfather clock

standing next to the front door chimed one o'clock. Churchill looked like he was ready for a break.

"Just one more question. Did you ever suspect Carmen might have been skimming off the top?"

"You mean stealing from her husband?"

"I noticed at the awards show you had to ask her about the ring she'd forgotten to leave with you the day of the robbery. I was wondering if there were other items."

"There were times I noticed her delivery didn't match up with the list of jewels Diaz was selling. Sometimes I suspected she was taking things. For the most part, I considered it a cost of doing business. The ring, however, was an unusual piece. It's believed to have once belonged to Spain's Duchess of Alba, who recently died. I'm afraid I couldn't let that pass."

I thanked Churchill for his time. With the inscribed jeweler's loupe in my hand, I had found the proof I needed. I walked out of Henry Westin's feeling victorious. As for Carmen, I still wasn't certain how much she knew when she died. However, I was beginning to believe the reason she was killed wasn't so much because Donatella wanted to be the next Mrs. Umberto Diaz de la Roca, but because Carmen had discovered the truth about Diaz's team, and Donatella couldn't have that.

CHAPTER 32

I called Nina from my car on the way home. The reception up Beverly Glen through the canyon could be pretty sketchy, but I wanted to talk with her about Tomas as soon as possible. I figured with all the time she spent at the barn she had to know something about him. Where he was from. How he came to work for Diaz. I clutched the jeweler's loupe in my hand as I drove, too excited to let it out of my sight. The inscription, showing both Celine and Tomas' names on the loupe, had to be proof Tomas was connected to Ms. Pero. In my opinion, the jeweler's loupe, in addition to Liz Taylor's pearl necklace found on her body the morning of the robbery, was one more nail in Ms. Pero's coffin, pointing to her being the inside contact for the Westin's robbery.

After several rings, Nina answered the phone. She sounded breathless. "Carol! I'm so glad it's you. I was just about to call. You won't believe what's happened. The police are back."

"Are you at the barn?" I hoped so. Another set of eyes and ears at the ranch might be helpful right now.

"Yes, and Diaz is going crazy. I've never seen him so upset. The police are talking to Donatella." I heard a click through on the line. Someone else was trying to reach Nina. She sounded impatient. "Can you hold a minute? I've got another call."

Nina put me on hold while I imagined the scene at the ranch with Diaz. I wasn't surprised the police had gone back to talk to Donatella. If Eric had wanted me to broadcast that sources close to the investigation found no reason to delay Diaz's return trip to Europe in hopes of shaking things up, I figured this was them doing more of the same.

I doubted they were going to arrest Donatella. Proving Bunny's death hadn't been an accident was going to be difficult, but I knew the cops would make a scene of it. Do what they could to make Donatella think they suspected her and hope it makes her nervous. Enough so that she would believe she was about be left behind when the team left on Sunday, and maybe even confess.

An enthusiastic Nina came back on the line. "That was Mimi. I told her the police were here and she's all excited. This is good news, right?"

"I don't know, Nina. But that's not why I called. I want to talk to you about Tomas. Have you seen him around?"

"Not since before Bunny's accident. Why?"

I didn't have time to explain to her that Tomas was the Wigged Bandit or how I knew. Instead, I said, "I need to know what you know about him."

"Only that he's one of Diaz's teammates. I don't know any of them very well. They live in the guesthouse on the ranch and they stick to themselves. They're thick as thieves. What's going on?"

I paused at Nina's word choice before answering. "I was wondering if you knew how he came to work for Diaz." There was a long pause. Long enough that I wondered if our connection had been lost as I drove through the canyon. "Nina?"

"It was after the accident in Florida. Diaz couldn't get anyone to work for him. Like I told you before, everybody thought he was jinxed and he was depressed. I had never seen him so dark. He was drinking and for a while I thought maybe he'd go back to Europe and disappear. Then one day, he told me Donatella had heard about a group of equestrians performing with a traveling circus in Europe. They had fallen on hard times and were looking for work. Next thing I know, Diaz flew home to Europe and suddenly he's got a new team together. He loved them right away. He thought Tomas was a genius, and his team was magic with the horses. They could get them to do anything he wanted. He said it was like Tomas could speak their language."

"Do you think maybe Donatella might have lied about just

hearing about a group of equestrians looking for work? That maybe she knew Tomas before the accident and arranged for Diaz to meet him because of it?" The line went quiet again. "Nina? Are you there?"

"Are you saying what I think you're saying? That Donatella may have had something to do with the death of Diaz's horses? That she used their deaths to introduce Diaz to Tomas?"

"I don't know, Nina. Did she know about drugs Diaz made up to treat the horses for exhaustion when they traveled?"

"Probably. The team traveled regularly and the horses were her responsibility. They had to be injected after every trip, before a game. She could have easily tampered with drugs without his knowing. He trusted her implicitly."

"You think she'd actually do that?"

I wasn't so sure. I could easily have pegged Donatella for a fortune hunter or maybe even part of a ring of international jewel thieves, but for someone to deliberately kill twenty-one horses seemed extreme.

"I think Donatella tried to kill my sister, Carol, and she succeeded. And the cops aren't here right now because they want to talk with her about riding lessons. I think they suspect she had something to do with Bunny's death too, and I have trouble believing anyone—particularly a trainer—would leave Diego in the crossties alone."

I paused. Nina sounded so sure of herself. I couldn't help but think how similar I must have sounded to Eric. But without any witnesses or real proof, it was all conjecture, nothing that could secure an arrest or stand up in court. I needed more. I asked, "Did you know that Donatella and the woman who died in the explosion at Westin's had the same last name? It was Pero."

"And you think there's a connection?"

"I'm not sure. Maybe it's a coincidence, but I think there's something there. I've just been to see Mr. Churchill at Westin's. He gave me a jeweler's loupe that had been hers. And there's an inscription on it. 'To Celine, from Tomas with love.' I think Tomas is the same Tomas you have at the barn, and that he and Celine may have been lovers."

"And you think Donatella's related?"

"I do. And that they're all in this together." I explained how after the robbery in Beverly Hills, Kari Rhodes had invited Detective Lewis on the air to talk about the recent rash of robberies, the history of some of the bigger jewelry heists, and the mindset of those involved. "He described them as a very different bunch, highly trained and knowledgeable in their craft. They're known to take their time to plan and as a result seldom get caught, and the jewels nearly always disappear."

"If you're right, then Donatella was after a whole lot more than just Diaz."

"I think Donatella might have been bait for Diaz. That it didn't take too much to imagine he'd find her attractive—she looked a lot like Carmen—and that whoever she's working for figured she'd fit right into his world. All she had to do was play along. And once the horses were dead and Diaz's riders left him, it was easy for a new team to slip into place, and Donatella knew exactly who that should be."

"If Donatella never wanted to marry Diaz, why kill Carmen?"

"I don't think she meant to kill Carmen. I think she wanted to scare her. The coroner's report said the copper sulfate alone wouldn't have killed her. Your sister died because she choked to death. It's still murder, but I think your sister may have noticed every time she made a delivery for Diaz that the store was robbed shortly after. It probably seemed a little too coincidental at first. She may have even recognized Tomas in his various disguises and started to put two and two together. If Tomas knew Carmen recognized him, he may have been afraid she'd go to Diaz and tried to blackmail her. Or maybe the other way around, Carmen may have attempted to blackmail Tomas. Like you said, your sister wasn't above skimming off the top of Diaz's deliveries, and maybe she saw a way to get even more. After all, if Carmen divorced Diaz, she walked away empty-handed. But this way, she may have thought she'd have something. We may never know, but either way, I think Carmen was killed for what she knew, or what Tomas and Donatella thought she knew."

"And what about the police? What do they know?"

"I know there's a big investigation going on, and things take time. But if I'm right, this police visit to the ranch to talk with Donatella is nothing more than an attempt to shake things up. See if they can't scare her and maybe get her to lead them to Tomas."

"And if it doesn't?"

"Then Diaz, Donatella, and his team are going to get on a plane on Sunday and we may never find out who murdered your sister or stole the jewels."

CHAPTER 33

Kari was back on the air Friday morning. She was feeling better, and while still quarantined, she had managed to convince Tyler she was well enough to broadcast once again from the bedroom of her Hollywood Hills home. Today's hot topic: Celebrating the holidays in a time of stress. With her on the air, via the magic of phone patches, was the famous pop psychologist Dr. Murray Merriweather, a bowtied busybody whose column frequently appeared in the *Beverly Hills Courier*.

I entered the studio filled with the sound of their voices and took a seat behind the console. I had twenty minutes until my top of the hour news report, and I wanted the time alone to process the recent chain of events and organize my thoughts. In the absence of either Kari or Bunny, the studio felt empty, cold, and gray. Just two days ago Bunny stood right where I was sitting, dressed in her moss green camouflage fatigues, and read me the riot act. Telling me I didn't have the chops or the wherewithal to do the job she was going to do. That I let my personal relationship get in the way of my career.

Losing Bunny hurt, and so did the truth. Bunny wasn't entirely wrong; I had played it safe, and I was determined to change that. While Kari and Dr. Merriweather chatted on the air, I pulled up my notes. I wanted to include news about the robberies in my morning news break, something new, something our listeners didn't know, that might prompt Tomas to call the station. I picked up the inside studio line and called Detective Lewis.

From within the news booth, I cut the sound so Kari, Dr. Merriweather, and KCHC's listeners couldn't hear my conversation.

I needed to recap with Lewis the crime as I understood it. While the FBI couldn't talk freely with me, there were things Lewis could talk about. His role with the robberies had been altogether different. He wasn't working undercover with the FBI, but jointly on the robbery task force. As long as he didn't reveal what the FBI was doing, he could talk about the robberies in a more general sense, specifically those he'd studied internationally. If I was lucky, he might have something I could use as an update for today's report.

I reached Lewis on his cell. He told me he was in Beverly Hills at the Bouchon Bakery waiting for a box of French pastries to take home to his wife.

"You got a minute?"

"What do you need?"

I wasn't sure how much Lewis had heard about what happened after I'd left Westin's the morning of the robbery, so I recapped it quickly. I told him how I'd *accidentally* run into the Wigged Bandit as she was headed back to the parking structure and that afterward she, or he, had begun calling the station, using the name Tomi. From the way Lewis laughed, I suspected this wasn't the first time he had heard of my involvement, and that I'd become the subject of a little cop-shop humor.

"You really have got yourself into the middle of it, Carol."

I cringed, my head sinking beneath my shoulders as I pressed the phone closer to my ear. "Not intentionally," I said.

"But it certainly gives you a little inside advantage. You must have some understanding of what's going on."

"I'm not so sure. But I do have a few questions about some of the things you discussed on the Kari Rhodes show—about the Pink Panthers and the Paris robbery."

"Understand, I'm not saying they're connected, Carol. Only that the thieves who undertake such an operation are constantly trying to one-up the other. The more elaborate the crime, the bigger their bragging rights. They consider themselves to be above the law and what they do is frequently a team sport."

"That's what I want to talk to you about, this team sport

concept. I'm curious if you and I are on the same page." I explained how I knew Ms. Pero had been the Wigged Bandit's inside contact for the robberies, and that they were possibly lovers. And that I also knew the Wigged Bandit was Tomas or Tomi, my mystery caller, and that both he and Donatella worked for Diaz.

"I'm impressed. You'd make a good detective, Carol."

"I'm afraid hearing you say that doesn't make me feel any better. I still managed to get myself into the middle of it all, and it appears I helped Tomas get away with the jewels."

"I wouldn't beat yourself up. From what I hear, you've been an asset to the case. Because of you, the FBI now knows the Wigged Bandit's identity. Your ID that day at FBI headquarters confirmed he's Tomas Seville, an international jewel thief, wanted both here and in Europe. And I understand you broadcast a message we hoped to get out on air in attempt to lure him out. Something about the FBI clearing Diaz and his team to return to Spain on Sunday. It's the only reason we haven't issued a BOLO report. We don't want him to know that we know. So I suppose we owe you a little professional courtesy, and long as you keep this to yourself, I'll share with you a likely scenario of what we think happened that morning."

"I'd love to hear something."

"It's likely that by the time our Wigged Bandit rushed outside of Westin's with the jewels that another member of the team was waiting, grabbed the jewels, and passed them on to someone else. And that someone may have even passed you on the street after the bomb went off. By the time you finished your report and found Tomas, or who you thought was a little old lady struggling with her packages, and helped her to the parking structure, the jewels were long gone."

"You're telling me it was like a relay race? And I was right in the middle of it."

"In a sense, yes."

"And you think Tomas' teammates—the other polo players riding for Diaz—that they were all in on it?"

"Possibly, which is one of the reasons we've had such a tight lid on the investigation. We're getting close. We suspect four of Tomas' team have been traveling undercover as members of Diaz's polo team."

"And Donatella? She's the linchpin, right?"

"We suspect that someone, maybe Tomas or Ms. Pero, set her up from the very beginning. You have to admit, she was perfect. She looks a lot like Carmen and Diaz likes the ladies. It didn't take much to know he'd find her interesting. Once she got close to Diaz, it was her job to come between him and his polo players, convince him they didn't have the talent he needed, and introduce him to Tomas. Who then brought on his own team of thieves and that's when the games began."

"Except there was the accident with the horses in Florida. And much as I don't like Donatella, I have trouble thinking anyone could kill a whole string of polo ponies."

"She didn't do it. Like I said before, these groups pride themselves on pulling off these jobs without any violence. And when we went back and researched the case, they couldn't prove Donatella had anything to do with their deaths."

Lewis explained Diaz's team of polo ponies had died as a result of a pharmaceutical error. A tragic mistake. It seems Diaz had sent a list of ingredients he wanted to have prepared to help the horses with exhaustion from the long overseas flight. At the time, there was a drug, widely used in Europe, that wasn't available here in the U.S., and Diaz figured it wouldn't be a problem to have a custom concoction of it made up here. But the veterinarian misread the instructions and the results were devastating. "The vet admitted to the whole thing. So if you think this is connected, you'd be wrong."

"But what about Carmen and Bunny? They didn't both just die accidentally."

"The coroner's report is pretty clear, Carol. Carmen didn't die because she was poisoned, she choked to death. Not that that would prevent the police from filing murder charges against whoever attempted to poison her. But until we have proof, there's not much we can do. All we know for sure is that it looks like someone may have wanted to frighten Carmen—put a little copper sulfate in her drink, possibly to send a message. Unfortunately for Carmen, it literally scared her to death. But until we have actual proof it was Donatella, all we have is a theory."

"And Bunny?" I told Lewis about the voicemail I'd gotten on my home number warning me a friend of mine was becoming a nuisance. "I know it was Tomas. He said accidents happen, and the next thing I know, Bunny's dead."

"Her husband says she'd left the house early that morning. He thinks someone called her, and for whatever reason she went out to the ranch. We think someone, maybe Tomas, knew Bunny would be coming by the barn. Maybe even suggested she sneak in early in the morning, exactly like she did. If Tomas was worried about her, he may have even promised her it'd be worth her while. Whoever it was—whether it was Tomas or Donatella—they placed a bag of copper sulfate at the rear of the crossties, behind the horse's hooves, maybe knowing she'd be looking for it. But proving it, that's another matter."

"So there's no hard evidence that this was anything but an accident?"

"Not yet, there's not."

"One more question. You think the thieves actually had a shopping list? That they came here, when they did, for specific items?"

"Absolutely. In the Paris robbery they missed a lot because some of the more valuable jewels were here in LA for the big shows. There's no doubt in my mind that's why they chose Beverly Hills at this time of year. Not only could they target selected jewelry stores, but also some of the celebrities' homes like they did the night of the awards show. Broke into that actor's home in Studio City and stole one of Liz Taylor's bracelets. Annabelle's Auction was just frosting on the cake. They knew exactly what they wanted and got it."

"So they were all connected. Just like Bunny thought. They came shopping with a list."

"In a way, yes. They knew exactly what they wanted and where it was."

"And now Tomas is missing and Diaz and his team are getting ready to go home."

"That's right. And unless the jewels are already out of the country, they're probably taking home better than a hundred million in jewels."

"Isn't there any way the police or the FBI can stop them?"

"Not unless we find Tomas or the jewels. And right now, between you and me, it's not looking good. Come Sunday, if something doesn't change, Diaz, Donatella, and his team will take off."

"And all this will be old news before the end of the day." I hung up the phone and looked down at my notes. Since Bunny's death, Tyler was no longer riding me to stick with the chick-lite news. I flipped back on the sound so I could hear Kari's interview with Dr. Merriweather.

"So in essence, Doctor, it's on us. If we want the holidays to be special, we have to take charge. Make plans. Surround ourselves with friends and family and reach out to those who make a difference in our lives."

"Tell someone how important they are to you, Kari. You never know what a difference it will make."

"You hear that, Carol? We need to tell our listeners how important they are to us. Anyone you'd like to reach out to?"

Without thinking about it, I said, "I'd like to thank all our listeners and callers, particularly Tomi. You've called a couple of times recently, and I just want you to know what a difference you've made in my life. If you're listening, you know how important you are to me. And I have something special that belonged to someone close to you. I'd like to give it to you. Please call."

CHAPTER 34

I met Sheri for dinner at Wally's in Beverly Hills. Ordinarily on a Friday night, if Charlie was out with his dad, Eric and I would hook up. But tonight, Eric was missing in action, chasing after my elusive Wigged Bandit, and with the way things were between us, I had no idea when I'd hear from him. When Sheri learned I was going to be alone, she insisted we meet for dinner. Wally's was a wine warehouse turned trendy restaurant on Canon in Beverly Hills. It offered wine by the glass, tapas, and best of all, required no reservations.

A hostess showed us to one of Wally's long tables, where we were seated family style with a group of well-dressed strangers. Everyone was happily imbibing. It was Friday night, and bottles of fancy imported and domestic wines were lined up and down the table between small plates with tastings of meats and cheeses. As we settled ourselves on high stools, Sheri leaned over and asked me how it was going.

"The truth?" I picked up my empty wineglass and stared at the bottom.

Before I could replace it on the table, Sheri had signaled the waiter and my glass was filled with a warm Bordeaux from the south of France, pricier than the So-Cal wine I would have ordered on my own.

"You're paying?"

Sheri smiled and placed her black Amex card on the table. "From the look on your face when I walked in here, I think I need to. So 'fess up, girlfriend, how's it going?"

"Going?" I said sharply. "Not good. I feel like I'm striking out everywhere I turn. The men in my life are all either unavailable or hiding from me. Charlie's with his dad. Eric's off chasing this Wigged Bandit. Tomas or Tomi or whatever he wants to be called hasn't called me back. I've got nothing, and right now, nobody's returning any of my calls."

"It's that bad, huh?"

"Worse," I said. "Eric and I haven't had so much as a casual conversation in days. He's off in his world, and I'm in mine. And that leaves a lot to be desired." I took another sip of my wine and glanced back at the glass. This wasn't just a good bottle of wine, it was excellent. "What is this we're drinking? And how much is it?"

Sheri lifted her glass to the light and smiled. "Good, isn't it?"

"That would be an understatement." I swirled the glass beneath my nose, releasing the wine's fragrant bouquet, warm, earthy with a hint of dark berries. It even smelled expensive. "What is this?"

"It's a 2012 Contet-Pontet from Bordeaux. And you don't want to know the price."

"Sheri..." I tried to sound authoritative. I didn't want my best friend dipping too deeply into her well-lined pockets. A simple bottle of Zin would have been just fine. "It's just—"

"Don't." Sheri held her hand up in front of my face while she took another long sip. "This here," she pointed a finger at me and then back at herself, "is cheaper than therapy. Besides, need I remind you, things like robberies and murders, they never happen to me, they happen to you. So let me live vicariously, okay? A hundred-dollar bottle of wine is well worth it." Sheri picked up her glass and clicked the rim to mine.

I knew what Sheri was saying was true. Maybe that's why we were such good friends. I loved to talk and tell stories, and she liked to listen. She kept me grounded and I kept her entertained.

"To therapy," I said.

"And if I could offer a little advice with regard to your lack of *casual* conversation with Eric, one doesn't always have to talk,

Carol." She raised her eyebrows and looked at me knowingly. "In fact, sometimes it's better when you don't."

I took another quick sip of wine. "Yeah, well, if you're referring to my love life, let me just say that since my last romantic encounter with Eric in Carmen's hotel room, I'm sad to report I think that appears to have been tabled. Rubber-stamped officially off-limits by the FBI. At least, until the Wigged Bandit is caught, and even then I'm not sure. So much has happened."

I could tell the wine was already having an effect on my empty stomach. I couldn't remember when or if I'd eaten today, and I was starting to feel lightheaded.

"So, what's next then, Carol? Diaz and his team just go home? Fly off, and that's the end of it? There's nothing you can do?"

"It appears so. Unless something happens and the Wigged Bandit is found, it's bon voyage. Bye-bye, Donatella. Goodbye, Tomas and his well-trained team of jewel thieves." I raised my glass above my head in a mock salute to their success, the frustration bubbling out of me like an uncorked bottle of champagne. I couldn't help it. One glass of wine and I was wobbly.

"And the jewels?" Sheri asked.

"They're probably halfway around the world right now."

The waiter filled my glass again. I shouldn't have had a second. Not on an empty stomach. But the warm wine and the cheese plate with dates and nuts he placed on the table looked beyond good. I didn't refuse.

I waited for the waiter to finish filling my glass, then raised it to Sheri in a toast. "To the jewels, wherever they are."

Sheri ordered a second plate of cold cuts. It arrived looking like something from the south of France, with artisanal bread and thinly sliced cuts of saucisson and bresaola. She lightly buttered a piece of the bread with a seeded mustard sauce and topped it with prosciutto.

"Then find them," she said.

"Find them? If the FBI can't, how can I?" I must have said it slightly louder than I intended. The couple seated at the end of the table looked over at me uncomfortably. I raised my glass again. "Great guys, aren't they? Can't live with 'em, can't live without 'em."

Sheri grabbed my hand and lowered my drink to the table. "Maybe you need to eat a little something?"

"You think?"

"And how about ordering a cola, and going easy on the wine?"

"No." I was thinking out loud. Sheri looked at me, surprised at my firm response. "I don't mean the wine. I mean the jewels. You're right about them. I need to find them." I took my glass from beneath Sheri's hand and finished off the rest of my wine. I was starting to feel good. Ironically, the wine had cleared my head in ways I hadn't imagined. "If they're not halfway to Europe by now, the jewels are still here. The FBI's going to search everything that gets on that plane on Sunday. Top to bottom."

"And if they don't find anything, it's going to take off."

"Right." I had visions of a big fat-bellied plane sitting on the tarmac. The horses loaded in the back with Diaz and the team waiting to load in the front. Their bags laid out beneath the aircraft, after being checked and rechecked. The pre-flight check would be extreme. They'd go through everything. Except...

I looked at Sheri. I doubted the FBI ever mucked stalls. As a kid, I'd spent summers at the local stable. Why hadn't I thought about this before? I knew a few things about transporting horses, and thorough as the FBI might be, they wouldn't check everything. If I was right, I knew exactly where the jewels were hidden.

"Sheri, there's one place they're not going to check."

"Where?"

I didn't trust saying another word. I was almost afraid to think it, for fear someone might read my mind and sabotage my plan. I'd already said too much, and the couple at the end of the table continued to look at me as though I were more than just tipsy.

"Sheri, come with me to the airport on Sunday. If I'm right, that plane's not taking off. Not with the jewels."

Sheri reached for my glass. "And you're not driving home tonight. I'm taking your keys and calling you a taxi."

CHAPTER 35

Saturday morning, I woke to the sound of a buzzing from within my purse. I had dropped my bag on the floor when I got home from dinner and fell into bed, exhausted and more than a little drunk. The wine had really gotten to me. All I remember was crawling under the covers and then *buzz...buzz...buzz*. Like an angry bee buzzing about my room. I swiped at the air above my head until I realized the sound was my cell phone.

I glanced blurry-eyed at the screen. It registered three missed calls. All of them from Tyler. The fourth call I answered mid-ring. I must have sounded groggy, like I was hollering from the bottom of an empty barrel. Tyler's reply came back at me like a shotgun.

"What, are you sleeping? It's nearly ten o'clock, Carol. I need to see you right away."

I squinted at the clock. "It's Saturday, Tyler. Why are you calling—"

"We need to talk."

Pushing my hair from my face, I told Tyler I was planning on coming into the station later in the afternoon, that I had left my car in Beverly Hills the night before. Sheri had said something about calling in the morning for a ride.

"If you can give me a little time I can be there by—"

"I'll pick you up." Tyler's impatience was blatant, like the ticking of the clock on my bedside table. I pushed it off onto the floor. Hungover on two glasses of wine. Damn, I was such a lightweight.

"We can grab breakfast at Nate 'n Al's in Beverly Hills," he said. "I'll drop you at your car afterward. If you still want to come by the station, you're free to do so." Tyler hung up, his usual goodbye, leaving me with the dull dial tone droning in my ear that matched the pounding in my head.

I grabbed a couple of aspirin from the medicine cabinet, splashed cold water on my face, and stared into the mirror. Who was this girl? I scarcely recognized myself. I was hungover, pale with puffy eyes and bedhead that looked like it had been ironed to my scalp. I hit the shower, washed my hair, and tried to imagine what it was Tyler wanted to talk about, on a Saturday of all days. What was he going to do? Fire me?

No way.

I dried myself off and determined no matter what the outcome of my conversation with Tyler, I wasn't about to give up, and I wouldn't come home. I was going to do exactly as I'd planned to do yesterday. Follow the story. Go to the station and hang out. At least then I could hear the police scanner. If the police found Tomas, I'd be the first to know. It sure beat the alternative. I wasn't about to sit around the house and wait until Sunday morning. It would drive me crazy. With nothing to do but watch the clock and check my phone for messages while counting the hours to Diaz's departure, I'd sooner eat worms.

Thirty minutes later on the dot, I heard Tyler's MG pull up outside my door and the rusty squawk from the horn.

"Get in."

With the top down and driving at the only speed I think Tyler knew—fast—we sped up Beverly Glen, over Mulholland and down into Beverly Hills, weaving in and out of traffic. I knew better than to ask Tyler what this was about. Behind the small wooden sports wheel of the car, he was like a young Mario Andretti. With the wind in my hair and the sound of the engine's roar, I couldn't have heard him even if I had headphones on. Between Tyler's lead foot and the gears grinding, conversation wasn't top on his list.

We pulled into an unbelievably good parking space directly in front of the restaurant. Only Tyler could have such luck. Parking in Beverly Hills at this hour on a Saturday morning, particularly right in front of Nate 'n Al's, was at a premium. But Tyler jumped out of the car as though it were no big deal, his skinny legs slipping over the door like a sprinter, while I pushed open the door on my side and, after a clumsy exit, slammed it shut.

I followed Tyler into the restaurant. Without a word to the hostess, he grabbed a menu off the counter like he was a regular and found an empty booth near the front.

"Thought you might like to know," he said, "we're dropping the chick-lite format."

I wasn't prepared for this. I felt like someone had ripped open the blinds in a darkened room and my eyes were burning from the bright sun. I squinted at Tyler and contemplated what it might mean for the station and me. Were the next words out of his mouth going to be "and with the format change, we've decided to let you go"?

Instead, I asked, "You spoke with Morganstern?"

"He's okay with a format change. In fact, he says it was Bunny's idea. They discussed it before she died and realized it was the only logical move. I'm going to make some personnel changes. I could use an assistant program director, and I'll need some help. You interested?"

I hadn't expected such news. I leaned back against the booth and took a deep breath.

"Program director?"

"*Assistant* program director, and it's temporary, Carol. Only until I get things straightened out." The waitress arrived and Tyler took one quick look at the menu and put it aside while he ordered.

"Pastrami on rye and a cream soda." Then nodding to me, he added, "She'll have coffee. You already ate, right?" I gestured with my hands, palms up, whatever, and waited for him to go on.

"Anyway, far as the position goes, don't get too excited. It's mostly a glorified administrative position. But..."

"But? What, Tyler?"

"I want you to think about taking on a one-hour show. Late night Sundays. I'd like to call it 'Inside LA with Carol Childs.' You can do with it what you like. Investigative reports, city news. I don't care, but it'd be in addition to your regular duties with the newsroom and top of the hour reports. And before you say anything, I know it'll be a conflict with your son, but fact is, Charlie's getting older. No reason he can't be alone on a Sunday evening for a couple hours. Plus, there's a little more money in the budget, and I'll swing some your way so you can hire a housekeeper if you need."

I couldn't believe what I was hearing. I was getting my own show and a raise?

"You mean a real format change? No more anniversary stories like National Crockpot Day? Or Key Lime Pie Day? Or chasing down Festivus interviews?"

"Don't get cute, Carol." Tyler didn't appreciate my reference to Hollywood's parody of a secular holiday that served as an alternative to the pressures and commercialization of Christmas. "I'm going to need you to focus on more serious matters, and I still have my doubts about you. You're still, in my opinion, the world's oldest cub reporter, but I'm giving you a chance. As for Festivus...this is Hollywood, Carol, what do you think?"

By the time I got to the office, it was midday. Things were usually pretty still around the station on weekends. There was a different vibe. Voices of prerecorded shows echoed in the nearly empty hallways. The studios, for the most part, were dark. The sales staff was gone, and the station operated with a skeletal staff. It was exactly the atmosphere I wanted.

I headed to the newsroom. Tyler had excused himself, grabbed a newspaper, and made his way to the men's room. A ritual I knew would allow me at least thirty to forty minutes alone. Enough time to listen to the police scanner and check the newswire uninterrupted. I wanted to see if there had been any new jewelry store robberies reported or something that might indicate the cops had picked up Tomas. There was nothing.

In less than twenty-four hours Diaz and his team would be on a plane winging their way back to Europe. I picked up the phone and called Nina. Maybe she had news. Perhaps Tomas had resurfaced at the barn.

"Nina, I called to—"

"Carol, you're not going to believe what's going on. Donatella's moved out of the big house she shared with Diaz and into one of the small trainer cottages below the barn."

"Did they break up?"

"Looks that way, but that's not all."

"It's not?"

I hoped the next words out of her mouth would be that she had seen Tomas, or perhaps that he was hiding in one of the small trainers' cottages as well. If he were, I could call the police and we'd catch him.

Instead, she said, "Mimi's back. She's moved into the big house and announced she's planning on going to Europe with Diaz. She says he was always hers, and now with Carmen gone, it's just the right thing to do."

Wow. I whistled. This was big news. I wondered for a moment if I had it all wrong.

"You don't think Mimi had anything to do with Carmen's death after all, do you?"

"No. Absolutely not. If you ask me, you were right. Donatella was after Diaz for his jewels. She and the polo team are nothing but a bunch of thieves who've been using Diaz as a cover to travel back and forth from here to Europe."

"Does Diaz know?"

"Mimi told me the police clued Diaz in when they were here to question Donatella about Bunny's death. They told him he had to keep it quiet until they could finish their investigation, but it definitely was the beginning of the end for Donatella. According to Mimi, Diaz staged a big fight with her over the way she was handling the horses and then he moved Mimi in right after. They're sitting out on the balcony of the big house right now. Mimi's still in her negligee. They're having breakfast."

I glanced at the clock. It was almost one p.m. "A bit late for breakfast."

Nina laughed.

"And what about Donatella?" I asked. "Do you think she knows Diaz is on to her?"

"That would be assuming the girl's smart. And he certainly didn't let on. I doubt Donatella has the faintest idea. She's convinced her job is done, at least as far as Diaz goes. Sooner or later she had to figure Mimi was going to come between her and Diaz. I'm sure she thinks that's all it is and doesn't really care. Like you said, it was all an act with her, and now I think she's looking forward to going home and being done with him."

"And Mimi? Can she be trusted not to say anything?"

"Mimi's got one thing on her mind. She wants to be the next Mrs. Umberto Diaz de la Roca. As far as she's concerned, she's got it all: Diaz, his money, and the jewels. She's not going to say or do anything to interfere with that."

CHAPTER 36

Sunday morning started early. Sheri and I arrived at the cargo transport hangar off Avion Drive, just north of the airport, before sunup. An oversized building big enough to contain several football fields and tall enough to easily house a jumbo jet backed up to the airport's international runways and specialty cargo loading areas. A small nondescript white metal door with an orange awning above it indicated this was the entrance for Triple-A Animal Transport. Deliveries were to the left, through a sliding gate large enough to accommodate a semi. We entered through the front door and were met by a pimply-faced security guard who looked like he was barely out of school and surprised to see us. I explained I was a reporter on assignment, and needed to speak to Mr. Diaz, who I knew was here prepping his team for a flight to Spain.

"Sorry, ma'am." He shook his head as he checked the roster. "Your name's not here."

"It's important. He's expecting me," I lied and looked over his thin shoulders through a filmy glass window and into the hangar behind him. "I have to talk to him before they finish loading the plane."

"Hate to be a pain, but we're understaffed. Right now, we're a ways away from loadin' Mr. Diaz and his horses. Things out on the tarmac are a zoo. We just loaded an eight-thousand-pound elephant onto a plane and she's nervous as hell. Pilot won't take off 'til she settles down. 'Til then nothing's movin'."

Sheri stepped forward and peered over the counter and into the hangar behind him. "What's she doing, rocking the boat?"

The young guard didn't look amused and took a step to block Sheri's view of the hangar behind him. "Hey, it happens."

"I'll bet," I said. I was trying hard to find some middle ground, anything that would get me out on the tarmac. "Why should animals be any different than humans? Gotta be a tough job. Make an interesting interview. Don't you think, Sheri?"

Sheri nodded and I noticed security-boy checked his clipboard again.

"Reporter, huh?"

"Yeah, ever listen to KCHC's late night Sports Talk?" A wild guess on my part, but not uneducated. A number of KCHC's late night audience were male, age eighteen to forty-nine, and enthusiastic followers of the show.

"Sometimes. Hey, any chance you can get me tickets to a Lakers game?"

I wasn't surprised by the request; in fact, I'd counted on it. A lot of listeners, once they find out I work for radio, asked about tickets. At times, I feel more like a vending machine than a reporter.

"Nothing's impossible, but I really do need to get out there and see Mr. Diaz."

"Let me check." He motioned to a couple of cheap folding chairs by the front door and said he would be back in a few minutes. But he didn't sound very encouraging, and I wasn't about to sit and wait. The moment he left, I leaned up against the heavy glass doors and cupped my hands around my eyes, peering through the filmy window into the hangar. There was a giant menagerie of cages, caged animals, and large wooden cargo boxes, each tagged for a different part of the world. At the far end, sunlight and a bay of oversized garage doors yawned open to the tarmac. I could see an army of activity beneath the belly of a plane. Screw waiting. I wasn't going to get stuck in some stuffy little room while Donatella and her band of thieves escaped.

I pushed through the glass doors with Sheri behind me. Together we dodged any two-legged human security types that patrolled the hangar, hiding behind large freight containers and sneaking our way down the aisles and onto the tarmac. The young security guard was right. It was a zoo.

Ahead of me were two huge cargo jets, one slightly behind the other. The plane closest I figured was for Diaz and the horses. The second, a wide-bodied 767, had begun slowly taxiing away from the hangar and towards the runway. I could only assume this was the elephant express, and that the animal had finally calmed down enough for the pilot to take off. To my right, more activity. An eighteen-wheeler, Diaz's mobile transport for his horses, was beginning to unload. The horses, each haltered and accompanied by one of the airline's animal transport officers, were slowly escorted one at a time from the truck and up onto the plane's loading ramp.

Securing the area, I counted six blue-jacketed FBI agents. I noticed Eric, his back to me, along with three other agents. In front of them lay a line of tack boxes, duffle bags, and backpacks, like a trail of birdseed from the back of the horse trailer to a forklift parked beneath the plane. It was exactly as I imagined it to be. Agents on one side of the bags and members of Diaz's team on the other. They eyed each other suspiciously. I could tell from Eric's stiff posture they didn't have anything. Whether it was a sixth sense or some form of nonverbal communication people close to one another share, I knew. His shoulders were squared and his jaw clenched. He wasn't happy.

Farther to my right, I noticed Diaz's black Hummer. It was parked in front of the horse trailer, and standing next to it was the man himself. He was dressed in a camel cape, looking like a forties noir film star. Next to him, tucked coquettishly beneath his arm in a symphony of white like she was about to embark on her honeymoon, was Mimi. The smile on her face said it all. She had just won the lottery. Perhaps she had. The woman finally had everything she wanted, the man *and* his money. I suggested to Sheri she go stand next to Diaz and congratulate Mimi. I had work to do.

I looked back at the plane. A custom-built Boeing 727, designed to fly horses like first-class passengers around the world. Beneath the belly of the plane, a cargo trolley loaded with saddles, horse blankets, lead ropes, and miscellaneous gear for the trip waited to be loaded onboard. Between the cargo trolley and the line of tack boxes and bags belonging to Diaz's team was Donatella. She was sitting on one of Diaz's monogrammed hunter green tack boxes and dressed as I had never seen her before, in a short skirt, cowboy boots, and jean jacket, staring at her cell phone.

It was as plain as the early morning sunshine on the tarmac that Donatella was distancing herself from Diaz as well as her band of thieves. She sat with her back to them all as she stared at the phone in her hand. She had to know something was up. The FBI was searching through luggage, and despite the fact they hadn't found anything, the flight had been delayed. But I had to give it to the girl; she was holding on to her charade for all she was worth, playing the jilted girlfriend, sulking like a broken-hearted school girl as she texted.

Wait. Who was she texting?

I looked back at the line of men, Diaz's grooms and riders, waiting patiently next to their bags lying on the tarmac from the horse trailer to beneath the plane. The men were all trim and fit, dressed in jeans and comfortable shoes for the flight home. I noticed three of them had formed a small group beneath the wing. They stood more closely together than the others. One was staring at a phone in his hand while the other two appeared to be reading over his shoulder.

Was it just a coincidence, or was Donatella texting one of the three men beneath the wing of the plane? I studied the grouping. These had to be the same three men I had seen in the barn with Donatella the day of Carmen's memorial. I scanned the tarmac. If Donatella was here, Tomas had to be somewhere on the airfield. Just like Carmen's funeral, he was probably silently watching. Waiting. I could feel it.

I took the jeweler's loupe Churchill had given me from my

jacket pocket and placed it around my neck. If I didn't spot Tomas, maybe he'd spot me. My hope was the jeweler's loupe might catch his eye. A quick tell, no matter what his disguise, man or woman, would reveal his identity. It was a long shot. But it was all I had.

I approached Eric. "Any sightings of Tomas?"

Eric shook his head, surprised. "How did you manage to get onto the tarmac, Carol? I left word with security at the gate—"

"Don't ask. But I think you're going to be glad I'm here. I know where the jewels are hidden."

Eric looked at me without saying anything, his eyes narrowed.

"After the accident with the horses in Florida, Diaz was devastated. He never trusted anyone. His loss was too great. I've been thinking about it, and if I was Diaz, no way would I risk someone messing with my horses' meds ever again. Or their food or water, for that matter."

"What are you saying, Carol?"

"I think Diaz travels with his own hay and medical supplies. Usually, the transport companies provide food and water and sometimes even basic meds. I know because when I was a kid I used to hang around a barn and ready the horses for the shows. The transport always came with everything. All we had to do was load the horses. But both Tomas and Donatella know how Diaz feels about that, and they would have arranged to transport everything, including their own food."

I pointed to the cargo cart beneath the plane. Loaded on the back end, crated and ready to go, were several bales of hay and barrels of water.

"I'm not certain, but it'd be pretty easy to hide the jewels between the bales." I added how I had seen Nina feed the horses at the barn. They were fed flakes of hay. Each flake, the size of a doormat and weighing about five or six pounds, was a couple of inches thick, and they piled ten or twelve together into a bale for transport. "My guess is if we check between the flakes of hay, the jewels might be there."

For a second, I thought Eric was going to kiss me. Instead, he yelled to one of the agents to pull the hay off the end of that loader and start going through it. "Straw by straw if you have to."

Within minutes, the tarmac beneath the plane was covered in hay. Beneath the plane's giant wheels, hay was tossed and quickly discarded, while agents tore through the bales searching for the jewels.

There was nothing. I walked beneath the plane. Like a kid tearing through Christmas wrap, I searched everything. The jewels had to be here. I couldn't be wrong.

"Try the med packs," I said.

Again, agents pulled off the prepacked medical kits from the cargo trolley and went through each pack, piece by piece.

Nothing.

I felt as though we had been looking for a needle in a haystack and come up empty. I thought for sure the jewels had been hidden in the food. They had to be. Where else could they be?

"What about the water? The bottoms of the buckets, they're insulated. Maybe the jewels are hidden in the space between?"

I knew before they finished pulling apart the last water bucket I was wrong. I felt defeated. Stupid. Dammit, Tomas and Donatella were going to get away with it. I stared over at Donatella, seated atop the tack box. She was still on the phone.

"Eric, the tack box Donatella's sitting on, did it come off the horse trailer this morning?"

"We checked everything. All the bags, the tack boxes. Right as they came off the trailer."

"But what if the box Donatella's sitting on didn't come off the horse trailer? Look." I pointed to the tack boxes lined up beneath the wing, waiting to be loaded onboard. "They all look alike. They all have Diaz's logo on them, and there are at least twenty. One for each horse. With all these boxes on the tarmac, it'd be easy to mix them up. But if the box Donatella is sitting on didn't come off Diaz's rig, but came off the trolley cart, then—"

Eric and I both had the same thought, at the exact moment. "Then if the jewels are here, Tomas can't be far away."

I glanced back at the cargo hangar.

"Or wasn't." Eric nodded to the abandoned cart parked outside the warehouse. The door was standing wide open.

"And Donatella's sitting on top of the jewels," I said.

Eric whispered quietly into a wrist microphone he was wearing as he signaled the three agents closest to her. Donatella sat unsuspecting with her cell phone still clutched tightly in her hands as they approached. Then suddenly she stood up. She knew she had been caught. I could see the color drain from her face as she started screaming.

"It's not my fault. I didn't know anything."

"Stand up." Eric grabbed Donatella and shoved her into the hands of a waiting agent, then opened the trunk. Inside was an assortment of equestrian necessities, brushes, halters, a hoof pick, and miscellaneous riding gear. "Well, what do you know? Look what we have here." Eric held up an unopened bag of copper sulfate. "Planning on treating any other horses for thrush, Donatella? Or were you saving this for another *attempted* poisoning?" The sarcasm in his voice caused me to almost laugh out loud. I bit my lip and turned my head away.

"I don't know why that's there."

"I'm sure you don't."

Eric nodded for the agents to cuff her while he began emptying the trunk. We all watched as he removed several more items, a pair of stirrups, horse pads, and a halter, until there was nothing left inside. Then he reached inside and felt the bottom.

Eric addressed Donatella one last time. "Anything here you want to tell me about? 'Cause something else is here. There's a false bottom. What am I going to find? Some hidden treasure maybe?"

Donatella shook her head, her eyes bulging. She knew she'd been caught. We all leaned forward.

"Bingo." Eric ripped out a thin piece of plywood and tossed it on the ground. Beneath it was a pirate's treasure chest of jewels. Gold bracelets, diamond earrings, necklaces, and rings, all wrapped in cellophane, heaped upon one another. "We've got it."

With nothing more to say and the jewels clearly in her possession, Donatella looked helplessly in the direction of the line of the men waiting to board the plane, as though she were waiting for someone to rescue her.

Eric asked her, "Anyone you might like to reach out to?"

Before she could answer, three of the men who had been standing together staring at the cell phone took off, running across the tarmac in the direction of the runway.

Eric and four agents followed in quick pursuit, leaving me with Donatella and one of the agents to watch.

Within seconds, Sheri, Diaz, and Mimi were beside me, all of us watching the chase out onto the approaching runway.

Diaz leaned into me and whispered, "I guess I owe you a thank you, Ms. Childs. Your friend here's been telling me all about you and what you've been doing and how much help you've been."

Sheri smiled back smugly.

"I don't think anyone needs to thank anyone until we've got your men," I said.

"They're not going to get far. The airport's fenced and security's not going to take kindly to them running across a runway." Sheri pointed to the fencing surrounding the runway.

"I doubt they'll get that far," I said. "Look."

Already Eric had grabbed one of the men, and the two others weren't going to be much of a challenge. Coming in their direction was a huge Airbus A380, a double-decker cargo plane. The men stopped cold in their tracks and turned back towards the agents, their hands in the air.

CHAPTER 37

Four days after the arrests, I met Eric for lunch. We hadn't talked in the interim. I knew he'd be busy with reports and debriefings, and I thought perhaps we each needed a little space until we were ready to center back into our personal lives. He'd finally called me today at work and said we needed to meet, that it was important. We had things to discuss, both personal and professional. He suggested The Blvd inside the Beverly Wilshire Hotel. The same hotel where Annabelle's had held their Huguette Clark auction. I thought the location curious and slightly overpriced. He said I'd understand the significance later.

When I arrived, security was everywhere. Annabelle's was preparing for another auction—this one with a selection of jewels by designers Rene Boivin and Suzanne Belperron, along with vintage pieces from Cartier, Van Cleef & Arpels, and Henry Westin's. I wondered if this was the significance at which Eric had hinted.

As I entered the hotel, a plainclothes security guard spotted me. He was dressed in an ill-fitting blue suit and looked like a former linebacker with a small audio piece in his ear. "Ms. Childs? If you'd follow me, please."

Without waiting for an answer, he turned, and I trailed behind a set of broad shoulders past the hotel's Christmas tree that looked like it could have answered Irving Berlin's dream for a White Christmas in Beverly Hills. The dining room, a luxurious old-world affair with its dark mahogany furniture and gold chandeliers, had been decked out with Christmas wreaths and garlands. At least three more plainclothes agents were inside the room, their backs to the walls and eyes on the door. Eric was seated by himself at a table. He stood up as I approached.

"I've missed you." With both hands he reached for mine and pulling me close, kissed me lightly on the cheek, like an old friend. Appropriate for a public place, but not quite what I was hoping for. "It's good to see you."

Good to see me? I seated myself and took an immediate sip of water. I couldn't explain why I suddenly felt uncomfortable. Was it the location, the fact Eric and I hadn't been alone to share a meal or anything else more intimate in what seemed like forever, or that I sensed we weren't alone? I glanced back at the door and the security guard standing next to it. "I take it we've got company?"

Eric didn't answer. Instead, he said, "I promised after everything was settled, I'd give you the whole story."

"I thought I had it all." Eric had emailed me an unclassified document outlining the investigation, the FBI's undercover role, and their work with the LAPD's robbery-homicide task force. After the robberies in Paris, the FBI had begun to suspect something more might be about to happen here in Hollywood before the big awards season and began shadowing Carmen. Her deliveries were too coincidental to the robberies taking place and drew their suspicion. At first, they believed Carmen might actually have been a target. It wasn't until the FBI was well into their investigation that they began to suspect Diaz's polo team might be involved. And then, after I uncovered information about Carmen's safe deposit box, they started to think of her as not only a target but also a possible suspect. In the end, her role was still somewhat unclear. I supposed we'd never know if she was a victim or an accomplice. But after reading the report, other than Tomas' whereabouts, I felt it was pretty much a closed case and I knew everything.

"There's more. It's a bit more personal than what was covered in the report, and I thought you should know." Eric reiterated that the easiest way for the FBI to get close to the operation was to infiltrate one of the escort services Carmen used. "And, as you know, I wasn't supposed to be in the field the day I saw you in front of Henry Westin's. I'm sorry about that. I'm sorry for all the confusion it's caused between us."

Eric's blue eyes searched mine, his face like a hurt puppy. How could I refuse such an apology?

"Yeah, me too," I said. "I mean, who knew? In a city of more than thirteen million people, what are the chances I'd see *you* coming out of Henry Westin's with Carmen that morning?"

"Small world sometimes." Eric looked uncomfortable. He fiddled with his collar, undoing the top button beneath his tie.

"Particularly between reporters and law enforcement, right?"

Eric reached for the glass of water in front of him and took a sip. "How about we table that conversation for the moment and talk about Tomas first?"

"You found him?"

"No, but just like we suspected, he was at the airport on Sunday. After we arrested Donatella and her three cohorts, we got a look at their cell phones. She was texting him that morning. Unfortunately, Tomas' phone was a burner. We found it later in the trash, but he was there all right."

"I knew it. I had a feeling. Where was he?"

"Operating the cargo trolley. We found the real driver tied up and hidden inside one of the cargo crates. It seems Tomas snuck into the hangar earlier in the morning, claiming to be looking for a lost dog. He got by that same new hire you got by at the front desk—no surprise there, huh?" Eric smiled and shook his head. "Then he attacked the trolley driver and stole his uniform."

"So he delivered the tack box Donatella was sitting on?"

"He did. Right under our noses. You were right about the tack boxes. There were twenty of them, all monogrammed with Diaz's logo and looking exactly alike. It was perfect. Just what a master thief and magician like Tomas Seville loves, a sleight of hand trick, right in front of us."

I remembered the scene in my mind. Tack boxes and bags all lined up beneath the plane, just feet from where the cargo trolley was making deliveries. It would have been easy.

"And not one of us noticed that just three feet from the boxes Diaz's team unloaded was another matching trunk. Our treasure chest, if you will. Tomas brought it in on the back of the cargo trolley about the same time Diaz's horse trailer came in. There was a lot of activity going on—another big plane taxiing out to the runway—and we weren't concerned about the delivery of food and water. We missed it, and then after we searched Donatella and her bags, she went over and sat down on top of the trunk. Everybody assumed it had already been searched."

"So Tomas must have been waiting around to board once everything was loaded."

"And once he saw us arrest Donatella, he took off. He either slipped out through the warehouse or managed to double back and climb onboard the plane to Europe. Either way, we lost him." Eric exhaled and looked down at his hands on the table. I could tell he wasn't happy; the case hadn't gone as he'd hoped and he was still blaming himself.

"But you did get the jewels," I said.

"We did," he said. He smiled at me. "Which is one of the reasons I wanted you here today. It's almost Christmas, and it's not every day you get to celebrate."

"Celebrate?" I hadn't expected this to be a celebration. There was so much that had been left unsaid between us since the start of the investigation, it just didn't feel right. I wanted to say I thought we should talk. But I didn't get a chance.

"Carol, before you overthink this, there's something I want to—" Eric stopped midsentence, glanced nervously around the room, then took a small blue velvet ring box from inside his coat pocket and slid it across the table. "I've never done this before. Go ahead, open it."

"Eric? I..." I froze, staring at the box in front of me, unable to move. What was he doing? "What is this?"

"Just open the box, Carol. You'll see."

Slowly I picked up the box and lifted the lid.

"Oh my God. Eric!"

Inside the box was the largest square-cut diamond I'd ever seen. I had no doubt whose ring this was. It sparkled back at me like my own personal Milky Way, a thousand twinkling little shimmers of light dancing across the table.

"You can put it on if you like."

"Oh yeah, I like." I slipped the ring onto my finger and held my hand up to the light. "Is this it? Is this Huguette Clark's ring? The two-and-a-half-million-dollar diamond? The one Carmen had in her possession the entire time?"

Eric nodded. "Only Carmen didn't know it was Huguette Clark's ring. She thought it was the ring Diaz brought back from Europe and had asked her to carry into Westin's the day of the robbery."

"But she didn't. Instead, she put it aside, or maybe conveniently forgot about. So she could keep it for herself."

"That is, until Churchill reminded her the night of Mimi's party, and she sent me back to her hotel room to get it."

I stared at the ring. I had never dreamed I would have something so big on my finger. It dwarfed my hand and was beyond gorgeous. Big. Square. And sparkly. The kind of thing that could turn a rational girl silly. I took a deep breath and forced myself to concentrate.

"So Carmen had this ring in her possession the entire time and never knew it?"

"Let's say she never knew the value of it." Eric took another sip of his water and nodded. "And if she had given it to Churchill like she was supposed to and waited for him to check the jewels she had brought into the store that day, she would have known it wasn't the ring Diaz had given her, and so would Churchill."

"But she didn't." I kept staring at the ring. "She kept it back and was probably going to put it in the safe deposit box with the other jewelry pieces she'd been skimming off the top."

"And until then she was just enjoying it. Exactly like you are now." Eric winked at me then stared back at the diamond on my hand.

I thought about the history of the ring. I wondered how often Miss Clark had worn it and where. How Tomas had been caught on videotape right here at this very hotel as Annabelle's was readying for a private showing of her jewels. How Diaz had come in with Donatella to compare his lesser-value estate sale ring with the ring now on my finger and never noticed Tomas switch the two, and later gave the ring to Carmen to take to Henry Westin's. How Tomas had expected it to be with the jewels she gave to Churchill. Or had he known Carmen would take it? Was it a payoff for her silence? I supposed I'd never know. The ring possessed as much mystery as it did brilliance.

Eric leaned across the table and gently took my hand in his. "You probably shouldn't flash that around quite so much."

"Why? Are you worried someone will steal it?" I laughed nervously and glanced over my shoulder.

Eric shook his head. "There's more security in this room than you know. It's why I wanted to meet you here, and Annabelle's is fine with it."

I stared back at the ring and took my hand from his. "All the same, I suppose I should take it off."

"It does look good on you. You've got the hands for it, Carol."

I put the ring back in the box and looked into Eric's eyes. At one time, I could have locked into his gaze forever and built my life around him. I knew he was thinking the same thing. If this had been an engagement ring, another time, another place, we could have been perfect together.

"I've thought about it, Carol. You know, asking you. Making this thing between us permanent." He took the ring box, his eyes going from it to mine. "Not with a ring like this, but maybe something slightly smaller."

We laughed. I felt tears forming behind my eyes.

"Our differences with this case, Carol, weren't the only reason I've been so distant. I've been doing a little soul searching."

"Eric." My throat tightened. I couldn't hear this. "It's just—"

"No. Hear me out. I need to say this." Eric grabbed my hands between his and squeezed them. "This case, it hasn't been my best work. I've made mistakes, lots of them. I've been preoccupied. Hell, Carol, I've been thinking about you. What you were doing. What trouble you might be getting yourself into. It's killing me and it's not good. I'm a take-care-of kind of guy, and you're a take-charge kind of woman. But dammit, Carol, I love you. Marry me."

I felt my heart stop. I knew we had both been dancing around the issue of something more for some time. An exclusive relationship has to grow, but this couldn't. I loved Eric, but the timing just wasn't right.

"I wish I could, but I can't, Eric. It's not right. We both know that. We're always going be on the opposite side of things. I can't give up my work, and you can't either. It'd never work. It's like Tyler said, cops and reporters, we're strange bedfellows. And much as I love you, I can't marry you. Even for a ring like this."

I let go of Eric's hand and felt the warmth of his touch slip from beneath my fingers. Eric put the box back in his pocket.

"I didn't think you'd say yes. I could wish it might be different, but you're right. We both know we can't change. And I could never ask you to give up who you are so I could go on being who I am. You're too good of a reporter. Better than even you know. And you should never give up on who you want to be."

I sat back in the chair feeling strangely whole. I knew we'd done the right thing. Ten, fifteen years ago it might have been different, but not now.

I thought about the show Tyler had offered me and the excitement I felt growing in the pit of my stomach about a new venture. And I thought about Bunny and how she'd wanted to start over. Maybe if she'd never left her career and married Morganstern, or if things had been different between them, she'd have gone on to be the woman she wanted to become, instead of dead from trying to be someone new.

I looked back at Eric. I thought I could see a bit of relief in his face. I smiled. "But you and me, we're still good, right? Even if we don't tie the knot?"

"We'll always have a connection, Carol."

"But not like it's been, right?" I was smiling, but tears formed in my eyes. I couldn't let them fall.

"We both know it can't continue. Not like it's been. But I do have something for you." He reached back into his coat and took out another small square velvet jewelry box.

I wiped the corner of my eye. "What's this?"

"Think of it as a Christmas present. The people at Annabelle's wanted you to have it. Without you, Carol, we wouldn't have found the jewels. It's a thank you for all the work you did."

I opened the box. Inside was the Phoenix brooch.

A month later I got a call while I was in the studio. I had just wrapped my first Sunday night show when Matt, now my producer, said the caller insisted on talking with me. I told him to put the call into the studio on speaker. I'd take it while I packed up my reporter's bag.

"Carol, my love." I stopped what I was doing instantly. "You know who this is?"

I sat down behind the console. I felt as though the floor were about to fall out from beneath me.

"Tomas?"

"I've missed you, love. I'm afraid I had to cut my trip short. Complications with travel. You know how difficult it is these days. And to top it off, I had to leave without my bags. Dreadful timing."

"Where are you?"

"Oh, now, you know I can't say. That would ruin all the fun."

"You can't keep running. The police, the FBI, they'll find you."

"Well now, much as I'd like to chat on, I called for a purpose. You have something of mine. The jeweler's loupe? You were wearing it at the airport last I saw you. I was hoping you'd do me a favor and hold on to it for me."

"You've got to be kidding."

"I don't kid, Carol. Least of all about business. I'd like to have it back. It's not worth a lot, just sentimental value. I'll pick it up next time I'm in town."

"But—"

"Until then, love, I'll be listening. Or should I say, I'll stay tuned. Ciao."

An empty dial tone droned into the studio and I pulled the plug, silencing the earsplitting echo in my head. He wasn't going to get away with this. Not with me.

"Yeah, Tomas, stay tuned."

AUTHOR'S NOTE

Huguette Clark, pronounced oo-GET, has always fascinated me. For years, I'd drive up the California Coast Highway through Santa Barbara and catch glimpses of her summer home, or rather the tree-lined walls that surrounded Bellosguardo. The white mansion with lush green lawns that rolled to cliffs with panoramic views of the Pacific Ocean was never quite visible, and I was intrigued. Who was this woman who had left this mansion in pristine condition sixty years ago, as though she might return at any moment, and never did?

My research revealed she was the wealthy daughter of a former U.S. Senator and industrialist, who had remained largely a mystery. She was from an era I only knew about from black and white photo albums and stories the locals would tell. Rumors of an elaborate doll collection she preferred to people; a paranoid, reclusive heiress who spoke only French to those closest to her for fear of being overheard, and a rare collector of art and jewelry that might rival some of the richest estates in Europe.

It wasn't until she died in 2011 that any of the media was allowed their first look inside the estate, and while I was not lucky enough to be one of them, I understand it was like stepping back in time. Visitors who saw inside her home for the first time after her death report it was a time capsule, the perfect preservation of a life from a bygone era. Ms. Clark's perfume bottles remained on her dressing table, and rings and jewelry were as though she just left them and planned to return and place them upon her hands and fingers and join a party in the lavish great room that overlooked the ocean. Game tables with cards and a chess set sat at the ready. My imagination ran wild. I would have loved to have known Huguette Clark. Records indicate she was married once and then divorced quickly after that. She never had children and her older sister died when she was just seventeen. Ms. Clark lived most of her life alone and when she died, much of her estate was auctioned off by Annabelle's in New York with the proceeds going to various charities and the support of the newly founded Santa Barbara Foundation for the Arts.

While none of Ms. Clark's jewels were ever auctioned in Beverly Hills, as they were in my book, it was the mystery of her being and her jewels that stuck with me as I wrote *Without a Doubt*. I couldn't resist the urge to include something about this fascinating woman and her fabulous estate as the mystery unfolded. I tip my writing quill to her and thank her for her generous donation to the Southern California art community.

In addition to Huguette Clark, I must also salute the wonderful people who allowed me to tour the Diamond District in Holland. Most of the world's cut diamonds come from Amsterdam and while there, I must confess this mystery writer's mind went to the dark side. I became very curious about the crimes and business of jewelry theft. And of course, I wasn't disappointed. Our tour guide shared story after story of thefts and attempted thefts and I was fascinated. Jewel thieves are a breed of their own, creative and extremely competitive. The bigger the heist, the riskier the stakes, the more unusual the stories become. This was a writer's dream. And if there's one thing I learned about jewelry theft, it was that while the crooks may be caught, the jewels are almost never found. It didn't take much for me to see how a group of thieves who had perfected their skills in Europe might follow the money and resurface in Hollywood in time for an awards show season.

Thank you,
Nancy Cole Silverman

NANCY COLE SILVERMAN

Nancy Cole Silverman credits her twenty-five years in news and talk radio for helping her to develop an ear for storytelling. But it wasn't until 2001 after she retired from news and copywriting that she was able to sit down and write fiction fulltime. Much of what Silverman writes about today she admits is pulled from events that were reported on from inside some of Los Angeles' busiest newsrooms where she spent the bulk of her career. In the last ten years she has written numerous short stories and novelettes. Today Silverman lives in Los Angeles with her husband, Bruce and two standard poodles.

**The Carol Childs Mystery Series
by Nancy Cole Silverman**

SHADOW OF DOUBT (#1)
BEYOND A DOUBT (#2)
WITHOUT A DOUBT (#3)

Available at booksellers nationwide and online

Visit www.henerypress.com for details

Henery Press Mystery Books

And finally, before you go...
Here are a few other mysteries
you might enjoy:

CIRCLE OF INFLUENCE
Annette Dashofy

A Zoe Chambers Mystery (#1)

Zoe Chambers, paramedic and deputy coroner in rural Pennsylvania's tight-knit Vance Township, has been privy to a number of local secrets over the years, some of them her own. But secrets become explosive when a dead body is found in the Township Board President's abandoned car.

As a January blizzard rages, Zoe and Police Chief Pete Adams launch a desperate search for the killer, even if it means uncovering secrets that could not only destroy Zoe and Pete, but also those closest to them.

Available at booksellers nationwide and online

Visit www.henerypress.com for details

PRACTICAL SINS FOR COLD CLIMATES

Shelley Costa

A Val Cameron Mystery (#1)

When Val Cameron, a Senior Editor with a New York publishing company, is sent to the Canadian Northwoods to sign a reclusive bestselling author to a contract, she soon discovers she is definitely out of her element. Val is convinced she can persuade the author of that blockbuster, The Nebula Covenant, to sign with her, but first she has to find him.

Aided by a float plane pilot whose wife was murdered two years ago in a case gone cold, Val's hunt for the recluse takes on new meaning: can she clear him of suspicion in that murder before she links her own professional fortunes to the publication of his new book?

When she finds herself thrown into a wilderness lake community where livelihoods collide, Val wonders whether the prospect of running into a bear might be the least of her problems.

Available at booksellers nationwide and online

Visit www.henerypress.com for details

A MUDDIED MURDER
Wendy Tyson

A Greenhouse Mystery (#1)

When Megan Sawyer gives up her big-city law career to care for her grandmother and run the family's organic farm and café, she expects to find peace and tranquility in her scenic hometown of Winsome, Pennsylvania. Instead, her goat goes missing, rain muddies her fields, the town denies her business permits, and her family's Colonial-era farm sucks up the remains of her savings.

Just when she thinks she's reached the bottom of the rain barrel, Megan and the town's hunky veterinarian discover the local zoning commissioner's battered body in her barn. Now Megan is thrust into the middle of a murder investigation—and she's the chief suspect. Can Megan dig through small-town secrets, local politics, and old grievances in time to find a killer before that killer strikes again?

Available at booksellers nationwide and online

Visit www.henerypress.com for details

FATAL BRUSHSTROKE

Sybil Johnson

An Aurora Anderson Mystery (#1)

A dead body in her garden and a homicide detective on her doorstep...

Computer programmer and tole-painting enthusiast Aurora (Rory) Anderson doesn't envision finding either when she steps outside to investigate the frenzied yipping coming from her own back yard. After all, she lives in Vista Beach, a quiet California beach community where violent crime is rare and murder even rarer.

Suspicion falls on Rory when the body buried in her flowerbed turns out to be someone she knows—her tole-painting teacher, Hester Bouquet. Just two weeks before, Rory attended one of Hester's weekend seminars, an unpleasant experience she vowed never to repeat. As evidence piles up against Rory, she embarks on a quest to identify the killer and clear her name. Can Rory unearth the truth before she encounters her own brush with death?

Available at booksellers nationwide and online

Visit www.henerypress.com for details

KILLER IMAGE
Wendy Tyson

An Allison Campbell Mystery (#1)

As Philadelphia's premier image consultant, Allison Campbell helps others reinvent themselves, but her most successful transformation was her own after a scandal nearly ruined her. Now she moves in a world of powerful executives, wealthy, eccentric ex-wives and twisted ethics.

When Allison's latest Main Line client, the fifteen-year-old Goth daughter of a White House hopeful, is accused of the ritualistic murder of a local divorce attorney, Allison fights to prove her client's innocence when no one else will. But unraveling the truth brings specters from her own past. And in a place where image is everything, the ability to distinguish what's real from the facade may be the only thing that keeps Allison alive.

Available at booksellers nationwide and online

Visit www.henerypress.com for details

Made in the USA
San Bernardino, CA
19 January 2017